Rowan's Well

C.J. Harter

Published in 2013 by FeedARead.com Publishing –
Arts Council funded

A CIP catalogue record for this title is available from
the British Library.

Cover design by Mike Martin

www.redherringcg.com

For my parents
Ken and Mavis Johnson
with love
Per ardua ad astra

2003: Ten Years After
Chapter 1

"Can I tell you one more story before we finish?"

In his head, Dutton punched the air. "Yes, of course."

Mark Strachan remained where he was, looking out of the window at the upper floors of the high-security wing opposite. He thrust his hands into his pockets.

"This happened a long time ago. I must have been about five or six. I hadn't been in school long, anyway. We made these collages. These autumn collages. With leaves and twigs and stuff, you know? We went on a walk to some woods nearby to collect things. I remember it was cold. My fingers went red and tingly. I remember running about looking for the most colourful leaves. Then we brought them back to school, and we put them in a big pile on the teacher's desk. I remember it looked like a bonfire - a great big bonfire, you know? And the smell of it - God, I can smell it now, all damp and earthy. It was great. We got to choose what paper we wanted for our pictures. I think they used to call it sugar paper. Never worked out why. Anyway I chose this green sheet. This rich shade of green. I could picture my bonfire burning all bright and fiery on that green. We got to pick lots of bits of leaves and twigs and beech nuts and acorns and all that, to use in our collages. And I built this amazing bonfire on my sheet of green. I stuck it all down with that white glue we used back then. It smelled rank. Like fish, if you remember?" He cast him a quick glance.

"Yes, that's right."

"You had to apply the glue with those little plastic spatulas and it got all over your hands and your jumper and everywhere. And I remember thinking my mum was going to be cross about that. But then I thought, no, she wouldn't be because I was going to give her my picture, my beautiful bonfire, and she would be so pleased she couldn't be cross." He paused. Bowed his head. Dutton held his breath. "The teacher - Miss Pickmere? Pickford? something like that - she was thrilled when she saw what I'd done. She helped me make some flames, cut out of red and orange and yellow cellophane - her idea - and I stuck them on. It looked fantastic. All earthy and shimmery and fiery. And nobody else got to use the cellophane that day, because my picture was special. Miss Pickmere said I could take it home to show my mum and dad, but she asked me to bring it back tomorrow because she wanted to put it up on the wall for our autumn display. God, I was so proud, I can't tell you." Another pause. "So I came running out of school with my picture. I had to hold on tight to it because it was windy, and the picture was big, and I was scared it would fly out of my grasp. I ran to my mum. She was standing further up the road. She never stood with the other mums. And I showed her the picture and she took it from me and she said - she said: "Come on, I don't have time for this nonsense. I've got to be in work in half an hour. Hurry up." And she shoved my picture into her bag. Not carefully. No. She scrunched it up in her hand and she shoved it, all screwed up, into her bag. And she grabbed me by the wrist. And - and I don't remember any more after that."

6

PART ONE

1981: Twelve Years Before
Chapter 2

Mark watched his parents' silver Volvo pull out of the leafy car park. He didn't wave. Nor did they. He slung his rucksack over his shoulder and picked up the suitcase. He turned to face his new home. A red-brick three-storey building. Not old, not new. Surrounded by trees, but austere and impersonal. His guts clenched. Stay calm. Breathe. He smelled food. School dinners. His mouth watered in defiance of the cabbage. He reached into his donkey jacket for the letter, sellotaped where it had fallen apart along the creases. Report to the Porter's Office to be assigned a room. Hareton Hall. The university's only all-male hall of residence. He applied so late, he'd have to share a room. Probably with some sweaty-socked rugby nut.

He approached the building trying for an air of confidence. He looked up when a window above the entrance opened. Music blasted out. Spandau Ballet. A boy about his own age sat on the windowsill smirking down at him.

He pulled his shoulders back. The lobby was busy. New students hanging around in subdued huddles with parents and younger siblings. Mothers trying to give kisses and hugs, pushing greasy hair out of their sons' eyes. Fathers offering last-minute advice. Brothers and sisters shuffling feet, looking at the floor. He was relieved his parents had abandoned him outside.

He strolled as nonchalantly as he could across to the windowed reception desk.

"Name?" The black-sweatered, thin-haired man at the counter didn't look up.

A grey corridor. His Doc Martens squeaked on the shiny lino. A strong smell of disinfectant and polish couldn't disguise the reassuring odour of changing rooms. Stale sweat, rubber and mud blended with a hint of something more animal. Music escaped from the doors on either side, clashing in the air around him. His nostrils flared as he picked up another, sweeter smell. He relaxed a little. He'd track down its source later. He paused at an open door. A skinny kid was pulling clothes out of a stuff bag. He looked up. "Hi."

Mark nodded and walked on.

Thirty six was fourth on the left. Spandau Ballet and that familiar smell were coming from the room opposite. Laughing boy. Interesting. His own room was unlocked. He opened the door wide and stepped inside, bumping his rucksack against the frame. He saw a clean-looking narrow bed with a blue duvet. He'd never slept under one of those before. Two desks, two small wardrobes and a sink. A large window with a view across a leafy quadrangle to other windows. And, partially obscured by the open door, another bed with someone lying on it. He closed the door and took in the muddy ex-army boots, crossed comfortably one over the other, the torn and faded jeans, the lime-green rugby shirt, the thick neck and large round face. The messy light brown hair. Pale green eyes peered through a shaggy fringe at him.

He stepped forward. Caught his foot under a duffle bag on the floor. He fell and struck his chin on the metal bed frame. It hurt. Badly. Pinned by his heavy

10

rucksack, his legs tangled in the duffle bag string, he struggled to get up. The rucksack was lifted from him. A hand gripped his arm.

"Are you ok? Sorry, I should've moved that. Shit, you're bleeding."

He wiped his chin and looked at his hand. A lot of blood. "Fuck's sake. Are you some kind of moron?"

"Yeah. Stupid place to leave it. Let's have a look?"

He batted the hand away and scrambled to his feet. He kicked the offending bag.

"Watch out - it's dripping. You need to stick it under the tap." The boy tried to steer him towards the sink. Mark snatched his arm away. "Oh, ok. Only it looks bad. You need to clean it up."

He pulled from his pocket the handkerchief his mother had rather disturbingly foisted on him that morning. He held it to the cut.

The Arsehole sat on the bed. "D'you think it needs stitches? Should I get someone? See this?" The boy pointed to a pink scar on his cheek close to his ear. "Stud. Rugby. Four stitches. No anaesthetic. Wrecked."

He examined the now throbbing cut in the mirror above the sink. His chin was covered in blood. It was all down the front of his new white teeshirt. He shrugged off his jacket and let it drop to the floor. He ran his handkerchief under the tap and cleaned the wound. Now it didn't look so bad. As he watched, more blood oozed from it. The cut was small, but it hurt. It stung when he touched it. Worse, there was an ominous dull pain beneath the surface.

"Shit."

"D'you want me to get someone?"

"Who?"

"Dunno."

"Arsehole."

"Sorry."

He dabbed some more. The blood was pumping now. His face had gone very pale against his floppy black fringe. It made him think of Snow White. Was he getting delirious? Or hysterical?

"We need to get that seen to."

"You think?"

"I'll go get someone." The Arsehole was out of the door.

He sat on a bed and pressed the handkerchief to his chin. He felt a bit nauseous. The handkerchief was sticky now. How much blood could you lose safely? He went back to the mirror. The cut seemed to have stopped bleeding but it looked deep, like a second little mouth gawping under his bottom lip. It knocked him sick to look at it. Carefully, he pinched together the two edges of the wound. When he let go, it remained closed a moment but then it opened up again, slowly, like a goldfish gasping. The hole quickly filled and a ruby red tear rolled onto his chin. He pressed the handkerchief to it and went to the door. Would the reception guy have a car or would they send an ambulance? The door at the end of the corridor burst open and the Arsehole strode through followed by two other boys. He shouted: "Couldn't get any help. Massive queue. But it's ok cos James has booze" – a blond-haired boy waved a bottle of Jack Daniels above his head – "and Rob's-"

"Robbie."

"- Robbie - right- Robbie's got a sewing kit."

Robbie was gangly with wild red hair. The Windowsill Smiler. He disappeared into the room opposite.

"So we can fix you up. If you want, like. Or would you rather go to hospital? I'm easy." He looked embarrassed. "This is James, by the way. We just met. In the lobby. He's down the corridor with -?"

He looked at James.

"Peter. He's from Rotherham. I'll give him a shout."

The skinny kid answered the call and came running. Arsehole shook his hand: "Will Cooper. And this is -", he turned to him with a comical look of astonishment. "Shit, I didn't even ask your name!" He laughed.

"Strachan. Mark." He backed into the room. The others followed. "What d'you mean, fix me up?"

"My brother stitched this." Will Cooper tapped his cheek. "Mum and Dad were away, and Mike said he wasn't farting around with hospitals. So he made me drink half a bottle of tequila, then he got Mum's sewing box out. Like I say, it wrecked. D'you want me to have a go?"

"What?"

"D'you want me to – y'know – stitch you up?"

"Are you fucking mad?"

"That'll be a no, then?"

"Too fucking right. If you come anywhere near me with a needle - "

"Point taken. So you'll go with the lifelong disfigurement?"

James chipped in. "You should stitch within an hour of injury or septicaemia can set in."

"Bollocks." He tried to stay calm but the little git sounded like he knew something about it. "What are you? Doing medicine?"

"I am, as it goes."

"Bollocks." He took a last look in the mirror. "Ok. Do it. Not you, Dr Kildare. William Cooper, you do it."

Cooper rubbed his hands trying to look like some kind of expert. "Ok. Good. Better start on this, while we sterilize the instruments." He handed him the Jack Daniels.

"Do you actually know what you're doing?"

"Yeah. Well, sort of... How hard can it be? We've just got to make sure everything's clean and we're sweet."

He took a swig from the bottle. "Want some? Steady your hand?"

Cooper shook his head, serious. "Not before I've worked out how to do this." He sized up the room. "We need more light."

"I've got a desk lamp. Just unpacked it." Skinny Kid flitted out the door.

The Windowsill Smiler - Robbie? - came in with a small plastic pouch in one hand and the biggest spliff Mark had ever seen in the other. "Here. This should knock the edge off." He chucked the sewing kit on the bed and lit up. "Come over to the window."

He followed him. The JD was kicking in. Despite the throbbing in his chin, he could feel his earlier tension slipping away. He drank some more.

"Hey, leave some of that for the workers. You're on this now." Robbie dragged on the spliff and handed it to him. The hit was immediate. The leaves outside the window brightened. The whispering back in the room condensed into clear utterances. "That one's thinner." "Yeah, but what if it snaps? It's kind of like sewing leather. We need a strong one." "How d'you sterilize the cotton?" "You don't." He took another drag and looked round at the preparations.

Cooper came at him with the needle and thread. "Whoa! Hang on! Let's think about this."

The medic - the one called James - was drinking the Jack Daniels. "Chicken?"

"Merely a strong survival instinct."

Cooper drank from the proffered bottle, and wiped his mouth. "Ready when you are. It's still bleeding so we better not hang about. Lie on your bed. Peter, hold the lamp over his face. No, higher. Robbie, you kneel down there and waft that spliff about a bit. Mark, deep breaths. Eh, James, don't drink it all, mate. We might need it."

"Wait a sec. Let me psyche myself up." Then the pain bit. He fought to keep still, crushing the new duvet in his fists. Cooper said he'd been through this. How hard could it be? Hard. He squeezed his eyes tight shut. Tears streamed down his temples and into his ears. Bright lights stabbed at him inside his closed eyelids.

"Here." Someone shoved the spliff into his mouth. He bit through it. "A novel approach." Robbie's accent. Edinburgh? Weird, what you noticed when you were dying. Glasgow, maybe. And now he'd never know. Heigh ho.

"Robbie, get your hand out of the way." Cooper sounded older. In control. "Keep … really… still. Nearly done. Last one. Seven. Think that should hold it. What d'you reckon?"

He pushed away attempts to help him up and sprang off the bed. "Jesus fucking shit. What kind of sadist are you?" His face in the mirror was paler than he'd ever seen it. The black cotton, now fused woozily with his flesh, matched his hair. It looked like some pathetic attempt at a goatie. But the gaping little mouth was closed and seemed to have stopped bleeding. "Thanks. I think."

"Sit down. You'll be a bit shaky. Drink this."

More drink appeared. The repaired spliff did the rounds. Someone put Led Zep on. Cooper sat on the bed next to him.

"Cosy, in't it? Ever shared before?"

"No."

"Where're you from?"

"Manchester. Place called Altrincham?"

"I know it. Bolton, me. That's probably how they put us together - both coming from round Manchester, like? How's the cut?"

"Painful. I need vodka! Wanderers, right?"

"You into football?"

"United, naturally." His smile pulled painfully at the stitches.

"Nay!" Cooper fell back against the wall, as if fatally shot, thudding his head. "You rag bastard!"

He passed the spliff. Cooper passed it on without partaking. "You're vicious, William Cooper."

"You're welcome, mate."

A few weeks later. Their daily session with the guys from the corridor. Mark could do without it today. He had a couple of essays on the go and Robbie had disappeared again so there was no-one to dilute the Polish Twat.

"You know he's not Polish. And anyway what if he is? That just makes you a racist twat, mate. A racist twat who fancies the same girls as the Polish twat. No, hang on, a racist twat who never gets a look in with the girls who fancy the Polish twat. We're going."

Where did William get that silver-tongued persuasion?

Their table was full of empties before the conversation turned to Robbie. Some sort of record?

"Mark, what do you reckon to this?" Greg nudged Luca. "Go on. Tell him what you told me."

Luca glowered at Mark. "Nah."

He glowered right back.

"Go on." Greg nudged him again.

Luca took a cigarette from the pack William was offering round. He leaned forward for a light. Sat back. Inhaled deeply. Wanker. "You know he's been mithering me to get him into the D.R?" Luca was always going on about the Dissecting Room. Mark yawned. "I took him in yesterday. It's always quiet on Saturdays. Minimal staff." He took another leisurely drag on his cigarette.

"And what did he do? Just watch you, like?" William seemed to be all ears.

"No. I thought he'd ask to have a go, you know, dissecting. We're doing the thorax right now. But he didn't."

"Tell them what he did. Go on." Greg looked around the table with a big stupid grin. "This is sick, this is."

"He wandered about for a bit, looking at the specimen jars and that."

"Sick." He yawned again.

Luca cast him a sour look. "I left him to it. Got on with my cadaver. But then I heard this whispering. It was him." He paused. The others leaned forward. "He'd pulled back the sheet on one of the cadavers. He was whispering to it."

William put down his glass. "How d'you mean, 'whispering'?"

"Whispering. Talking quiet?"

"So what was he saying?"

17

"Dunno. He was whispering. But when he'd finished chatting to that one, he covered it back up and moved on to the next one."

Greg butted in. "He uncovered every single body and had a chat with it. How sick is that?"

"There's over fifty cadavers in there and they're all hacked about," Luca said.

"Some of them don't have heads." Greg lowered his voice. "And some of them don't have faces."

He couldn't resist: "That would follow from the lack of a head."

"No, but you know what I mean. He was talking to a - a bloody pulp."

"They're not bloody, in fact," Luca said. "They're pumped full of preservative. Formaldehyde."

"No, but you know what I …"

"Yeah. It is weird, is that. What was he playing at?" William said.

"Christ knows. He's a nutter, if you ask me. I'm not taking him in again. No way."

William turned to Mark. "What do *you* think?"

"I don't."

"You must have an opinion."

"Must I?"

William pulled a face at him and said to Greg. "What do you make of Robbie? I mean all that dying his hair red. And the Doctor Who coat and scarf. I don't get it."

"Me neither. He gives me the creeps."

"You're quick enough to smoke his dope, though." He hated all this psychoanalytical crap.

"Yeah, and he's quick enough to charge through the fucking nose for it, isn't he?" Luca said.

William glanced at the clock over the bar. "Eh, we mustn't forget that washing."

18

Mark set the alarm on his new digital watch.

"Let's have a look." Greg leaned over.

He raised his hand. The chrome strap caught the light. Greg whistled. Luca looked impressed, but tried to hide it.

"He's an only child," William said.

He snatched his hand back. "What's that supposed to mean?"

"It's just something people say."

"Not about me."

"Ok. I'm just saying…"

"You'll just say too much one day, my friend."

"Here we go again." Luca used an undertone loud enough for him to hear.

"Got something to say, Lech?" His face felt hot. Luca squared his shoulders.

"Come on, Luc." Greg looked over at William. "We said we'd meet the others at the union. You two coming down later?"

"Yeah, probably. When we've done the washing."

"You're a wanker!" He couldn't help himself. Luca raised his middle finger without turning back.

William said: "You know you're never going to win friends and influence people that way."

"Who says I want to?"

William drummed a tattoo on the table. "Right. Shall we go and see to that washing?"

He tipped his last half pint down his throat, wiped his mouth and stood up. Mark followed him.

While they were pulling their laundry out of the washers, William said: "What did you think of Luca's story? D'you reckon Robbie's a bit mad?"

"He's a drama queen. It's all done for effect. Like when he locked himself in his room in Freshers' Week. He likes the attention. He likes being talked about."

19

"That's all it is?"

"He's ok when you get to know him a bit. And he can get hold of some fine dope."

"That's why you hang around with him, then?" William slammed the door on the tumble dryer.

"It's not just that." This was difficult to put into words. "Let's face it. When he's around I come off relatively sane. Frankly, William, he makes me look good."

William laughed. "Fancy joining them down the union later?"

That night Will hooked up with a girl he knew from the swimming pool. Sally, she was called. He spent a pleasant hour trying to persuade her out of her knickers. He was frustrated but optimistic when he was gently pushed from her room in the early hours, with a kiss and the promise of a second chance the following night. He took a long route home to let his passion subside. He'd sobered up considerably by the time he got in.

Despite his own intimate relationship with cigarettes, he was hit by a coughing fit as soon as he stepped in the room. The sickly sweet smoke went straight to his head. He was greeted by feeble cheers and pitiful attempts at whistles which dissolved into giggles.

"Hey, Will, my man! Was she good?"

There were no secrets on this corridor. He smiled enigmatically at the assembled company, and headed for the kettle.

"Anyone want tea?"

"I could murder a cup of tea." Luca was sprawled on his bed. Bloody cheek.

"You sound just like my Gran." That was James, curled in a tight ball on the floor at the bottom of the bed.

"Gran Schman."

More laughter.

"There's some J. D., or there's cans in the sink." Mark stood up unsteadily to offer him a nearly empty bottle. "We're a bit stoned."

"No shit, Sherlock." He went to open a window. When he turned around, Mark was doubled over, hugging his belly, and emitting a weird squeaking sound. He bent down, and took the bottle from him. "Mark, are you ok, mate?"

"No - shit - Sherlock," Mark gasped between strangled giggles. "No shit - Sherlock." He collapsed to his knees. "I must remember that." He looked up at him with tearful eyes. "Remind me."

He flopped forward, laughing. That set the others off again. He opened all the windows. He had to step over several helpless bodies to get back to the door to fan it to and fro. He waited for the hilarity to subside. He had that pain in the top of his nose. He was going to end up with a mad headache. Mark had promised he wouldn't do this in their room again.

"Look guys, I want to get some sleep. D'you mind if we call this a day?"

He didn't expect them to take the slightest notice. He wasn't disappointed. It was the usual gang. Luca and Greg from next door, with James and Pete. And, of course, Robbie on the floor by the sink, hogging the spliff. Robbie was always at the centre of these little get-togethers. They were his version of tupperware parties. He always used their room because he could get more people in. Mark often accused Will of being naïve, but when it came to Robbie, he was pretty gullible himself. He didn't begrudge him, though. It was hard for Mark to make friends.

Suddenly Robbie sprang to his feet with surprising agility for one so gangly. His rich Edinburgh accent rang out: "I'm going to fly! I really am. I'm going to do it!"

Shit. He'd left the big window wide open. Robbie was standing with his back to it, right in front of it, flapping his arms about like a scarecrow with a strong work ethic. All he had to do was sit on the sill, swing his legs over and he'd be out. Shit. He moved fast. Stepped smoothly over Greg. Tried not to spook him. As he reached him, Robbie dropped to the floor with all the grace of a condemned block of flats. From the pile of struggling limbs at his feet, Will deduced that Mark had somehow pulled Rob's legs from under him, and was now regretting it.

"In the name of all that is holy, William, a little help here!"

He couldn't resist a smile.

Will finally persuaded their guests to leave. He'd aired the room, and now he gazed at the darkened ceiling, the duvet tucked under his chin. He loved this part of the day when they talked about everything and nothing, often well into the early hours. Tonight they'd discussed the relative merits of Charlie's Angels and argued about their wildly differing England dream teams. But Will was missing home. Especially his mum. He knew he was rambling on but he couldn't help it. He praised her sense of humour, her ferocity, her favourite perfume, her cooking, her all-round sound parenting. He told Mark about the time when he was five and the whole family, all eight of them, went to Blackpool to see the illuminations. He'd been walking down the prom, gazing up at the strange, colourful lights. Suddenly his brother was no longer holding his hand. He was alone in the crowd. It was a big, jostling crowd. He stood perfectly still, petrified but remembering what his mum had taught him. Always look for something lost in the last place you had it. He knew if he stayed put his mum would come back for him. And she did. It seemed like hours before the family returned, but they maintained it was no longer than a couple of minutes. Will laughed.

"Then she went into overdrive, drilling me to chant out my name, address and phone number every five minutes. It got to be a bit of a party trick with me. Oh, and she started introducing me to every policeman we ever saw, getting me to look out for them when we were shopping and that. I still do it now." He fell silent. Mark hadn't spoken for a while. "So what's your mum like? You don't talk about her much."

"Not much to tell. We don't get on."

"Oh?"

"Your mum sounds great. I'll have to meet her."

"Yeah, I'd like that."

Mark went quiet again. Will was about to say goodnight when he spoke.

"It's weird, because something like that happened to me too."

"Yeah?"

"My mother took me shopping in town - I was about seven, I think. I was bored. I wanted to go home. I wouldn't go in Marks and Spencer's. She got angry. Told me to wait by the door while she went in. So I did. But she was ages, and I went inside to look for her. I couldn't find her so I came back out. But she still didn't come. Funny thing is I remembered that same thing as you. About looking for something you've lost in the last place you saw it? Mrs P - remember the cleaning lady I told you about? - she told me that. So I stayed put." He paused. "I suppose it has to be something you really want to find, though. I was there for hours. I remember I was confused, thinking maybe I was wrong and it'd only been a few minutes. Anyway, I noticed there were fewer people shopping and I started getting funny looks. I kept looking inside the shop. Eventually there was no one in there except a woman with a vacuum cleaner." Will heard him sigh softly. "She came out. Asked if I was ok. I said yes, and walked away. I was scared I'd be in trouble for hanging around. Problem was, I'd never been in town on my own before. I had to work out how to get back to the car park. I must have been panicking a bit too which made it harder to think, you know?"

"Yeah." Will heard the quiver in Mark's voice. This wasn't a family story trotted out at every get-together.

"I remember thinking, she must be waiting in the car for me. She'll be at the car park. I managed to find my way there. But the car park was empty. That's the first time I had one of those panic attacks I told you about." The bed creaked as he shifted position. "It was scary. Shit, when I think about it … Anyway, I got a grip. Told myself I'd have to walk home. It was only about two miles to my house, but to a little kid that's a long way, you know?"

"Course it is."

"So, yeah, I got a grip and set off. I remembered the way from there. You had to go past the firm where my dad worked and then past the football ground, and then turn left and just keep straight on. When I got to Dad's work, the security man was standing outside, having a fag. He said hello. I said hello back, but I

24

remember he was looking at me funny. I think I was crying by this stage, so he probably realised something was wrong. I carried on and eventually I passed the football ground and turned the corner. That was when I saw my mum's car coming down the road. God, I was fucking relieved. I got in. She wouldn't look at me. I said sorry. Kept saying sorry. She said: 'You will be'."

He stopped.

"And then what?"

"Nothing."

"But what happened next?"

"Can't remember. Don't remember it ever being talked about. Don't think my dad got to know about it. Or if he did, he never said."

Will was out of his depth. What kind of mother would leave her small child alone and drive home without him? He'd wondered why Mark hadn't yet been home. As far as he knew, he hadn't even phoned home. Maybe he had good reason not to.

"I don't know what to say."

Mark laughed. "You don't have to say anything." Will heard him roll over. "G'night."

"Night." Will lay awake a long time.

Chapter 3

The road unravelled before the short beam of the mini's headlights. Will tried to concentrate. He didn't like the way the car seemed to be veering about. He felt sick. Maybe Robbie shouldn't be driving. Maybe he'd had too much to drink. Why did they agree to come out here with him in the first place? Robbie was a head case. A lunatic driver. But Mark said it would be a laugh. He wanted to try the Furnace Inn, famous for its real ale.

They'd spent all evening there, getting pissed on the landlord's many and varied offerings. It was cosy in front of that huge log fire on a cold winter night deep in the Derbyshire hills. Will was thrilled by the sense of independence, freedom from parental constraint, with him still well into this second term at university. The knowledge they could go anywhere and do anything was almost as intoxicating as the Black Sheep on tap.

But they must have got a bit loud because the landlord came over. He said they'd had enough for one night. Then he saw the car keys on the table and asked who was driving. Mark jumped in before Robbie could open his mouth, and said he was. He always drank halves so he was well behind their six pints each. Will was sure the landlord hadn't believed him, and now he cursed the guy for not saying something. He should have stopped them leaving. Called them a taxi or something. That was supposed to be his job, wasn't it? And anyway Mark couldn't even drive, the tosser. Will rested an elbow on the back of each seat. How come he had to sit in the back? He'd been in the back on the way there too. He rubbed his face. He should try to concentrate on the road. One of them had to. Once they were outside the pub, Mark had chucked the keys to Robbie. He missed them. Scrabbled about in the dark for ages before he found them. He was obviously pissed as a fart. Why the hell did he get in the car with him?

Mark and Robbie had fallen silent. In the dim light of the instrument panel, Will saw Mark's head droop forward and jerk up. He was falling asleep. That bastard couldn't hold his drink, either.

"Hey Will!" Robbie shouted.

Will jumped. He'd been drifting off, himself. "What?"

"Ever seen that 'Twilight Zone' episode where the guy turns the headlights off on a road just like this?" He wiggled his eyebrows at Will through the rear-view mirror. His voice was going in and out of tune. Will was definitely falling asleep.

"Wasn't there a monster or something on the bonnet when he turned the lights back on?" Mark sounded suddenly wide awake.

"Well, boys and girls, why don't we try it and find out?" Robbie flicked off the headlights.

Will was fully awake now. "Shit, Robbie. Don't. Put them back on. It's too dark." The mini was bowling along into total blackness at about forty miles an hour. He reached forward for the switch but Robbie batted his hand away. "There'll be a bend. Turn them back on!" The sound of his own voice, high and staccato, frightened Will all the more.

Mark snorted and said: "Wanker" under his breath. Who did he mean? Robbie laughed. Insanely.

"Now, ladies and gentlemen, I shall restore the lights and we'll see what we shall see!" He flicked the black switch with a ringmaster's flourish. A big white sheep hurtled into view right in their path.

Everything seemed to slow down. A deafening roar filled his ears. He glanced over his shoulder to see what was making the noise. Idiot. It was his own blood rushing through his veins. He turned to face the windscreen in time to see Mark throw up his arms in front of his face. Robbie yanked the small steering wheel down to the left. He leaned right over onto Mark. He must have been braking hard, because there was a screech of skidding tyres. The wheels locked. A loud boom and a shudder as the back of the car swung round and impacted with the sheep. Will opened his eyes, expecting to see blood and bits of dead animal everywhere. They were still moving. Going down a slope fast. Shit. They'd left the road. They were careering over rough ground. The three of them were flung around as the car leaped about crazily. What were all those bangs? Robbie fought to control it.

"Hold on!"

Will was lifted from his seat. Hit his head. He put one hand up to the roof. Pressed against it. With the other, he gripped the back of Robbie's seat. Braced himself for the crash. This wasn't real. This couldn't be happening. It was like some mad nightmare.

"Stop! Stop!" he heard himself shout.

"I can't. Brakes have gone." Robbie sounded dead sober now.

"Wanker!" Mark grabbed the hand brake. He yanked it. The car lurched. Slowed. But the descent was getting steeper and still they did not stop. All Will could see through the windscreen were greenish grey hummocks of grass emerging from the darkness, rushing past them, like waves cut through by the prow of a ship in rough seas. Where the hell were they? He tried to picture the journey out from town that afternoon. The landscape had been hilly but to the sides of the road was scrubby moorland, wasn't it? He struggled to remember. Fear fogged his mind. Were they going to hit anything? What did they need to avoid? He forced himself to think. Trees? Stone walls? Oh, shit - The car was airborne. No more banging. How much would it hurt if they landed upside down? There was a tremendous splash all around them. They came to rest. The engine had stalled. Blackness. Eerie silence. Then he heard Mark's voice.

"We're in the lake. We're in the water. Listen. We haven't got long. It's going to fill up. I'm going to open my window …"

"No, don't!" Even as he spoke, a terrifying cold gripped his ankles. "It's in, it's in!" He drew his feet up out of the water - one of them, anyway. His right foot was stuck fast. Full of pain. He was trapped. He was going to drown. He bent forward. Searched with his hands in the still shallow but freezing water. His foot was pinned under something. The driver's seat seemed to be sloping as if the runner holding it up had collapsed. His foot was wedged underneath it. It must have happened when they hit the sheep. The impact had caved in the whole side of the car. "Fuck." The water was up to his knees now. A loud gurgling noise as the car tipped forward. The weight of the engine and two bodies in front was pulling it down nose first. He strained to see. It was like staring into a solid black wall. The only noises were the rushing of the water, sounding cruelly like a bath emptying, and Mark's voice. He was still bloody talking:

" … for the pressure to equalise, then we can open the door. Get ready to hold your breath."

"What?" Will scrabbled in the surging water. This could not be happening. He was going to drown. "Mark, I'm stuck."

"I'll open the door. Get ready to hold your breath. William! Do you hear me?"

"Yes, hold my breath. Hold my breath." He pushed himself up, his head pressed against the roof to keep his face away from the encroaching water. His mind fled to home, his mum. Then he thought of Robbie. He'd gone quiet.

"Rob? Mark, is he ok?"

Mark didn't answer. Will heard him moving. The water in the car chopped about more. It covered his face. He coughed. He heard a groan. The back of Robbie's head hit him full in the face with a hollow thud. He yelped. Robbie groaned again. Mark must have shoved him backwards in his seat. Will heard the panic in Mark's voice: "Knocked himself out - bleeding - it's coming up - hold your breath."

He was under water. Terror rose in him. He fought to keep his mouth closed. He opened his eyes long enough to see the passenger door open. The interior light had come on. By its blurry glow he saw a shape disappear upwards out of the car. He yanked his foot one last time. It came free. He was still alive. How much longer could he hold his breath? How long had it been? He opened his eyes again. Black. He gripped the back of the passenger seat with both hands. He wriggled and squeezed himself through the narrow gap between the top of the seat and the roof, forward into the space vacated by Mark. He pushed past Robbie's inert body. Shoved him aside. He had to get out. He felt something pull his coat collar, guiding him out of the tiny space. He could hold his breath no longer. He was exploding. He opened his mouth. Choked on the water

30

that reached in searching for his lungs. Then, unbelievably, he felt cold clean not-water on his face. He coughed. Gulped in fresh air. He went under again. The hand still gripping his collar pulled him up.

"Stop struggling. Can't hold on if you kick." Mark's voice was barely a whisper. It was close. Right in his ear. "We've got to swim. Can you do that?"

He gasped. He breathed in a mouthful of water. Sank again. Pain seared his chest. He choked and spluttered. He felt a hand under his chin. Mark lifted his face clear of the water.

"William? Ok? Can you hear me?" He twisted his neck. It hurt. "Answer me, you bastard!"

"M'ok - m'ok," He retched. Mark's arm wrapped around his chest and shoulder. He was pulled close to his friend's face.

"Listen to me. Keep still. I'll hold you, ok? We're going to be ok. It's not far."

How did he know how far it was? It was pitch black. He didn't care. He just wanted to let go. "Ok." He drifted into a strange sort of sleep. The intense cold formed a soft and comforting blanket all about him.

He jolted awake. Mark's voice in his ear. "Put your feet down. You can touch the bottom."

Reluctant, he did as he was told. There was solid earth beneath his feet. He wasn't dead, then? Maybe he wasn't going to die, after all? The water was chest deep. Suddenly he was very scared. He stared into blackness. He pulled away from Mark. He couldn't see.

"Shallower this way. Come on, William. Got to get out of the water." Mark's teeth were chattering. He could barely get the words out.

Then it hit him. Robbie was still in the car. "Robbie!"

31

"We can't. It's too late. We can't help him. William, please. Please …"

Mark dragged him. He was crying now. Will stopped resisting. He let himself be led. They waded, stumbling over unseen stones on the bottom, the reservoir gradually relinquishing them to the night air. They reached the shore. There was no beach. Only a wall of eroding earth. He reached up. It was like the side of a swimming pool. Mark let go of him. He heard him push up onto the bank, with a grunt.

He was completely done in. Desperate for sleep. "I can't."

"Give me your hand." He reached up again. Mark grabbed hold of his arm: "Help me, you fat bastard." Will dug his toes into the side of the bank. He pushed himself up. Sharp pain shot through his foot.

"Agh. Shit."

He slumped onto the tussocky grass, face down. There was something badly wrong with his foot, but right now he couldn't make himself care. Mark was gripping his collar again. The weight of his arm across Will's back was comforting. He turned his face out of the grass toward the area of black where he knew Mark lay exhausted at his side.

"You just saved my life."

"Aha."

Will reached into the dark and touched Mark's face. It was convulsing, the lips trembling. Will raised himself on his elbow. He leaned closer.

"D'you think he's dead yet?"

The sobs came harder. He stroked Mark's cheek. Then he let his elbow give way beneath him and surrendered to a deep dark sleep.

Chapter 4

"Look son, we need to know how the car came to hit the sheep."

Detective Sergeant Nicholson tapped the nib of his biro on the table. The boy held his gaze. They'd been here over an hour already. He shouldn't let the lad get to him. He tried again: "Was Robert distracted? Did something happen in the car to make him take his eyes off the road?"

The boy, Strachan, shifted his gaze to the wall. "Not that I can remember. It was just dark."

He spoke calmly, with a reasonableness that verged on patronising. Who the hell did this kid think he was talking to? DC Finch shifted in his seat. He wanted in, but Nicholson wasn't finished.

"Ok. Let's leave that aside for now. Take us forward to when the car hit the water. You and William managed to get out." Was that a flicker of a reaction? Did the lad's mouth twitch? "What about Robert?"

Strachan raised his eyebrows. "What about him?"

Nicholson swallowed his irritation. "Why didn't he get out of the car?"

"Have you ever been trapped in a car under water?"

"No."

"No," the boy said, looking him full in the face.

"So enlighten me."

"He was unconscious. He must have hit his head. I couldn't see. It was dark."

"Look, Mark. We know Robert had been drinking. We know you and William had been drinking. So why don't you stop pissing us about and tell us exactly what happened in that car?"

The boy's startled look was quickly veiled. He was good.

"Ok." Nicholson put down his pen. "We'll leave it there for now. Thanks for coming in. We may need to speak to you again, after we've talked to William."

When the boy had gone, Finch vented his displeasure. "You should've let me have a go at him."

"Why? Everything he says makes sense."

"Yeah, but - it doesn't feel right."

Nicholson sighed. "I know. He's way too calm. Controlled. I mean, he barely survived, himself."

"Hiding something, you reckon?"

Nicholson drew a circle on his notepad. He added heavy black arrows pointing in at the circle, surrounding it. "Not sure. It's not like he's overcompensating. There's none of the usual bravado." He added circles within the circle. "It's more like he's genuinely detached from what happened - you know? Like he's denying his own emotions about it."

"Just a nutter, then?"

"Dunno. If he's cut himself off so effectively - well, maybe there's a reason for that?"

"Something he doesn't want to face up to?"

"I think we need him back in, Finch."

"I think you're right, gov."

Will's stay in hospital went by in a haze of pain relief and visits from family. He snatched sleep during the day. He spent the nights trying to stay awake for fear of the dreams. When he was discharged, he moved with his mum and dad into a local hotel. He didn't get to see or even speak to Mark until nearly a week after the crash. He finally managed to get hold of him by calling their corridor payphone at Hareton.

"Mark! Where the hell have you been? I've tried to get you every day. Are you ok?"

"How are you?"

"All right. You know."

"Yeah, I know."

"Were you in hospital too? I kept asking, but no one would tell me anything."

"Only overnight. I came to see you, but you were sleeping. I met your mum and dad. They took me out for a meal. I like them."

"Yeah. They're getting a bit much now, though. I wish they'd go home really, but they're waiting for the - you know."

"The funeral? Yeah, well, that's good of them. Appreciate it."

"I do. It's just - I don't know. It's all so -" Will struggled to keep his breathing even. "It's all so intense. I've never even known anyone who's - who's died before, let alone -"

"I know. It's shit. Look, have the police spoken to you yet?"

"No. Why? Have they spoken to you?"

"Yes."

"And?"

"They're asking about what happened. They know we'd been drinking."

Will went cold. "Mark, are we in trouble?"

He didn't answer straightaway. "I don't think so."

"What does that mean? What should I tell them?"

"Just tell them what happened. William? It's ok. Don't worry."

"I don't know about you, but I need to talk. Will you meet me later?"

"Course. Where? Here?"

"Christ, no. I can't face everyone yet."

"William, my friend, listen to me. Words of one syllable: you haven't done anything wrong."

"Anything's got three syllables actually, and haven't's got -"

"Piss off. I'll come to you. Three, ok?"

He hung up without waiting for confirmation.

He replaced the receiver. He didn't like the way William had sounded. He'd talked very fast. His voice had been tight and tense. How would he cope with the police? He hoped they'd be easier on William than they'd been on him. James came down the corridor, giving him a wave and a stupid grin. Not now. He hurried back to his room. He closed the door behind him. He was keeping it locked, surviving on black tea and digestive biscuits. He ventured out only to use the toilet and talk to the police. He didn't blame William for not wanting to come back to the hall yet.

Will lay on the hotel bed, waiting for Mark to come. He tried to ignore the film of the accident playing on continuous loop in his head. There was a knock on the door. His dad stuck his head in.

"You awake, son? There're some policemen here to see you."

He sat up with difficulty. Couldn't get used to this bloody plaster cast on his leg. He rubbed his eyes. "Policemen?"

"You don't have to talk to them yet if you don't want. It'll keep."

"I don't know. What do you think I should do?"

"'S'up to you, lad."

"I'd better get it over with. They've already seen Mark."

"So I believe. D'you want me or your mum to stay with you? Bit of moral support?"

Did he? "No thanks, Dad. I think I'd rather do it on my own."

"Understood. Will you see them in here?"

He glanced round the anonymous beige-papered room. "I guess so. Good a place as any."

"Right you are. I'll go and get them."

"Eh, Dad!" His father popped his head back in the room. "If Mark arrives, can you keep him entertained?"

His dad winked. "I'll see what I can do, lad."

There were two policemen. Why had they sent detectives? The lack of uniforms was unnerving. A bit sinister. They introduced themselves. Detective Sergeant Nicholson and Detective Constable Finch. They shook hands with him. They seemed friendly enough. When he reached for his crutches to stand up, they motioned him to stay put on the bed. The constable pulled up two hard-backed chairs. He pictured how he must look to them - an invalid. Helpless and weak. He tried to sit up straighter.

"How are you feeling, William?" Sergeant Nicholson asked, as if reading his mind.

"Better, thanks."

"You understand we need to ask you a few questions? When a death occurs, it's important to get all the facts straight, yeah?"

"Yes, of course. Course it is." He nodded, eager to show he wanted to help.

"Ok to start now?" He nodded again. "How is your memory of the events of the night of the twentieth?"

37

He swallowed. He felt sick. He'd been dying to talk about it all, to get it off his chest, off his mind, but he wanted to talk to Mark, not these strangers. "It's good. I remember it all. Up to getting out of the water, anyway."

Constable Finch looked up from his notepad, pen poised. "You don't recall anything after that? Who picked you up? How you got to hospital?"

He hadn't given these questions a moment's consideration until now. That ever-repeating loop in his head would end abruptly when he lost consciousness on the bank of the reservoir, and always took up the story again from when they left the pub. Now he came to think about it, he didn't know how they got back. "I'm sorry. I don't remember any of that. Sounds stupid, right?"

"Not really. You were in shock." The sergeant took over. "I want you to take us through the events of that evening, as you remember them. Take your time. There's no hurry."

"Where shall I start?"

"How about from when you got in the car at your hall of residence?"

"Right." He took a deep breath and began. Finch took notes. He did all right at first. Gave as much detail as he could. He was sure he blushed when he said how much they had to drink. When he got to where they hit the sheep, he broke into a sweat. He swung his good leg off the bed.

"D'you mind if I get a drink? Only -"

"No problem. I'll get you one." Finch disappeared into the en suite and emerged with a glass of water. "There you go."

He gulped it down in a single draught. His hand quivered like an old man's as he put the glass on the bedside cabinet.

"Better?" the sergeant asked. "All right to carry on? Say if you're not."

"I'm ok. I just feel a bit sick. Can I ask *you* something?" He said it before he could stop himself.

"Fire away."

Finch looked up from his notes.

"Robbie. Did he -? I mean, was it -? Would it have been -?" He was dizzy. He was right back there. Waiting to be engulfed by the lake water. "He got knocked out. Unconscious. He didn't - He wouldn't have -felt anything, would he?"

He got the words out, but couldn't control the tears. He ducked his head. Nicholson came to him. He placed a hand on his shoulder, just as his mother knocked once and burst in. She must have been listening outside the door.

"Do you mind if we draw this to a close, gentlemen? I don't think he's up to it yet," she said in her most teacherly voice.

"Of course." Nicholson moved toward the door. "Would it be possible to see you again, William, either tomorrow or the day after, at the station? We do need to get this all written up fairly sharpish. For the coroner," he added, turning to his mum. "Thanks Mrs Cooper. See you later in the week, then."

They left.

His mum sat on the bed next to him. "All right, love?"

"No." He could hardly see her for the tears. "What am I going to do, Mum?"

She brushed the hair out of his eyes. Stroked his cheek.

"It'll get easier, love. It will, I promise."

Finch took over the questioning. "Are you sure he was unconscious? How do you know?"

Strachan shifted slightly in his seat. "Because he didn't speak after we hit the water. I shook him. He didn't move."

Finch scribbled a note, then asked: "How did you get out of the car?"

Nicholson sat back to observe the boy's interaction with his DC. Maybe Finch would have better luck. Strachan glanced at him. Was that a smile?

"Didn't we cover this already? Maybe you should consult your notes."

"Humour me."

"I wound my window down to let the water in. Then when it was in over our heads I opened the door."

"Simple as that?"

"If you say so."

"So you got out."

"We've gone over this already."

"Then you dived back down and pulled your mate out." Strachan stared at the wall behind their heads. "Well?" Finch was losing patience too.

"Look at your notes."

"Just answer the question, please."

"Yes."

That was enough. Nicholson leant forward. "Word to the wise, Mark. You're making this a lot more difficult for yourself than it needs to be, yeah?"

Strachan shrugged and looked straight through him.

Finch had also had enough by the sound of it. "Ok. We'll go over it one more time, so I can write it up. Then you can sign the statement and we can see the back of you."

Strachan stared at him, impassive. Nicholson felt a chill down his spine. Something about this boy gave him the creeps.

"I said I'd be here at three. Why aren't you ready?"

"I am ready."

"I'm not going out with you looking like that. Get a shave, at least."

He looked Mark up and down. "New jeans? And you've ironed that shirt."

"Of course I've ironed it. When have I ever not ironed a shirt? It's linen, for Christ's sake. It creases."

He laughed. He hobbled to the en suite. "You're a living breathing Burtons window, you know that?"

"Better than looking like some shitey old wino, my friend."

"You're too kind."

"Will your dad drop us off at the Botanical Gardens, d'you think?"

"You're joking. Why there?"

"Because it's dead. Quiet, I mean. No one we know, anyway."

Parlour palms. Bright sunlight. Posh. And, most important, empty except for two old ladies gossiping at a table over the far side of the café.

"It's quite nice, is this," Will said, looking up at the glazed roof. "Like a big greenhouse."

"It's a conservatory. Don't suppose you have them in Bolton."

"I'll have to bring my mum and dad."

"Yeah, it's that sort of place."

The waitress came over and Mark ordered the full works. Cucumber sandwiches, scones with jam and cream, fancy cakes, tea and coffee. When she'd gone, Will leaned across the table: "How are we paying for this?" Mark threw him a disdainful look. "Because I am not doing a runner from here, got it?"

"Keep your hair on." Mark pulled a wad of bank notes from his pocket and threw it on the table. He smiled. "D'you think that'll cover it?"

"Where'd you get all that?"

"Parents. Came the day after - the day after it happened. Left the day after that. Guilt money, I suppose. Still, ours is not to reason why etcetera, etcetera."

Will knew better than to ask more. His mum and dad were waiting at the hotel for a phone call to come and pick them up whenever they were ready. Like parents should. They sat in silence until the tea arrived, all silver cake trays and fine china.

"Shall I be mother?" Mark pursed his lips and pushed up imaginary boobs with his folded arms, like Les Dawson.

"Give over." He laughed. Watching him pour the tea, it hit him how much he'd missed Mark this last week. How much he'd needed him.

They ate. He took the plunge: "So how have you been? Really?"

Mark kept his eyes on his plate. "It's like some weird nightmare. And I can't wake up."

"Yeah? Me too! I was beginning to think I was going mad."

"You're not mad. You're just bad and dangerous to know." Bit of a low blow, mate. "Sorry, William. That was a stupid thing to say."

"True, though."

"No. We didn't do anything wrong. It was an accident. Look, William. It was an accident. If anyone *is* to blame, it's Robbie. He was driv -"

Will brought his fist down on the table. "Don't say that! Just don't, all right?"

Mark put up his hands. "Ok, ok."

"We left him there, Mark. We left him in that water." The old ladies were looking. He dropped his voice. "Why did we do that? Why did we leave him? We could've gone back for him. There was time. Well, wasn't there?" He grasped Mark's arm. Shook it. "Wasn't there?"

Mark pulled away. It was his idea to go to that pub. He'd been the only one of them sober enough to realise Robbie was too drunk to drive. He should have taken the keys from him. He could have driven them home himself. He didn't have a driving licence, but he'd had a few lessons for his seventeenth birthday. If only he had taken the keys …

William was waiting for an answer.

"No. There was no time. At least, I didn't think there was. All I could think of was getting you out. Get you safe. I didn't have a plan after that. I'm sorry." William was staring at him. "All I remember thinking is 'I've got to get the door open'. When it was, I got the fuck out of it. But then I remembered you. So I went back down. Grabbed hold of you. I don't remember pulling you out. I think you got out by yourself. Then we had to get out of the water. We were going to freeze. That's all I remember. I didn't even think about Robbie. Just me. And you."

He watched William stir his tea.

"It's weird trying to remember it all, in't it? It's kind of like a dream. Like it didn't really happen.

43

Except it must have. Otherwise Robbie'd be sitting here with us right -" William swallowed. "He'd be with us now. Laughing about it, probably."

He doubted that. He couldn't see Robbie sipping tea in the Botanical Gardens. He reached for a silver tray. "Here. Eat."

"Cheers." William munched, staring into the middle distance. Not much wrong with his appetite. "It's funny though, because the thing I do remember is Robbie. I didn't forget him. I pushed him out of the way to get out. Did you know that? I squeezed right past him. I kicked him when I was getting out the door. I felt it. I think I kicked him in the head. It felt like it. So I could have helped him."

"How?" Mark said. "How could you? Do you remember what it was like in there? We were under the water, for fuck's sake. It was black. Freezing. We were drowning. We almost died."

"Yeah, I know. It's just -"

"Just *what*?"

"I'm here instead of him, aren't I? You could have got either one of us out, but you chose me."

"It wasn't like that, ok? I didn't think. I didn't choose. I just went for you. It's not your fault." William frowned. "Look, I'm sorry, William. I'm sorry I saved your life. Please forgive me." He lunged across the table. The china tinkled. He grabbed William's hand. "Forgive me!"

"You're a right plonker, Strachan." Will pulled his hand away. He couldn't smile. He suddenly felt very afraid for Mark. Why did he always have to mock? This thing was too big for that. It was like he couldn't feel it as he should. Surely that wasn't healthy?

They fell silent. Tucked into the remains of the tea. When they'd done, he wiped his mouth and said: "I owe you. Big time. I won't forget it."

"Nay, lad. Don't be soft." Was that supposed to be Bolton? More like South African.

"I mean it, Mark. Now pay up, you tight bastard."

The funeral was held a week later. Will and Mark spent the intervening time together. Will's parents upgraded his room to a twin and invited Mark to be their guest. He accepted gratefully. He didn't want to be alone anymore. He found he enjoyed this brief bask in reflected familial love. The week passed quickly. They were kept busy. All five of Will's brothers visited, with various wives and kids in tow. Mark rose to the challenge of remembering all the names. That was exhausting, but not as bad as the final interviews with the police. Robbie's parents wanted to meet with them. They couldn't face it. Not yet, Will said. Not ever, Mark thought. The Coopers stepped in and met them instead.

They took a taxi, just the two of them, to the crematorium. Arrived late to avoid bumping into the parents. Mark asked the driver to pull over at the gates. They waited until the coffin was taken in, then attached themselves to the back of the large crowd of mourners. They were the last to file into the chapel. They stood by the door. William shifted his weight awkwardly on his crutches. His mum waved to them. She'd saved seats. Mark smiled thanks and shook his head. A man stood up from the back pew. It was DS Nicholson.

"All right, lads? William, take a pew."

He obeyed. Nicholson took his place standing beside Mark.

"Thought you'd finished with us," Mark said, under the cover of the recorded organ music. He didn't turn to look at him.

"Paying my respects, if that's ok with you?"

He shrugged. "Free country."

Frustration. Suspicion. That's what this kid roused in Nicholson. But he had to look at the facts. The lads had done nothing more than get pissed too far from home. Who hadn't done that at some time or other? There but for the grace of God, and all that. Besides, the Cooper boy insisted Strachan had got himself free of the car, and had then gone back in for his mate. That took guts. There were no two ways about it. There was no prosecution to be had here. Accidental death would be the most likely outcome at the inquest.

The vicar stepped up to the lectern. Nicholson glanced from one boy to the other. He could see only Cooper's back from where he stood, but that told the full story. Hunched forward. Shoulders sagging. Head down. He appeared to have lost weight even since last week. Strachan, however, looked calm and detached, as he had during questioning. It beggared belief he was only eighteen. Standing straight and tall, taller than Nicholson, he gazed steadily ahead, at the vicar. Or maybe at the coffin in the alcove. As the inevitable sobbing began, there was not a trace of emotion in his young face. He might as well have been carved of marble. Placed on a plinth above the rest of the mourners. He shivered. Christ, this boy could be capable of anything.

Eleven Years Before
Chapter 5

"It sounds like a whole load of bullshit to me." Mark bent over his desk. He was studying Megarry's 'Real Property, Real People' for his Land Law module.

"Listen." Will sat on the bed. He flicked ash from his cigarette into the coffee mug at his feet. "They've done it a few times now and the same thing's happened."

Mark scribbled a note.

"Are you listening, or what?"

"I'm working."

"They're shitting it. They're going to do it again tonight, and they want us to go round. So what d'you think? Mark!"

"What, for Chrissake? Can't you see I'm trying to work?"

"And I'm trying to talk to you, so just bloody listen, will you?" He reached across to the other bed and hurled Mark's own pillow at him.

"Desist, Arsehole." Mark turned his chair away from the desk and put his booted feet up on the end of Will's bed. "Don't the English Department give you *any* work? Come on, then. I'm all ears." He stretched and put his hands behind his head.

"They're doing the Ouija board again tonight. D'you want to go along?"

"No."

"Why not?"

"Because it's bollocks."

"Yeah, but it'll be a laugh."

"Watching Little and Large next door crapping their pants over a board game is not my idea of a good night out, my friend."

"Well, I'm going."

"You do that."

Will took long sucking drags on his cigarette. Mark watched him.

After a while, Mark tipped his chair onto its back legs, bracing his feet precariously on the bed. "Did you know it's a little known fact that eight of ten people who use a Ouija board actually make contact with Henry the Eighth?"

Will laughed. He swallowed some smoke, and started coughing.

"True, my friend. Busy fellow, old Henry."

Will grinned through teary eyes.

Mark righted his chair. "So what exactly happened?"

"Well. They were -"

"Who's 'they'?"

"Luca and Greg. James and Peter were there, too. Anyway, they were -"

"Where did all this happen?"

"Don't you ever listen? Next door, in Luc and Greg's."

"Ok. Gotcha. Do carry on."

"Gee thanks. Anyway, they were doing the Ouija thing and -"

"What with?"

"What d'you mean 'what with'?"

"What were they using?"

"I just pigging told you. A Ouija board."

"Yes, but was it a real Ouija board, or did they make their own?"

"Christ, *I* don't know! Does it matter? Look, do you want to hear this story or not?

"Yes, and yes."

"Don't be a twat, Strachan. One minute you're ridiculing the whole thing and the next you're saying it really matters what kind of pigging board they use? Make your sodding mind up."

"Your point is eloquently made, as ever."

Will reached for his cigarette packet. "D'you want to hear this, or not?"

"Go on. I'll stick the kettle on." He went over to the sink.

"It was really creepy, Pete said. And the weird thing was, he said, it felt dead cold in there."

"It's been snowing." Mark flicked a dripping teabag into the bin.

"Well, yeah, I know. I thought that, too. But even so…"

Mark passed him a huge mug of dark brown tea. His own smaller, cleaner-looking mug contained a much paler drink. He sat down opposite Will and swigged his tea. "Carry on."

"You know all this shit they keep going on about? About Led Zep and 'Stairway to Heaven'-"

"Oh, dear God! Please spare me. Not all that crap about subliminal messages again."

"It wasn't 'Stairway to Heaven' this time, it was - well, I suppose it was sort of 'Stairway to Heaven' -"

"Get on with it."

"I'm not saying this actually happened, right? I'm just saying this is what they told me."

"Ok. Roger that." Mark saluted.

"So. You know how on 'Led Zep Four' they've got those symbols on the inside cover?"

"No."

"Yeah, you do. Those symbols for each member of the band? I'll show you."

"Please don't. Get on with it, before I lose the will to live."

"So you know those symbols?" Mark nodded. "The only one that represents a word is Jimmy Page's symbol, right? 'Zofo'?"

"If you say so."

"It is. And last night, that's what the board spelled out - sort of."

Mark guffawed into his mug, spraying tea everywhere.

"It beats Henry the Eighth, I suppose. And Jimmy Page isn't even dead. What do you mean 'sort of'?"

"It actually spelled out the letters M-O-F-O."

"So, not Jimmy Page at all, then. Must have been some other motherfucker."

Mark rolled on his side, laughing uncontrollably.

They knocked on next door at around ten that evening. Mark heard scrabbling, whispering and the flick of a light switch from inside. The door opened slowly, apparently of its own volition.

"Enter, all those who dare!" Luca's voice boomed.

"Twat," Mark said. The room was dark. He walked straight into the little coffee table, striking his shin.

"Ah! Shit! What the hell's that doing there?"

"Oops. You all right, my friend?" Like he cared. "That's vital apparatus."

"Let's put the light back on for a bit." Greg sounded nervous. The room flooded with stark light from the overhead bulb. Mark noted Greg's look of relief.

"Where d'you want these?" William held up the cans of lager.

"Nice one. Stick them in the sink with the others."

Mark looked around the unfamiliar room. Page 3 posters. So predictable. He flopped onto an unmade bed. Shoved aside a pile of textbooks which looked like they'd been tipped out of the filthy wet rucksack that lay on top of them. The room smelled of damp clothes and baked beans. This was going to be a long night.

"Who else is coming? Or is this it?" William had sat in a chair by the window.

"Not sure," Luca said. "James and Pete said they might come along. But I think last time shat them up good and proper. I don't think they'll show."

William drummed his hands on his thighs. He gawked at the girlie posters. Greg kept glancing towards the window, as if he expected the others to arrive that way.

Maybe he could have some fun tonight after all. "It feels really cold in here. Is your radiator broken? Our room's much warmer than this, isn't it, William?"

"Mm?" He dragged his attention away from the girls. "Oh, yeah. Yes, it is." He wrapped his arms around his chest. Good man.

"I told you, Luca. We shouldn't be doing this. We don't know what we're messing with." Greg, small and sparrow-ish at the best of times, was pale. He peered about like he was afraid something might creep up behind him. Yes, this could be quite entertaining.

"What's the drill? How do we do this?" William said.

51

"This is the board." Luca indicated the shiny formica coffee table on which Mark had barked his shin. He grabbed a pack of playing cards from the desk. Mark looked at William. He grinned back. "It's basic, but it's got all the essentials. I've read up on it. And we use this glass." Luca picked up a thick stubby tumbler. He laid out the cards face down around the edge of the table. Written on the back of each was a different letter of the alphabet. The cards placed at twelve and six o'clock were marked 'Yes' and 'No'.

"That's very nice, Lech. Did *you* make those?"

"Laugh all you like, Strachan. We know it works. You can piss off if you're not going to take it seriously."

"Tell us again about last time," William said.

"It was scary, wasn't it, Luc? The temperature just dropped. Much colder than it is now. The glass kept moving round the centre of the table, and it shot off a couple of times." Really? "But nothing much happened until Pete screamed."

Of course he did. "How come *we* didn't hear him?"

"Well, maybe not screamed. It was more of a yelp. He said someone touched his shoulder. And he heard whispering. That's what he said. And then all the candles blew out."

"Cool!" William was leaning forward in his chair. He shivered. "Jesus, it *is* cold in here."

"Try closing the window."

"It's not open, dickhead." Luca pulled the curtains wide.

"Close them." Greg said this in a breathy whisper. Mark placed his back more squarely against the chill wall. The exposed, dark glass reflected the brightly-lit room. Their four faces stared back at them. What if a pair of uninvited eyes peered back too? Luca yanked the curtains closed. Mark looked around at the others. His ears tingled with tension. He waited to hear tapping, or worse, scraping at the glass.

The moment passed. Greg resumed his story. "So the candles went out. Then you put the light on, didn't you?" He glanced at Luca. "But this is the really scary thing. Pete swears when the light came on he saw something."

"What?"

"Did you?"

They spoke simultaneously.

"No, I didn't see anything. You didn't either, did you Luc? But afterwards James said he might've."

"So, what was it?" Greg's eyes strayed to the window. "Come on, for Chrissake! Just tell us."

"He said it was kind of misty and red. But it looked like the face of an old man. An evil old man. In the window."

William let out a squeak. Not cool. He jumped up from his seat by the window. He came and sat next to him on the bed. He pressed his back against the wall. Mark ruffled his hair. "You stick with your Uncle Mark, lad. I'll look after you."

William turned to Greg and Luca. "Do you believe him? What about you, Luc? Wasn't he winding you up?"

Luca's broad shoulders slumped. "Possibly. But you should have seen him, Will. I mean he was terrified. Crying and everything. And he hasn't come back tonight, has he?"

Greg stood up. Shifted from foot to foot, like an institutionalized chimpanzee. "I don't think we should be doing this." His voice was high and tight. "We're messing with stuff we don't understand. What if - what if -" He rubbed his face. He was sweating. Didn't he say he was cold? "D'you believe in the Devil?"

"Oh, give me a break. Come on. If we're going to do this, let's get on with it. Lech?"

Luca pulled the coffee table into the space between the beds. He placed the tumbler upside down at its centre. From the shelf over the sink he retrieved a handful of tealights. He arranged them at each corner of the table.

"Matches," he said, like a surgeon demanding a scalpel. He held out his hand to William. He obeyed, mute and attentive as any theatre nurse. Luca lit the candles. "Lights." Greg flicked the switch. They plunged into semi-darkness. The feeble flickering candlelight lent their faces a halloween glow. "Now we sit."

The Pole was loving this starring role. He lowered himself gracefully to the floor to sit cross-legged at the table. Like a big blond buddha. They all followed his example. Mark sat with his back to the door. William and Greg squeezed in opposite each other between the table and the beds.

"Now we hold hands."

"Why?"

"Shut it, Mark," William was getting into it.

"To generate the energies. To create an inviting atmosphere. To raise the spirits!"

Luca flung back his head. For a moment he sounded exactly like Margaret Rutherford in those black and white films Mrs P used to make him watch with her during the school holidays. His laughter subsided when he looked at the others. They stared at Luca in wide-eyed horror. He was jiggling about like he was loosening up before a drama class. His head had fallen forward. It lolled from side to side. For crying out

54

loud.   After a while, he came out of his 'trance' and said: "Hold hands."

Greg's palm was wet with sweat. There were better ways to spend a Saturday night. Luca withdrew his hands.

"Now we begin." He placed a forefinger on the upturned base of the glass. They copied him. "Do not apply pressure. Do not direct the glass. The glass will direct you. Now we address the spirits. Is there anybody there?"

He fought down laughter again.

They sat, their fingers resting on the glass. Nothing happened. Until William gasped. The glass vibrated. It started to move toward William. Slowly. Jerkily. He didn't resist the pressure from Lech. Otherwise he'd know he was on to him. He wanted to see what would happen. This was fun. The glass juddered across the board to the letter D, then slid swiftly back to the centre. It moved again, but this time it slid across the board much faster toward Mark. It targeted the O, then back to the centre. It moved again under his finger. He couldn't actually tell who was pushing it. It must be Lech. He began to feel a grudging respect for him. No wonder he'd shat them up. The glass set off again. It sped to each letter, then back to the centre before seeking out the next one. Finally it came to rest. It had spelled: D-O-U-B-T-E-R.

He looked at Lech. He was glaring back at him. He looked slightly unhinged. The glass flew from under their fingers. Mark didn't have time to move. It hit him full in the chest.

"Ow!" He clutched the spot where it struck. "Bastard! What was that for?"

Luca didn't react. Just stared at him with demonic eyes. William picked up the glass. It hadn't broken. "Are you ok?"

"No, I'm not ok! Twat!" It bloody hurt. He stood up. He kicked the table leg. The cards shifted.

"You'll break the energies." Greg sounded like a girl.

"Fuck the energies! And fuck you, Lech, and your pissing little game!"

"Come on, Mark. Don't you want to see what happens? Sit down." William patted the carpet.

"Try that again, Lech." Now the bastard wouldn't meet his eye.

"Come on, mate. Sit down?"

"It's bollocks." But he did want to see what would happen. He sat and placed his finger on the glass again along with the others. Luca looked up to the ceiling. He said in that melodramatic voice: "Spirit! Who are you?"

The glass started to move again. He must have been practicing for ages to be able to do this without even looking. What a sad bastard. Quickly - barely allowing time for thought? - it spelled out: M-O-F-O

Greg snatched his hand away. He cradled it to his chest. "I don't like this. Let's not carry on. Let's stop now."

The candles went out in a single puff. Mark was looking at Greg, so he didn't see Luca blow them out. But he must have. Out of the darkness, William's voice quavered: "Mark? Was that you? That's not funny."

"What?"

"Breathing on my neck."

The hairs on the back of Mark's neck stood up. He heard the table go over. The overhead light came on. He blinked. Greg cowered on the bed by the switch.

The table had tipped on William. The cards, glass and tealights were in his lap. Luca remained absolutely still. He fixed Mark with a look he really didn't like. Then he blinked. He shook his head like he was just waking up.

"Who switched the light on?"

"Me. Sorry. It was too much."

"You shouldn't have done that, Greg" The séance voice again. Luca turned that bright hate-filled look on the poor kid. "We didn't dismiss the spirit. We didn't send him back." He paused. "He may still be here."

Greg gasped. He flopped on the bed. He drew his knees up to his chin and covered his ears. He screwed his eyes tight shut, like a small child. "Stop it, Luca. Please don't." He was crying now.

Damn. He'd let this go too far. Greg - and William, too - had fallen for Luca's game completely. He should have seen it earlier. Who knew what damage this kind of crap could do to William? He wasn't over the accident. He often woke crying in the night. He'd lost count of the times they'd stayed awake into the small hours. Going over what happened. Talking about Robbie. Shit. Luca's little performance wasn't going to help at all.

He righted the table. "Ok, boys and girls. The show's over for tonight. Who fancies a beer?"

William looked at him as if he'd gone mad. "A beer?"

Enough was enough. Mark stood up.

"Don't go. Don't leave me. I can't stay here. Not if - not if - *he* might still be here." Tears and snot smeared Greg's face. His scrawny neck looked invitingly snappable. "Please stay. We've got to do it again. We've got to get rid of him."

"God give me strength!"

William sat next to Greg. "Come on, Mark. Let's try it again. He'll never sleep if we don't finish it."

"Christ, William. You do know it's not real?"

The door flew open. It knocked Mark into the table. Barked his other shin. James and Peter barged in behind him. "Have we missed anything good?"

This time James sat in Mark's place. Mark stood behind Luca. He had to stay, to look out for William. Besides, he wanted to know how Luca was fooling them. Peter didn't seem too keen to get involved. He sat hunched in the corner on a bed. He didn't take his eyes off the Ouija board.

"Is there anybody there?"

"How long do we wait?" James asked.

"As long as the spirits need."

There was Margaret Rutherford again. How could they take this seriously? He laughed. William frowned at him. He zipped his mouth shut. There was silence. For ages. He wandered away. Gazed at the poster girls.

He was miles away when William shouted. Over Luca's shoulder, he saw the glass speeding to and fro again. William's mouth gaped. His eyes seemed to bulge. But, still, he had his finger on the glass. From the centre, it slid toward Luca: B. Then back to the centre with hardly a pause before it swept to B again. No. Not even the Polish Twat would do that. But he saw from William's stricken face the previous two letters had been R and O. In the flickering candlelight, the glass continued on its way. Heading for the I.

"You fucking shit." He grabbed Luca from behind. Pulled him to his feet. He span him round. Drove a fist into his belly. He doubled over. Mark brought a knee up to his face. Hard. He grunted. Dropped to the floor. Mark stepped back to get a better kick in. Everyone was shouting. He heard himself roar: "You fucking bastard. I'll kill you."

He swung at Luca's crumpled body with his steel toe boot. James pushed him. Caught him off balance. He fell back. Hit his head on the radiator. Dazed. He tried to get up. He heard Luca rasping for air. He heard his own heart drumming madly. He heard another sound. It drained all the fight out of him.

"Ok. I'm done." He held up his hands. James stood over him, waiting for his next move. He grabbed the radiator and pulled himself up. His face felt wet. He dabbed his nose. It was bleeding. Who hit him? He pulled his shirt straight. "I don't want to fight. I need to get William out of here."

They moved aside for him. William was making an awful keening noise. Rocking back and forth.

"He's ok, isn't he?" Greg stepped forward.

Mark shoved him back. "Get away from him." He helped William to his feet.

James lifted the coffee table out of their path and held the door open. "Should we call the doctor?"

"Leave us alone." His throat was dry and sore. He could hardly get the words out.

They staggered to their room. He slammed the door in James' face with a backward kick. He helped William onto his bed. The frightening moans turned to sobs. Stifled gagging sobs. Not an improvement. He knelt on the floor beside him. Stroked his hair.

"You've got to stop this. Now. You can't keep blaming yourself. You can't let those wankers get to you. They weren't there. What do they know? They don't have a fucking clue. You've got to stop. D'you hear me? Stop this. Stop it!" His stroking hand turned into a fist. He clutched a handful of hair. William stopped crying. He let go. "Sorry. Shit. Sorry, William.

Are you all right? I didn't mean…" He stood up. "Try to sleep, yeah? I'll… I'll stand guard." He sat on his own bed. Afraid.

He'd dozed off. His cheek was on the pillow, wet with dribble. William was still crying. He must be exhausted. Someone was knocking on the door. Wide awake now, he reached up and turned the lock just as they tried the handle.

"Mark! Let me in." James rattled the handle. "How is he? Everything's ok. Luca's fine." Luca? "He's not hurt. You're not in any trouble." A pause. "We're worried about Will. Is he all right?" Whispering. "Mark, listen mate. We had no idea he was going to do that. Luca, I mean. It was meant to be a laugh. He went too far. We're sorry, ok? Mark? Come on. Let us in, will you?"

"Fuck off, James." He felt calmer now.

He heard them walk away.

William's sobs subsided. He lay on his side. His eyes were haggard.

"How you doing? D'you want anything? Water? Or a drink? I've still got some of that tequila -"

William grabbed his hand. "Don't leave me."

"Ok. I'll stay right here." He knelt beside him. Stroked his hair again. Felt that tensing up before William could hide it. "You know none of that shit was real, don't you? It was fucking Lech Walensa in there, winding us up. You know that, don't you? Come on, William. Talk to me. Please."

William closed his eyes. His grip on Mark's hand relaxed. He seemed to have fallen asleep. But then he opened his eyes. He said: "I know. They were arsing us about. But it doesn't matter that it wasn't real. It's real in my head. It's going on in my head all the time. All

60

the sodding time. He *is* haunting me. In here." He punched the side of his head before Mark could grab his wrist.

"Hey, don't do that."

"He's driving me mad. Look at me. I'm turning into a pigging nutter." He flung himself onto his back. Covered his eyes with his arm. "How do you cope like you do, Mark? How do you… get on with life?"

Good question. "It's hard. You've got to make yourself stop thinking about him. Stop going over it. It's finished. We can't change it. It happened. And we can't change it." William shook his head. He started crying again, but he had to go on: "It's not fucking fair it happened. Not fair on Robbie. Not fair on us. We didn't deserve it. But we can't let it ruin our lives. It's bad enough Rob died." William covered his ears. "But he did die." He put a hand on his shoulder. "He died, William. We can't change that. We couldn't save him then. We can't save him now. Going over and over it isn't going to bring him back. It's just going to kill you too, in the end. Don't you see that?" He squeezed his shoulder. "William?"

William cried for a long time. Finally he turned to him. His face was red and wet. "It's like it's happening all the time. In my head it never stops. I feel like I never got out of that car. I'm still in there." He paused. "God, I need help, don't I?"

"You need to tell someone how you're feeling. Someone who'll know what to do."

"Who?"

"Dunno. Doctor, maybe? Talk to your mum and dad?"

William nodded. He sat up. Wiped his eyes on his sleeve. "I've made a right dick of myself, haven't I?"

"No more than usual."

He smiled. "What time is it?"

He looked at his watch. "God, it's four o'clock." He reached up and flicked off the light. "It's starting to get light, see."

"Is it too early for an aperitif?"

He laughed. "Tequila?"

William began to get better. He went home to talk things through with his parents. They wanted him to give up university. Move back home. But their GP recommended a counsellor in Sheffield, so they reconsidered. She was old and lived in Beauchief. Bit school ma'amish, according to William. But she specialised in dealing with the effects of sudden trauma, and his mum liked her. So it was arranged that he would visit her weekly. For two months initially. After that, they would review the situation.

His mum and dad came to check out the counsellor and satisfy themselves William was going to be all right on his own.

Judith took Mark on one side. "I wanted to thank you, love."

"What for?"

"For being Will's friend. He's told us how you've been supporting him. And the Warden had a lot of good things to say about you too." Really? "But I don't want you to feel responsible for Will. You've got enough on your own plate. This all happened to you too. We've not forgotten that. So, if there are any problems, if you get worried for any reason - *any* reason," she repeated when he tried to interrupt, "give us a call. We'll be right over."

"Ok. I will."

"Good." She had the same green eyes as William. "There's one more thing, Mark. I want you to

62

know if ever *you* need anything - or anyone - Bill and I - just you give us a shout, sweetheart." She reached up, kissed him on one cheek and patted the other. She laughed. "You're such a handsome young man. You shouldn't gawp like that."

Was this what it felt like to be loved?

Ten Years Before
Chapter 6

Will shoved an extra jumper into his rucksack. More than eighteen months on, he still thought of Robbie every day. Dreamed about him sometimes. It embarrassed him. They'd gone through hell back then, but he could have handled it better. He wished he could have been more like Mark. Taken it in his stride. Mark was right. Mithering about it wouldn't bring him back. He closed the flap and tightened the straps.

October was not a good month to go camping. It was idiotic. But this would be their last chance before spring. And they had to camp. It was a matter of pride now. After all Mark's bragging about his prowess in the great outdoors, they couldn't back down. Olivia was holding Mark to his promise.

They'd met Olivia and Eloise Brooke during the summer. When they were out celebrating their twentieth birthday. Identical twins, with golden eyes and copper hair. He was amazed he'd never noticed them before. Turned out they'd never been in the student union bar before. They were on an adventure. Roughing it. They were posh girls. But northern so that was ok. Mark couldn't believe his luck. Kept hinting, to anyone who'd listen, at four-in-a-bed sex romps. Will was usually around to put people straight. So far the lies hadn't got back to the girls, so there was no harm in it. As long as Olivia didn't find out.

It turned out Eloise and Olivia were Girl Guides in their teens. Did all the badges. Mark wanted to impress them. It was Olivia who challenged him to go camping.

"Only if you agree to sit back and let us men do all the work," Mark said.

Will had spluttered into his beer. As far as he knew, Mark had never been camping in his life.

"I think we could live with that, don't you, Lou?"

"Course! Sounds lovely. Nothing to do all day but sunbathe? When do we go?"

The summer was over before Olivia's digs finally nettled Mark into organising a trip. He'd got Will to borrow the tents and equipment. He let Will plan where they'd camp. Typical.

Today was the day. They set off to the bus stop.

"What if the weather does turn?" Olivia said. "It's forecast snow later in the week."

Will laughed. "It'll not snow. It's only October."

"You clearly don't know Yorkshire." The girls came from a landowning family with a big house near Whitby.

"We're only going to be fifteen minutes bus ride away. What can go wrong?"

Olivia shifted the bag of food to her other hand. She pushed her copious curly hair out of her face. He loved it when she did that. "I can't possibly imagine. You're sweet, Will, but you're not the most practical person I've ever met."

They got off the bus at the Fox House Inn. The countryside here was beautiful in a bleak sort of way. It was a grey day. Burbage Moor extended out beyond the pub. The invasive bracken was well into its autumn shades. Just down the road, the landscape would change dramatically as the Derbyshire hills showed themselves in all their glory. The boys adjusted their heavy packs. They set off to pick up the footpath to Burbage Rocks.

"Here we go," he called. "Follow me, campers!"

"What a wanker! D'you see what I have to put up with?"

"I heard that, Strachan." He clambered over a stile in the dry stone wall.

They'd been up here together during the summer for Sunday walks. Eloise knew the area from her geography field trips. At weekends it was busy with walkers and rock climbers. Today, Tuesday, it was quiet. Maybe everyone else had taken the weather forecast seriously. He felt a little anxious as he headed to the base of the cliff. It was an easy, short walk from the road. Only one scramble up a steep stretch. The ground immediately beneath the cliff was smooth and even. He relaxed. It looked ideal.

"We'll camp here." He slipped off his rucksack. "Why don't you girls go and collect some firewood while we pitch the tents?"

"But you said you'd brought a primus stove," Olivia said.

"We have, but we want a campfire, don't we?"

"Of course we do. Come on, Livvy. We can play Secret Island." Eloise bounded off down the way they'd come, limbs flying like a colt's.

"Wait for me." Olivia plodded after her, arms folded.

"They really are chalk and cheese." Mark watched them go. "I bet Olivia's quite a handful though, isn't she?"

"Give over." He'd warned him off this subject before.

"All that crazy hair. It's positively pre-Raphaelite. And it smells gorgeous."

"I mean it, Mark." He flushed, angered and flattered in equal measure.

"Don't worry, my friend. She's way too gobby for me. Not my type at all. I like to be the boss with my women."

"Sign of insecurity that, mate. Classic." He tipped the contents of his rucksack onto the ground.

"And she never wears make up. Have you noticed? Funny that. Still, I bet she's... you know... isn't she? Just like her sister."

"Leave it out, Mark."

"You're no fun, you know that? Come on, let's get cracking." He tipped out the other rucksack and rummaged through the contents.

He hadn't helped with the packing, so what was he looking for? Time to intervene. "We'll put Richie's tent up first. That's this one."

"Ok." Mark already had the poles in a brown plastic bag. "Where's the fly sheet for it?"

They scanned the equipment. Mark laughed.

"Eh, it's not funny. Where is it?" He moved a few items about pointlessly. There was no fly sheet. "Bugger."

"Don't look at me. You packed it, my friend."

"Shut up." Think. "Could we all fit in the other one?" Mark looked doubtful. "Only it looks like it might rain. Whoever's in this one'll get soaked without the fly sheet."

Mark laughed again. "Olivia's going to go ballistic."

"Shit." She was. He looked at his watch. "It's nearly three already. It'll be dark soon. We'd better get a move on. What d'you say we put them both up and see how we go on?"

"Ok, Kimusabi."

67

"Maybe if Richie's tent is too cold, we could sleep in it and let the girls share the other one?"

"Not really what I had in mind. But needs must, I suppose."

They were putting the finishing touches to the second tent, when the girls came back with armfuls of twigs.

"Will these do?" Eloise was clearly pleased with her foraging effort.

Mark kissed her. "Clever girl." He relieved her of her load.

"What the hell's that?" Olivia said.

Mark smiled. "A tent?"

"You can see through it. I'm not sleeping in that."

"No, it's all right. We've got it sorted." Will fiddled with a guy rope. Mark laughed. He pressed on. "You two can have this one." He pointed to the blue tent. It was small but intact. "Me and Mark'll sleep in the other one." Olivia opened her mouth. He clapped his hands. "Let's get that fire lit."

They set about making camp. The girls arranged sleeping bags and blankets in the tents. He and Mark made idiots of themselves trying to keep their tiny twig fire alight. It was getting dark when Eloise said: "Oh! What about water?"

He'd borrowed a roll-up water bag from Richie. He hadn't thought about where the water would come from.

"The pub." Mark said. "We'll go to the Fox House for a drink and fill the water carrier in the bogs before we come back. In fact, let's eat there, too. It's getting bloody cold out here. Come on. Put that fire out, William. Eloise, grab that big torch. Where's the water carrier? Ah, here it is. Right, let's get going." He strode off down the slope towards the road.

"Hang on a minute," Olivia called after him. "Are we just going to leave all our stuff here?"

Mark walked on. Eloise ran to catch up with him, torch in hand. She pinched his bottom when she reached him. Mark grabbed her round the shoulder and pulled her to him in a playful tussle, not breaking his stride. They disappeared into the gloom. Only Eloise's shimmering hair stood out in the twilight.

"Come on, Livvy. The stuff'll be ok. There's no one around." He was cold and getting hungry. He grabbed her hand and kissed it. They ran together down the slope, laughing and shouting for the others to wait.

It was dark now. They bunched together to walk behind the beam of the single torch.

"We should've brought the other torch as well," Olivia said.

"Lighten up, love, for Chrissake," Mark said.

Mark knew she hated being called 'love'. She didn't reply. They walked in single file along the road. They were all in dark clothes. Without street lights, they'd be barely visible.

The pub was bright and warm. They were the only customers. They ate, and knocked back a couple of drinks each. After the meal they moved into the snug. There was a big log fire blazing.

"I could stay here all night." Eloise drew up her feet onto the seat and snuggled up to Mark. He put his arm around her, a big smug grin on his face. He clearly wasn't going to move.

"I'll get them in then, shall I? Same again?" It wasn't Will's round.

"We mustn't forget the water," Olivia said.

When he came back with the drinks, Mark said: "You know what, William? This place reminds me of the Furnace Inn. What d'you reckon?"

They'd never discussed that night with anyone else. What was he playing at? "I suppose so." He looked around for a change of subject.

But Mark wasn't finished. "We should go out there again some time."

"Why?"

He'd never go back there, and Mark knew it. Why was he even talking about it? Olivia caught his eye. She understood. She asked Eloise about the geography of the area. Eloise, as usual, was oblivious to the sudden tension. She warmed to her subject. She tucked her sleek bobbed hair behind her ears and leaned forward a little. Mark smiled like an indulgent father. He seemed to have forgotten the Furnace Inn. Eloise went on about the rock formations at Higger Tor across the valley and about the flora of the moor. "Did you know the reason there is so much public access in the valley is because it belongs to Sheffield council?" She looked around at them. "Yes, that's right. Not the Peak District National Park, as most people think. They were going to flood the valley and make a reservoir, but they never got round to it."

He watched Mark. What had brought on that outburst? Mark winked at him. Christ, he could be a right tosser, at times. He was winding him up. He was so bloody thick-skinned when it suited him. Well, he wouldn't rise to the bait. He put his arm around Olivia's waist. Pushed his hand under her sweater so he could feel the soft warm skin of her belly. He sat back to listen to Lou's lecture. He was glad Olivia was studying Philosophy.

A couple more drinks later, Olivia sat up and stretched. " I'm a bit tipsy, boys. We'd better make a move, hadn't we? I'll nip to the loo."

Eloise stretched too, reminding him of his cat, Bowie, back home. "Wait for me." She stood up and bumped into a stool. "Oops! We should've brought our toothbrushes."

"Well, if his lordship hadn't been in such a hurry…" Liv stuck out her tongue at Mark. He blew her a kiss.

"See, I knew you two loved each other, really." He settled back in his seat, warmed by a surge of tenderness and goodwill.

Mark laughed. "I'll go fill that water bag. Then we'd better go out the side door in case they don't like it."

Stepping out onto the car park, they pulled up short.

"Pigging hell."

A thick blanket of fog had descended, so dense they couldn't make out the road. And the temperature had dropped. This wasn't in the weather forecast. Eloise flicked on the torch, but its beam evaporated, reflected by millions of tiny water droplets.

"Wow."

"Shit." The cold air must have sobered Olivia. "How are we going to get back to the tents in this?"

"Carefully. Very carefully," Mark said. "Give me the torch, Eloise, and hold my hand. William, you take the water. Stay in single file. I'll lead the way. Ready campers? Let's go!"

He seemed sober, but Will caught the slight slur in his words. This was all a big game to him, a laugh, but the fog had cleared Will's head enough to know they could be in real danger walking back along the road.

"Mark, I'll take the lead, ok? Then the girls, then you bring up the rear. All right, mate?"

"If it please you, my friend."

Olivia tutted.

"You know this isn't fog. Technically, it's low cloud."

"Shut up, Lou. Not now." Olivia sounded scared.

They made their way along the road, Will holding the torch high. It was worse than useless. It couldn't penetrate and made the fog ahead seem even thicker as its beam bounced back at them. But he hoped any oncoming vehicles might see the light and steer clear of them. They reached the stile without encountering a car, but their problems were only just beginning. He took the lead, this time pointing the torch at his feet. They walked, enveloped in fog-muffled silence, for several minutes until Mark said: "This bag's cutting into my hand. William, will you take it for a bit?"

"Ok." Will waited for him to catch up.

Eloise loomed out of the fog, making him jump. "Guys, I think we've gone the wrong way. This doesn't feel right. The path's too steep."

Mark took her hand. "It's ok, babe. We'll be there soon."

"I'm not sure…"

"Come on. Let's keep going," Olivia said.

They walked on, stumbling over the rough ground, until Eloise protested again. "No. Stop everyone. This really isn't right. We've been walking for ages. We should've reached the camp by now."

Will had carried on walking, but turned now and rejoined the others. "You're right, Lou."

"And the cliff should be on our right, shouldn't it?"

"Yes, but we can't see a thing in this." Olivia said.

"No, I know, but it doesn't *feel* like the cliff's there, does it?" She looked at each of them crowded round the light. "I mean, there's a little breeze for a start, coming off the moor."

"I don't get you," Will said.

"We've taken the wrong path. We've come up on top of the cliff instead of below it."

"Shit," Mark said.

"She's right," Will said. "Which means the cliff must be on our left now. Jesus. We need to be really, really careful because that's about a thirty foot drop."

He was suddenly afraid to move at all.

"Shit."

"You said that already." Olivia's voice had a hard edge.

"Ok. Let's not argue," Will said. "We need to turn back and retrace our steps. Carefully. We'll leave the water carrier here. Mark, you hold Eloise's hand. Lou, you take Liv's hand. And Liv, you hold on to me. We'll take it very slowly, ok? Single file, one step at a time."

It was like playing a strange party game. A mixture of Follow My Leader and Blind Man's Bluff, but in slow motion and with all the tension of What Time Is It Mr Wolf? They walked back the way they'd come, or as near to it as they could in the obscuring fog. Will sucked in the dripping air and coughed. All he could hear were the sounds of his own uneven breathing and the others' hesitant footsteps. The rest was silent. Eerie. Was he really here in the arse end of nowhere, in the middle of the night, lost, drunk, with two girls to look after and in danger of plummeting to his death over an unseen cliff?

He felt a sudden cold updraught. His next step slipped as the friable soil gave way. Loosened gravel

73

and dislodged stones went tumbling over the edge, clattering loudly. He threw himself backwards onto Olivia. She fell under his weight. The clatter of stones resounded as they bounced off rocks far below.

"William!" Mark screamed.

"Stop! Don't move." His voice was shaking. "Fuck. We're right on the edge. I nearly stepped off." He slid off Olivia. "Liv, are you all right?"

"Think so." She didn't sound too sure.

"You ok, William?" Mark shouted again.

"D'you hear that? My teeth are chattering. Almost shat myself."

He scrambled backwards, dragging Olivia with him. He'd nearly gone over. Shit. He'd nearly fallen. "We should all sit down -"

"We can't. Not here." Olivia sounded close to tears.

He forced his voice to be firm. "Here. Where we are. We'll wait for the fog to lift. We can't see where we're walking. There could be gullies or anything. It's too dangerous."

Mark followed his lead. "Eloise, sit down. Exactly where you are. Don't move around."

On the wet ground, they felt for one another's hands, and clung on like they expected to be wrenched apart.

The grass was tussocky and so cold. "We'll have to cuddle up. But be careful. I'm not sure how close we are to the edge."

They moved together cautiously until they sat in a close circle. Will placed the torch, beam up, in the centre. Despite the clawing fog, the muted light caught in the girls' hair. It illuminated the water droplets clinging there, creating spangled halos. Like the print on his bedroom wall of Rossetti's Virgin Mary. Eloise nestled her head into Mark's shoulder and he wrapped his arms around her. Olivia leaned into Will. He hugged her tight. He hooked his free arm under Mark's elbow and pulled him closer. He responded with a reassuring squeeze. "Should we turn the light off? Save the batteries?"

"Yeah." Will reached forward.

In the dark, Olivia said: "I'm so cold. And my bum's wet."

It was Mark who comforted her. "You'll be fine, honestly. It's not long till morning. We've done this before, me and him, and survived. Isn't that right, William? And we were colder and wetter than this, weren't we?"

Will hesitated. "Yeah. You're not kidding."

He knew Olivia was curious about the accident. He supposed she had a right to be, considering how often she was woken by his nightmares. Now she said: "Will you tell us about it? Only if you want to …"

"What d'you reckon, William?"

"It'll pass some time on, I suppose."

So they did tell. Disembodied voices in the dark. They took turns, correcting and encouraging each other, as they had often done. But this time was different. They had an audience. They were finally sharing their story.

At first light, as the rising sun burned away the remaining rags of fog, they found they were sitting just a metre or so away from the cliff edge. They saw their camp, away in the middle distance towards the road.

"God, we came miles out of our way," Eloise said.

"You were right. Clever girl." Mark ran his fingers through her messy damp hair.

Will stood up stiffly. He offered Olivia his hand. "Let's get a move on. I can't wait to get packed up, get home and get a hot bath."

"Amen to that, my friend." Mark hauled Eloise to her feet. "This is the last time I ever go camping."

Nine Years Before
Chapter 7

He hears rustling, grunting in the undergrowth. He feels afraid. Why? He doesn't want to look, but finds himself peering through the bushes. There's Robbie, rummaging - no, *snuffling* - in the long grass. Relief and joy wash through him. Robbie isn't dead. It was all a mistake. Nobody killed him. Everything's going to be all right, because Robbie's safe. Will steps from his hiding place as the phone rings. The sound of it disturbs Robbie. He looks up - Will gasps - he looks right at him from empty sockets, nibbled and raw -

"Will! Phone! You can answer it yourself next time!"

Olivia squirmed to disentangle her arms from around his body. "Who's that? What time is it?"

It was dark. He turned on the light to see the clock. "It's the phone. God, it's only three."

He jumped out of bed. Who would phone at this time?

He slipped into some jeans he found in a heap of clothes on the floor and opened the door softly. He padded along the cold lino. It was bloody freezing. He should have put a jumper on. He picked up the dangling receiver. "Hello? This is William Cooper?"

A brisk female voice responded. "Hello, Mr Cooper. William? This is Hallamshire Hospital. Sorry to disturb you at this late hour."

His brain fizzed. Accident. Mum? Dad? But why would they be in hospital in Sheffield? Then it clicked.

"Mark. Is he all right? What happened? Is he hurt? Can I speak to him?"

"He's going to be ok, but he's in A & E. He's sustained a head injury. Not too bad, but they're keeping him in for observation. He'll be moved to a ward as soon as there's a bed free."

"Ok." Head injury? That sounded serious. "Shall I come, then?"

"Yes, I think that's a good idea. He's been asking for you. He gave your name as next of kin. But you don't need to rush. He'll be all right. And he's not going anywhere."

"Thank you."

"Pleasure, duck." She hung up.

Will ran back to his room.

"Who was it? What's happened, Will?" Olivia knelt on the bed, hair dishevelled, the duvet wrapped around her. How did *he* get to be with a girl that gorgeous? But he had to go. He started searching for clothes to put on. "Will!"

He looked up, startled.

"Sorry, Liv." He sat down next to her. "That was the hospital. Hallamshire. Mark's been in an accident. He's got head injuries. He's asking for me."

"Oh God. What about Lou? What did they say about Lou?"

He turned to her. "They didn't mention her."

"I bet they're trying to phone me at the flat." She leaped up and they both scrambled to drag clothes on.

"Livvy, they didn't mention Eloise at all. She might not even be with him."

"But you said an accident."

78

"Thinking about it, they didn't actually say it was an accident. They just said he had head injuries."

Olivia took the initiative. "I'll phone the flat. See if she's there." She ran out of the room, bare-legged, and came back. "Have you got 10p? Why can't you get a normal phone like normal people? Quick, quick!" She held out her hand and beckoned impatiently. He pulled a handful of change from his jeans pocket. She grabbed the lot and disappeared. He finished getting dressed and laced up his boots. Then she was back, talking fast as she pulled on her jeans and looked about for her shoes. "Lou's ok. She was in bed. They had a row. She left him in the Stonehouse. He said he was going on to the Leadmill." She gave him an accusatory look. "I bet he's been in a fight again. Where the hell are my boots?"

He scooped them out from under the bed. A fight. Yes. Mark had a frightening temper. Especially when he was drinking. Will first noticed it after Robbie died. He needed help. He'd told him so, but he didn't seem to get it. He'd have a reason, a logical explanation, for what had happened tonight - whatever it was. It definitely wouldn't be his fault. Never was.

"Come on, Will. We've got to go. I've called a taxi. It's picking Lou up first. Then it's coming for us. We'd better hurry."

Mark wouldn't see the girls, much to Eloise's distress and Olivia's ire. They stayed in the waiting area, hemmed in by leering Saturday night drunks and brawlers, while Will was shown into the grubby cubicle where Mark was waiting for a bed.

"We must stop meeting like this." His voice was thick and lispy. He attempted a smile, but his swollen mouth made it difficult.

"Yeah."

Mark's face was covered in bruises and cuts. There was bright red blood on the front of his white shirt. More blood, darker, caked about his nose. His right eye was swollen shut. There was a deep gash, freshly stitched, above his eyebrow. His knuckles were swollen and cut. His right hand was bandaged. He'd given as good as he got.

"You're a pigging idiot, Mark."

"Thanks for those few kind words."

"Eloise is outside. She's going to freak when she sees this."

"She's not going to see it. Take her home, will you?"

He picked up the chart from the end of the trolley and examined it. "What've they said? Are you ok? How long will you be in? Christ, Mark. What the hell's the matter with you? How many were there this time?" Mark looked away. "What if they'd had a knife? You're going to get yourself killed if you carry on like this." It was pointless. He was wasting his breath. "Are you moving onto a ward?"

"I think so. When they can find me a bed."

"D'you want me to bring some stuff in for you. Pyjamas? A towel?"

"I guess so. But don't go yet. Stay for a bit? I've been here hours. They gave me a painkiller. Said it would help me sleep. But I can't. It's too noisy. Will you keep me company?"

"What about the girls? Eloise wants to see you."

"They should go home. Get them a taxi, then come back in. Tell them I'll pay for it."

"They won't want you to pay for it, you tosser." He was angry for Eloise. Olivia was right. Mark was no good for her. She didn't deserve to be treated this way.

"Sorry. Look, tell her I'm a mess and I'm embarrassed - which is the truth. Tell her I'll be ok and I'm sorry and I'll see her soon. Will you do that?"

"D'you want anything while I'm out there? A drink or something to eat?"

"I don't think I could." Mark pointed to his mouth. "Anyway, they said not to. In case they need to do anything later."

"Like what?"

"Dunno. I think they're waiting to see if I keel over. You know - comatose."

"It's not funny, Mark." Not when he had to deal with Olivia's wrath.

While he was away, Mark thought about what William had said. He was right. He should do something about his anger before it got him into serious trouble. Thing was, he enjoyed it, fighting. William would never understand that. He wished he could talk to him about it. About how it made him feel. The control. The clean communication of it. There were things he'd never be able to share with him. Like what he did to Luca. William put it all down to the accident. Unresolved grief and guilt or some such crap. Psychobabble bollocks he'd picked up from the old woman he used to see. The rages were nothing to do with the crash. He'd always had them. It was simply that William had got to know him better since Robbie died. Unfortunately for him.

William came back with a Mars Bar, a Kit Kat, a bag of crisps and two coffees balanced in his cupped palm.

"They've gone home," he said, obviously disgruntled.

"You're not going to sit and stuff all that, are you?"

"Want some?"

"No."

"Then, yes." He sat down and unwrapped some chocolate.

Mark laid his head back on the pillow. A drunken row was kicking off not far away. He was tired, and he felt better now William was here. He would keep an eye on him while he tried to sleep. "Mind if I have a kip?"

"Knock yourself out."

William frowned at him over his Mars Bar. He closed his eyes.

Before university he'd lived for Saturdays and Manchester United. The best moment of his life, until he met Eloise, was the first time he laid eyes on the Old Trafford turf. He was fourteen. He loved the Stretford End. But he didn't care where he saw the match from or how he got into the stadium, just as long as he was there. He'd do anything to make sure he was at every home game. His parents never gave him pocket money. He had a paper round right up to leaving for Sheffield. That didn't cover his costs though, so he discovered shoplifting. Selling the stuff - razors and make up, mainly - in the pub before the game was a good earner.

Stretford Enders were notorious as the thugs of British football. They were caged in behind high metal fences. Not the brightest idea, but what did he know? What little violence he'd seen at matches (in the stadium, anyway) had never been in the Stretford End. It was always under the Scoreboard where the opposing fans were corralled. Once, he'd kidded a policeman on the gate he was a colleague's son and was let in the side paddocks for free. Inside, he saw a bloke being led away from the Scoreboard End by St John's Ambulance men. He was walking all right, but he had a dart sticking out of his forehead. It was embedded at least an inch into his skull. It knocked Mark sick. The man didn't appear to know what had happened to him. He chatted away to the ambulance crew while the crowds fell silent on either side as he passed by. His picture was in all the papers the next day.

There were more incidents in the streets outside the ground where the police had less control. One time - it was after they'd lost to Liverpool - he was walking to the train station. Anonymous in the crowd. They'd been held back by the police. Prevented from leaving the ground to give the away fans chance to get clear. He didn't mind. He had no need or desire to get home early. He could wait for the next train, or get the bus. So he didn't know why, when a group of lads broke away from the crowd at a run, he followed. They sped down a passageway, about fifteen of them, shouting and laughing. They came out on the concourse of a car showroom. They ran across the parking lot, but their exit was blocked by a mechanic manoeuvring a Rover into a tight spot.

"Come on! Shift it! Out of the way!"

They were good-natured enough despite a few kicks at the car's tyres and flat hands banged on its roof. Afterwards, he was sure nothing more would have happened if the bloke hadn't wound down the window and shouted: "Leave it out, lads!" in a broad Liverpudlian accent.

The gang's mood switched. The banging and kicking got harder, louder, rhythmic. The men started to chant. He joined in.

"Scouse. Out! Scouse. Out! Scouse, scouse, scouse. Out! Out! Out!"

Still, it probably wouldn't have gone further if he hadn't stooped to pick up a half-brick. He hurled it through the windscreen. It didn't hit the driver. Or maybe it did. There was blood on his face. What he remembered most was the look of hurt amazement.

He stood there. Why had he done that? The gang surged on the car. Pulled open the door. Dragged the driver out. Started kicking and punching him. Mark turned and fled. He ran full-tilt into the road from which they'd diverged moments earlier. He narrowly missed being trampled by a group of enormous police horses. They disappeared round the corner at a canter, in the direction of the showroom. The crowd parted in panic to let the mounted police through. It closed up again like a fast-healing wound and continued to file down the road. What should he do? He was shaking. Couldn't get his breath. He had to stifle an urge to laugh out loud. The crowd ignored him. He pushed his shoulders back, and stepped into the river of fans.

He opened his eyes. Screwed them up against the harsh white lights. William had picked up a Mirror from somewhere. He was desultorily flicking through it. Mark let his eyes close again. His head was killing him. He often thought about that particular act of casual and unpunished violence. Why had he done it? Looking back, he couldn't understand how he'd got away with it. Now, it felt like it was nothing to do with him. Or maybe that was how he wanted it to feel. Because it was to do with him. And it frightened him.

It was meaningless. He did it in the name of nothing at all.

PART TWO

1990: Three Years Before
Chapter 8

The phone woke him.

"Hello, is that Mark? This is Lillian Bewes, from next door. To your mother."

He picked up his watch. One o'clock. He sat up.

"Hello Mrs Bewes. Is everything all right?"

"No dear, I'm afraid not. Your mother is in hospital. They think she's had a stroke. We've had a terrible time with her. We've been here five hours already, poor old soul. I've just left her to phone you."

"Oh."

"So ... you'll come? She's in Park Hospital, you know, at Daveyhulme. She seems to be in good hands. They're – oh, what did they call it?" He could hear the old lady breathing. He moved the receiver further from his ear. "Assessing and monitoring. Yes, that's it. Assessing and monitoring her, but they say they're going to move her onto a ward as soon as they have a bed ready. So it's quite serious, dear. Mark, are you still there?"

"Yes."

"So ... when do you think you'll be able to get here? Only she's asking for you. She is conscious, you see. She's very distressed. And I'll stay with her as long as I can - of course I will - only -" Damn, damn. "Only I'm not family, you see, am I?"

"No, of course. Thanks, Mrs Bewes. Don't worry, I'll be in touch with the hospital. I'll take it from here. Thank you."

"So… you'll be here soon?"

"Thanks again. Bye now." He hung up.

He sat on the edge of the bed, waiting to react. He felt nothing. His mind seemed to have splintered on hearing Mrs Bewes' voice. The broken pieces had flown off in all directions leaving his head quite empty. He needed to think. One thing he knew for sure. He was not going to the hospital. Eloise stirred beside him. He turned to her. She was looking at him in the darkness, half asleep. Moonlight fell through a gap in the curtain and lit up her hair. She reached up to touch his shoulder.

"What's the matter? Come back to bed," she said, softly.

So she hadn't heard the phone. "I will. I'm just going for a pee. Go back to sleep, sweetheart."

He smoothed her hair where it shimmered. She murmured something and rolled onto her side, asleep again.

They were at Rowan's Well, Eloise's family home on the North Yorkshire coast, for the Easter break. He left the master bedroom. Padded barefoot down the big oak staircase, across the draughty hall and into the kitchen. As he'd hoped, it was warm in here. The ancient Aga pumped out heat into the small hours. Hopelessly inefficient devices. It was time Martha did something about that. His mother-in-law was throwing money away hand over fist on this old house. Why, God only knew. He'd tried to make her see sense, but it was a waste of time. And William never backed him up: he was as sentimental about the place as the women. Of course! William and the Cooper clan weren't here yet. He and Eloise were alone in the house. No-one had heard the phone. This was a real stroke of luck. William and Olivia would arrive with the children tomorrow. Martha had taken her two eldest grandsons to London for Easter to see their mother, so she wouldn't be gracing them with her presence at all over the holiday. Hallelujah.

He flicked on the kettle. The work surface was covered in crumbs from the toaster. He scooped them up and put them in the bin. He listened to the hushing sound of the sea. It was strange how it always seemed louder at night. He shook his head. He needed to plan. He'd known this day would come, but he hadn't imagined what form it would take. Why did she not have the decency to die cleanly without any drama? Like his father had. That time, it must be nearly two years ago now, he'd got the call from his mother…

"Mark? This is your mother. I'm afraid I have some rather bad news. It's your father -" Her voice had cracked and she cried. A harsh sound, devoid of emotion. He waited patiently for it to subside.

"What about Dad?" He knew, of course.

"We're at home. It was peaceful, in his sleep. He was cold when I woke up. The doctor's been, but there's a policeman here and there's so much -" Her voice wavered. "Mark, you will come, won't you?" She wasn't sure that he would. "Please?"

He let her stew for a few seconds. "I'll be there in half an hour." He put the phone down before she could thank him.

Eloise had insisted on going with him. "Of course I'm coming. He's your father. I want to be with you."

"Really, there's no need. It's just paperwork and formalities to deal with. You'll just be"- he was going to say "in the way"- "You'll just be hanging about."

He didn't want Eloise in the same room with his mother. In the two years they'd been married, he'd done everything in his power to ensure their paths barely crossed. And now he hated the thought of his beautiful wife breathing the same air as that woman.

"I'm coming, and that's final." She reached up and kissed him. "In fact, I'm driving, so come on, hurry up. Your mum's all on her own down there."

He knew whose fault that was.

When they arrived, there was indeed a police officer there, as well as the undertaker speaking in hushed tones with his mother. The policeman took them to one side and explained why he was there. It was routine in cases of sudden death at home. His mother had been too upset to give the officer much information, so Mark attempted to fill in the gaps while Eloise went to her. The policeman seemed unimpressed by his lack of knowledge of his father's recent health, but who the hell was he to judge? When he'd filled in all his forms, he said he would wait outside. He left the three of them with the undertaker to await the hearse.

The undertaker, small and balding, was fidgety. Clearly itching to get away. He soon left with assurances the hearse would arrive shortly. Eloise went to see him out. He was left alone with his mother.

"This is terrible, Mum. I'm so sorry. Can I see him?"

He made no move to kiss or even touch her. Without warning she sprang from her armchair and threw herself on his chest. She clutched his arms with her pinching fingers. She was smaller than he remembered.

90

"What am I going to do?" She sobbed into his shirt.

He looked down at her, his arms at his sides. This was unprecedented. There'd been a time in his childhood when he'd dreamed of a hug from her. But that was then. He took a step back. Still she clung to him, so he held her shoulders and carefully pushed her away.

"Don't do that, please."

"What? I - I don't understand." A bubble of snot appeared at her nostril.

Eloise came in and said something. He couldn't take his eyes off his mother.

"Don't insult me. You do understand. You know how it is between us. You've always known." His voice sounded menacing, even to him. "Give me the undertaker's details and I'll make the arrangements. He deserves that much from me. But please spare me the "loving-family-united-in-grief" routine, for Christ's sake."

His mother stood her ground. She held his gaze. Showed no reaction. There was so much more to say. So much more hurt to express, to inflict. But he couldn't bring himself to do it. It was too humiliating. It was all too sordid. His mother glared at him with those fierce dark eyes, so familiar from the bathroom mirror. She almost spat the words: "I don't need you. Please leave."

"Mark?" Eloise stood by the door.

"It's all right, love. Wait in the car. I'm going upstairs to say goodbye, then I'll come."

Eloise did as she was told.

"Am I at least invited to the funeral?"

She looked away first. "Yes."

He turned his back and left.

He did attend his father's funeral. He stood side by side with his mother after the service to receive condolences. He attended the small gathering of neighbours and former colleagues at her house. But, other than the expected social niceties, he didn't speak to her again. That exchange on the day of his father's death had been the last time he talked with her.

And now this.

He made himself some tea and sat down at the battered kitchen table. He heard a seagull crying close by. On the roof probably. It was getting close to dawn. He must think. He sipped his tea. He let thoughts drift through his head without grabbing hold of any of them, until it came to him with a start that he didn't know how ill his mother was. She could even be dead by now, with a bit of luck. He needed to ascertain exactly what the situation was before Eloise woke. Focused at last, he phoned the hospital and spoke to the sister in charge of his mother's care. She was poorly but comfortable. She was asking for him. He was non-committal. He ended the conversation with a vague mention of working away.

He put the phone down. His mother was still alive and wanted to see him. What did he think about that? What did he *feel* about it? Nothing. He wasn't sad or distressed. Or angry or glad. He was neutral. He wandered out to the cloakroom off the porch. As he peed, he gazed at himself in the mirror above the toilet. He was neutral, and it showed in his eyes. There was no passion there. They were empty. He remembered the day his father died, the way his mother had blasted him with her glare. She was a woman full of life and passion. He had to admit that. But none of that energy had ever been reserved for him.

He held his own cold stare. Was this the face he showed the people he loved? Was this what Eloise saw? And William? The children? Christ, he hoped not. He was a good-looking guy, he knew. His dark, almost black, eyes were a big part of his looks. He could intimidate and quell argument with a glance. But it wasn't passion in his eyes that commanded attention. It was the awful emptiness of them. He tried to recall when he'd first noticed that shuttered look, when he'd first experienced this weird sensation of seeing a dead person reflected back at him. It must have been a gradual process, this extinction. As a little boy, he surely had huge energy and passion. Otherwise, how had he survived the daily torments of those other boys?

He flushed the toilet. Suddenly he remembered looking down the length of this body another time when it was much smaller and soaked to the skin in wet mud. He smelled the rank, stagnant stench of the pool in the woods as clearly as if it rose from the water before him now. And it came to him. He first saw this closed-down look in his eyes on the day Fitz died.

He switched off the light. What was he going to do about his bloody mother?

He awoke to the cacophony of the Cooper children trying not to disturb them. Right outside the bedroom door.

"Mummy said no."

"Want to."

"No!"

"Ow!"

From a distance: "Hugo! Leave your sister alone."

"But she's -"

"I said 'Leave her'."

93

Time to get up. Now William and the kids were here, the holiday could begin. "Come in, you two."

The door flew open. It banged against the old pine dressing table, waking Eloise.

"No more spinach for you, Hugo. Come here, you little reprobate. And you, Annie. Wow! Don't you look beautiful? New hat?" Since he'd bought her that cute little cowboy hat last summer, he'd rarely seen her without headgear. It drove Olivia mad.

After breakfast, he and William did their spring tour of inspection. They checked out a large green stain under the guttering on the front of the house. It stood out against the flaking whitewash.

"Could just be the gutter's blocked. Need to get up there. Take a look." William loved all this hands-on stuff.

"That's the front spare room. We'd better check there's no damp on the inside. I'll bet she's not had it opened up since we were all here last. That'd be New Year, right?"

"The whole front needs a lick of paint, whatever."

The white facade dazzled them in the bright sunlight reflected off the sea. Mark breathed in the salt breeze, gentle this morning, even up here. The tide was in, but there was only a lazy lapping from below. A becalmed North Sea. That was rare. He shaded his eyes. "The gutter looks like it's come loose at that corner. It's sagging, see?"

"That's a scaffold job, with the painting too. Won't be cheap."

"When is it ever, my friend?" Good money after bad, this house. Why did Martha need such a big place? Even when they were all there, they didn't fill it. Eloise's father had been the local MP at one time. Needed the space because he entertained a lot, apparently. A bit too much, if you listened to the pub gossip. "These window frames are on the way out, too. That's going to be another shedload. We should go for uPVC."

"Won't get permission for that. Listed, remember?"

"She's going to have to think about B&B, William. She can't afford it, even with us all chipping in."

"If you want to raise it with her again, you're a braver man than me, mate."

They strolled to the back of the house where it was much quieter away from the sound of sea. The picket fence they'd put up two summers ago, to keep the children safe from the cliff edge, was holding up well. It created a little back garden. Before, the house had stood unenclosed on the cliff top. How Martha had raised five children without losing any over the edge, God only knew. She loved her new garden. And the fence. She was for ever painting it. It was currently lime green. He smiled. Martha was a one-off.

"William, do you know anything about old people's homes?"

Chapter 9

"She's *your* sister-in-law, for goodness sake! What are you shouting at *me* for?" Olivia slammed the cupboard door and span round to face Will. He wouldn't look at her. He scrubbed the casserole dish. Scowled at his reflection in the darkened window.

They'd just got rid of Will's brother John and his new wife Denise. John had met and married her in South Africa, from where they'd only recently returned. The dinner party had been an opportunity to get to know her. Will was beginning to think he didn't like her. She'd driven Mark away early with her unrelenting interrogation and plain rudeness. Like when she said to Olivia in a stage whisper, while Mark was chatting with John: "He's a bit of a social contraceptive, isn't he? Where's his sense of humour?"

He'd seen Mark's back stiffen and Eloise blush. They left shortly afterwards.

"You were egging her on." He remembered the kids asleep upstairs. Tried to lower his voice. "You know you were."

"I wasn't. It looks like once she gets the bit between her teeth there's no stopping her."

"She was trying to make him look stupid, and you were laughing."

"It was funny."

He slammed the washing up brush down on the drainer. "He was a guest in our house, Liv, and you tried to humiliate him. That's not what I'd call funny."

"Oh Will, lighten up, for God's sake. He's hardly a guest. He's never bloody away from the place. And he's not a child. He can look after himself. He doesn't need you to fight his battles."

"But you don't try to make a fool of someone you've invited into your home." He tipped the water out of the bowl. It spilled over the lip of the sink. "Shit." He bent to wipe it up. "Is that so pigging unreasonable?" His voice sounded high pitched and comical in his effort not to shout.

"No, I suppose not. Sorry, love." She landed a kiss on the top of his head. "D'you forgive me?"

He stood up and smiled. It was hard to stay angry when she pulled that stupid face. He stroked her hair. Twisted a lock of it around his finger. He liked to see it shimmer when he played with it.

But Annie's cry broke the fragile peace. "Now look what you've done." Olivia strode from the kitchen.

When she came downstairs ten minutes later, Will was in the living room. He'd poured himself a last glass of wine, and Olivia some juice.

"I thought you said you'd had enough." She stood in the doorway, cradling her round belly.

He patted the sofa next to him and held out the juice. "Might as well finish it off, eh?" She took the glass but sat down in the chair opposite. He sat up a little. "Has she settled down again?"

"Mm." She held her drink to the light and peered at it. "D'you realise, Will, that almost every row we've had recently has been about Mark?"

"Don't be daft."

"It's true. You think about it."

"No, you're talking daft now, Liv."

"Am I really?" He sat up straighter. "We can't do anything these days without consulting Mr Mark God

97

Almighty Strachan." This was turning into a rant. "And woe betide anyone who doesn't take care around him, because of course we all know how sensitive he is. We mustn't hurt his feelings, must we? Oh no! Naturally, he can trample all over everyone else's, but we must remember *he* is sensitive. And so misunderstood!"

"Olivia? What the - where's all this coming from?"

There was venom in her voice. "It's the truth. He's a complete arsehole, Will, and you treat him like he's some sort of bloody buddha." She flung her hands about as she spoke. She splashed orange juice onto the arm of her chair. She ignored the stain. "It makes me so angry, the way you hero-worship him."

"We need to wipe that up. It'll mark."

"Stop trying to avoid the issue."

"What *issue*?" He stood up to get a cloth.

"Leave it!" He stared at her. She was really whipping herself into a state. He sat down again. This could be the hormones talking. He said, as evenly as he could: "Liv, you're out of order. He's my best friend."

"So what does that make me? Your fucking housekeeper?"

"This is daft, Liv. It's a stupid argument. I can't deal with it now. I've had too much to drink. Let's just go to bed, eh?"

"I said what does that make me? Don't avoid the question." She glared at him, her golden eyes hard as amber.

He tried to think straight. What had he done to make her so angry? Other than pointing out her lack of manners earlier, there was nothing. He must tread carefully or this could be the whole weekend down the tubes. "Ok. He's my best friend. But you, you're my soulmate, Olivia. Is that not good enough for you?"

She stared into her almost-empty glass. Finally she looked up at him. Her eyes glistened. "Why do you always put him first? I don't understand, Will." She was no longer angry. She seemed sad and confused. "It's bad enough I have to put up with it from Lou. But he's her husband, so I respect that. You're *my* husband, Will. *I* should come first with you, shouldn't I?"

Despite his urge to ease her sadness, he felt hard done by. After all, why was it they spent so much time with Mark and Lou? It was mainly the twins' doing. Their need to be daily in each other's company. Sure, he and Mark enjoyed being together, but they could happily go days without contact. It was the women who threw them together so frequently. It was the women who needed to live in each other's pockets. He watched a tear roll down her cheek. They were a foursome. Always had been. That was how it was. He looked at the clock. It was nearly half past two. Time to knock this on the head.

"Olivia, I love you, you know that. And you love me. So let's make friends? Please? I don't want to fight with you."

She contemplated him a moment. Then she came over and sulkily dropped down into his lap. She draped her arms around his neck. He felt the baby give a little kick. She buried her face in his chest.

"Sorry," she said, softly.

Two Years Before
Chapter 10

"It's the way he's lied to me, Livvy. All the times I've asked after his mum, suggested we go and see her, and he never even told me she was ill. I thought she was still in Altrincham, for God's sake! She's been in that home in Southport for over a year!" Eloise's hand shook as she lit a second cigarette. "D'you mind?" Cigarette in mouth, she tossed the lighter on the coffee table.

"Your house." Olivia did mind, but Eloise didn't seem to notice. She pulled on the cigarette as if her life depended on it.

"God, they must have thought I was a complete idiot. There's me saying: 'But she isn't *in* Southport'. And the woman's saying: 'I'm sorry Mrs Strachan, but I'm stood right next to her body'. Jesus! How could he do this? Why wouldn't he tell me? What reason could he possibly have not to tell me? What the hell's *wrong* with him?" Olivia pursed her lips. "Oh, please don't start, Liv. I can't bear it." She drew on her cigarette which seemed to calm her. "He never tells me anything important. He never shares anything with me. He treats me like a child."

"Have you talked to him?"

"I haven't had chance. As soon as I told him about the call from the home, he was on the phone to them making funeral arrangements. And then he left to

100

go over there. That was yesterday afternoon. I haven't heard from him since."

"Stay with us tonight if you like."

"No, I'm ok here. Thanks."

Olivia listened to the tick of the clock and the crackle of the fire. She loved this little cottage. She liked to imagine herself living here on the moor with Will and the kids. It was the kind of home that deserved a family. It needed some heart. She watched Eloise take deep drags on her cigarette and blow the smoke upwards. She'd started smoking when she married Mark. When she gave up working for her Phd. She shrugged as if to shake off unpleasant thoughts. Olivia knew the gesture well. "Are you all right for time? D'you have to get back for the baby?"

"No. I've left some milk for her. Will can handle it. He'll phone if he needs me."

"Sure?"

"Mm."

They gazed into the fire. Olivia smiled at the way its light danced in Eloise's hair. She was so beautiful.

"What should I do, Livvy?"

"What do you mean?"

"I mean, is this too much? Should I put up with this? I mean, has he gone too far?" She was agitated now. She leaned forward to stump out the cigarette. Then she sprang from the sofa and stood with her back to the fire. "I can't trust him, can I?"

Her mouth twisted. Tears welled. She put a hand across her face.

"Lou, don't cry."

Olivia went to hug her, but she pushed her away gently.

"No, I'm all right. Really. Don't feel bad for me. I just need to talk."

Olivia stroked her arms and looked into her clear honey eyes. "I'm listening."

They sat down again. Olivia kicked off her sandals and pulled her feet up onto the sofa. Eloise sat upright, her hands clasped in her lap, her feet on the floor.

"I know I can't trust him, Liv. It's not just this thing with his mother. There's other stuff."

She looked at Olivia. Searching for a reaction? Olivia's stomach lurched.

"What -" Olivia cleared her throat. "What stuff?"

"Other women."

"He's been seeing other women?" She tried to sound surprised.

"Yes. Well, woman. Just the one, as far as I know."

"How do you know?"

"He told me." She reached for the cigarette packet, then tossed it back on the table with a grimace. "Ugh, I must give them up. They're vile, really. Mark hates them. Want a coffee? Come through."

She headed for the kitchen. Olivia followed, squinting against the bright fluorescent lighting and the shiny chrome surfaces. Unlike her own grubby, chaotic kitchen, Eloise's always looked immaculate. Like something out of a brochure.

"He told you what, exactly?"

Eloise busied herself with the coffee. "That he slept with his secretary." She gave a humourless laugh. "Golly, how unimaginative."

"Lou, no! He was winding you up."

"No."

"But -"

"No. And what makes it worse is he did it to get back at me." She handed Olivia a mug.

"What for, for heaven's sake?"

"For being overly friendly with Richard."

"*Our* Richard? *Richard Evans?* No, you're joking."

Richard was a friend from their university days. He was only a couple of years older than them but Olivia had always thought he looked and acted about fifty. He was extravagantly, celibately, gay. He reminded her of the randy uncle in 'Withnail and I'. But in a nice way.

"He was mad after we all got together at yours the other week. He said I'd made a fool of him." Olivia couldn't believe what she was hearing. "D'you remember when Rich went up to the loo? He was blundering around, so I went up to make sure he didn't wake the children? Well, that's when he shagged me, apparently."

Olivia burst out laughing. She spilled her coffee. "Oh God, I'm sorry, Lou. But that's just ludicrous!"

Eloise smiled, despite her distress. "I know."

"But so should he, the dozy bastard. Jesus! I mean *Mark's* more in danger of being seduced by Richard than you are."

"Gee, thanks, Liv."

"You know what I mean."

Eloise sipped her coffee. "Anyway, that's what he thought. So he went and screwed his secretary."

The words hung in the air between them.

"That can't be true. He wouldn't do that to you, Lou. He may be a royal pain in the arse, but he loves you." Olivia put down her mug and held her sister's hand. "He adores you, Lou. You know he does."

"I'm not sure anymore." Eloise's lip quivered. She put a hand over her mouth.

"When did he tell you this? How long have you known?" The arrogant, spoiled, self-centred bastard.

"Please don't shout, Livvy. It doesn't help." Eloise sniffed. "He came home and told me straightaway."

"So how long ago was that?"

"About six weeks. It was right after we saw Richard. The next day."

"Well then, of course it's not true! He was just saying it, Lou, to get back at you for flirting with Rich, or whatever. God, he's a selfish bastard. He said it to hurt you, didn't he? Even Mark couldn't be that fast a worker, hey?"

She tried to look in Eloise's eyes, but she kept her face turned away.

"I know. You're probably right. But I still don't know where I stand, what I should do. Even if it isn't true, I can't trust him anymore, can I?"

Olivia looked at the little puddle of coffee on the floor. "Let me wipe that up."

Eloise yawned. "Oh dear. Sorry! What time is it? Feels late."

Olivia consulted her watch. "Heck, it's nearly twelve."

"Look, you get off, love. I'll be fine."

"No. I'll phone Will to check in, but I can stay as long as you like."

"Really, Livvy, I'm ok."

The phone rang.

"This might be Will now," Olivia said.

Eloise went through to the living room to answer it. Olivia followed her into the warm firelight. It was Mark. Eloise blushed. "Oh hi, baby. How are you? Are you ok? I was worried…. Aha … Aha…. No, Livvy's here…. I miss you too, honey …"

Business as usual, then. Olivia slipped her shoes on. She pointed at her watch and kissed Lou's cheek. Eloise nodded, listening to Mark and smiling. She mouthed "Night, night". Blew her a kiss. Olivia shrugged on her jacket and let herself out.

In the cold night air, she breathed a sigh of relief. She had thought for a moment earlier on that Eloise was going to accuse her. She climbed into her battered Fiat and started the engine. She had done nothing wrong. The only thing she was guilty of was not telling Eloise and Will. And how could she tell them? It would hurt them too much. She pulled away from the curb onto the dark country lane. How she wished she'd never laid eyes on Mark Strachan.

It began to rain as she approached the town. Much as she loved the cottage, Olivia was always pleased to get back to civilisation, as Will called it. Street lights, corner shops, kids in bus shelters. She drove along the ring road towards home. She couldn't believe Mark would have risked his marriage by having sex with the first willing woman he came across. Eloise was so gullible. He'd been winding her up. Playing his ridiculous mind games. He was jealous of Lou's harmless flirting with an old friend, and had made up this story in revenge. She was credulous. She'd believe Mark if he told her the moon was a mint imperial. No. Mark hadn't been unfaithful. He might be a bastard, but he loved Eloise. There could be no doubt about that. Then that little voice, the little nag that had plagued her for years, commentating on her relationship with Mark, piped up: *Just who do you want to convince, your sister or yourself?*

She pulled into a side road. Switched off the engine. It was a fair question. Who was she kidding? The truth was she was angry not with Mark but with the other woman. She was jealous of the secretary. She caught her own eyes in the rear-view mirror and looked away. If Mark was going to stray, then it should have been with her. She clapped her hand over her mouth. She braced herself to meet her own treacherous gaze in the mirror. She shook her head. She must pull herself together. She was being hysterical. Of course she would never have sex with Mark. She didn't even like him, for God's sake. She looked away from the mirror into the middle distance. She was weak, feeble when it came to Mark. God, she hated him. He made no secret of wanting her. And he worshipped the ground her children walked on. And...

She pressed her cold hands to her hot cheeks. Dear God, her hormones must be raging if she was thinking like this. Yes, that must be it. After both Hugo and Annie were born she'd felt amazingly randy for the first couple of months. It had to be hormonal, because it defied all logic. She was knackered the whole time, singularly unsexy, dripping milk and smelling of baby sick. And she was painfully tender in all her formerly erogenous zones. If Will had so much as offered to satisfy her lust, she would have slapped him. But he knew her better than that. He'd started reading to her in the evenings, from Catherine Cookson and Georgette Heyer.

She couldn't blame her feelings entirely on post-natal hormone imbalance, though, because there *was* that barbeque last summer. She felt butterflies as she remembered how Mark had brushed his open palm across her breasts, reaching round her for a bottle of wine. Then he'd pressed her against the kitchen counter and kissed her. She'd returned his kiss. He stared at her with a strange mix of delight and disapproval. It had been a serious mistake. The only reason he hadn't pursued his advantage at the time was because she was pregnant. She blushed to think what might have happened otherwise.

She blinked hard. Stared at her hectic reflection. She restarted the engine and turned on to the main road. So Eloise believed Mark had been unfaithful, and despite that was willing to carry on as if nothing had happened. She crashed the gears. It was none of her business how Eloise chose to conduct her marriage. How would she like it if the situation was reversed and Lou started pontificating about her and Will? She ran the traffic light as it turned to red. How did he manage to manipulate her so easily? The steering wheel dug into her palms. Lou had never been like this before they met Mark. She'd been confident. More assertive than her. She'd eaten other boyfriends for breakfast. And even now she was self-assured with her family. It was only in Mark's presence that she changed. She became dependent. Needy. She transformed herself into what Mark wanted her to be. He was no good for her.

She pulled into the drive. The downstairs lights were on in the house. Will had waited up. She was glad.

Eighteen Months Before
Chapter 11

Eloise had slept badly. She listened to Mark's rhythmic breathing in bed next to her. She loved these long summer days, but detested the oppressive heat at night. Whenever she couldn't sleep she would find herself going over that conversation with Olivia, even though it was months back now. She stared at the ceiling. She wished she hadn't told her that stuff about Mark sleeping around. She wanted to set the record straight. But things hadn't been the same between them since then, somehow. She flung her arm back onto the pillow. She couldn't get cool. It seemed like Livvy had become more distant. Less her twin. She'd tried to talk about it, but Livvy always brushed aside her concerns. But her disapproval of Mark had become more pronounced. As if she was constantly judging him. Waiting for him to step out of line. She turned onto her side and pushed off the light cotton sheet, careful not to uncover Mark. She dreaded to think how Liv would react if she knew the other stuff about their marriage.

The stupid thing was he never had slept with that other woman. They talked it through, of course, but he had no need to explain. She trusted him. He loved her and she loved him. He was sensitive, that was all, easily hurt. He tended to strike out to inflict hurt in return. It was instinctive with him. He couldn't help it. Her family had never understood him. They thought he was arrogant and selfish. And she knew he was: she wasn't daft, contrary to popular belief. But he was so much more that they never got to see. She snuggled into his back, and pushed thoughts of Olivia's disapproval to a corner of her mind.

It was coming light. The casement window showed pale grey against the darkness of the room. She reached over and stroked his unshaven chin. He was so handsome. She could feel his beauty through her fingertips. She breathed in the sweet scent of his skin. She laughed softly. To top it all, the gauzy white curtains billowed before the open pane. That was exactly the effect she had sought and she felt a burst of excitement, like a little girl waking on Christmas morning. She was happy. This was her room, her own little house, her beautiful man. Her wonderful life. It was perfect. Almost perfect.

"Mark?" She half-hoped he wouldn't wake up.

"Mm?" He was mostly asleep. She could leave it for another time.

"Nothing."

He turned to her as she knew he would. His eyes gleamed, animal-like. They lay nose to nose, breathing gently and uninhibited into each other's nostrils. Like horse whisperers.

"See. My curtains do billow. I told you they would."

"Smartypants." He stroked her buttock. She let the warm rushing thrill flow through her, enjoying it but not responding except for a slight wiggle of her hips. This was enough for Mark. He pulled her close.

"Honey?"

"Mm?" His deep voice sounded like a lion's purr. He landed soft kisses all over her neck.

"Can we talk?"

"Mm." The kisses now lighted on her breasts.

"Mark?" She giggled and gently pushed him from her so she could see his face again.

"Can't we talk later?" So far he was only grumpy. Not yet irritated. She had to tread carefully.

"It's important." She pulled away from him. She needed to see his face. They lay, once again, noses almost touching, his face cradled in her hands. "Do you remember what you said before we got the cottage? That you wanted to feel settled? In the right place?" She waited for a response. There was none. "We have the perfect home now, don't we? Enough room and everything." She hesitated, but she couldn't stop now. "Let's have a baby."

She reached forward to kiss him but he drew away and got out of bed. He stood over her, silhouetted against the window. Damn, she'd gone too far. She'd ruined it again. She felt his eyes burning into her, though she couldn't see his face. At last she could bear it no more. She turned away, and sobbed as quietly as she could. She pulled up the sheet around her ears. She heard him stride from the room. Then she heard the shower.

When she came downstairs, her eyes swollen and itchy, he was sitting at the kitchen table, reading the Sunday papers.

"There's coffee in the pot," he said, not looking up.

She poured herself a steaming mug and clutched it in both hands, needing the warmth despite the weather. She stood at the counter, her back to him. She had to work out how to raise it again without him getting angry. Without her getting angry. She'd always backed down before, but she wasn't going to let it drop this time.

For once, it seemed he could read her mind. "Can't we let it drop?" He put the paper down. Held out his hand. She took it and walked round the table to him. She stood next to him, leaning against him. She stroked his hair.

"I can't, honey. I want it so much."

He kissed her hand. "I know you do, babes. And you know I'd do anything for you, anything - "

"Except this." Her voice came out flat and lifeless. She dropped his hand and stepped away from him, thinking hard. She looked at the photos on the fridge door. "Mark, please think about it. There's no hurry. You love children, you know you do. You're great with them, with Hugo and Annie and little Tessa. And what about Alex's boys? You adore them, don't you?" He looked at the photos. He did love her nephews and nieces. He wouldn't want to deny it. He positively doted on them. Spent every minute he could with them. He loved to babysit. He carried their pictures in his wallet. "Mark?"

He seemed to drag his eyes from the photographs. He looked at her with an odd expression. As if she was a child, or maybe a very stupid adult.

"They are not my children," he said, like this explained everything. She clenched her fist. "I love them, but they aren't my kids." Then he said something she would never forget. Not ever. "I don't want kids. And I don't want you to have kids." He folded the paper, got up and strolled out of the kitchen.

Her knees went weak. She sat down. What the hell did that mean? The tone of his voice chilled her. He couldn't dictate to her like this, the arrogant bastard. But what could she do? She slammed her hands down on the table. Enough was enough. She followed him.

111

He was about to go upstairs and he hesitated, his foot on the bottom step.

He said: "Thought we could phone William and Olivia. See if they want to meet for lunch? The Blundell Arms, maybe? They've got that ball pool thing. Our treat?" Did he really not give a damn how she felt?

"Forget lunch, Mark. We're going to talk about this whether you want to or not. Or at least you're going to listen. Sit down." He frowned, but he didn't move. "Please."

He smiled then and sat on the chesterfield.

"I want you to listen, Mark, because I am completely serious about this." He settled back, smiling in that patronising way. She struggled to keep her breathing even. "Before we got married, we talked, didn't we? I told you I wanted children. I talked about it a lot, remember? And you never, not once, said you didn't. You lied, Mark, about the most important thing in the world to me." Her voice gave out. She couldn't stop the tears. Damn.

"Oh come on, sweetheart. There's no need for all this."

He came and put his arms around her. She pushed him away.

"No - I don't want that. I'm ok, I'm just - so - angry."

"Baby, baby." He enfolded her again. He laughed.

She shoved him hard this time and he staggered backwards, nearly falling over the low table.

"You condescending bastard. How dare you! See if you're still laughing when I'm walking out the door!" She made for the stairs, but he grabbed her arm. She caught her breath: he was angry now. "Let go of me!" She tried to pull away. He tightened his grip, twisted her arm, forced her round to face him. The pain was intense, but she didn't cry out. She had to save her energy. Anyway no one would hear. She looked into his blank eyes. She had good reason to be afraid. But it was not yet too late. Maybe she could still distract him. "Mark, please - ." She let herself go limp. He caught her up, releasing her arm. He placed her on the sofa and knelt by her.

"Oh God, Eloise, I'm sorry. Are you ok? Baby?"

She couldn't believe it had worked once again. Her elbow throbbed. How many more times could that trick protect her? She had his undivided attention now so she lifted her head, weakly.

"I'm sorry, Mark. I don't want to hurt you, I really don't. But I am going to have a baby. I want more than anything to have one with you. But if you can't, if you won't, then I'll have to find someone who will."

Mark flinched as if she'd hit him.

Nine Months Before
Chapter 12

Much as she loved her elder sister, Olivia found her hard to cope with for longer than a few days at a time. Things always went out of kilter when Alex was around. She didn't fit into the Rowan's Well routine. She didn't fit into any routine.

"Carl is such a darling, Mum. You must meet him." Alex leaned against the kitchen counter. Olivia watched her. She was willowy, red-haired, like them, but full of expansive gestures and elegant in a way only money could buy. She moved slightly to let Olivia get to the sink. "He's much older than me of course, but he's - how can I put it?"

"Loaded?" Olivia said. She rinsed the lettuce.

Alex laughed. "You little cynic, Livvy. No, I was going to say 'full of fun'. But since you mention it: yes, he is loaded. How did you know?"

"Educated guess." She winked at her mother. She turned back to the Aga to stir the bolognaise.

Alex played with the gold bangle on her wrist. "Stop it, both of you. I've only just arrived and you're already having a go."

"Oh Alex, don't be silly, sweetie. It's wonderful to see you and we're very happy for you." Olivia looked at her mum fondly. Martha was the template for her daughters with copious once-red hair, now faded to a delicate strawberry blonde which belied her age. Plenty of women paid good money to acquire hair like that. Martha hugged Alex. "Of course we are, aren't we, Olivia?"

"Yes. Did you get parmesan when you went into Whitby, Mum?"

"In the fridge. So how is London, Alex? Tell me all about it."

"Later. First I want to see my beautiful sons. Where are they? And I want to hear all the gossip about Lou. I couldn't believe it when she phoned to tell me she's expecting. I was beginning to think it was never going to happen."

"I don't think it would be, if it was up to Mark."

"Really?" Alex raised an eyebrow and smiled. "So the delectable Mark has a weakness, after all. Tell me more."

"Olivia, that's enough. You girls are the absolute limit. You shouldn't be talking about your sister like this."

Olivia pulled a face. "Be fair, Mum. I have to let off steam once in a while. Otherwise I might explode right in front of him one day. And you wouldn't want that, would you?" She slammed the cutlery drawer with her hip.

"I've told you before, Olivia. Your sister made a choice, just like you did. And now she has to live with it. For better or for worse."

"Yes, but the difference is Olivia had the good sense to choose Will."

"I know that, dear. But Mark isn't - isn't -"

"Isn't what?" Olivia laughed.

"I was going to say, he isn't all that bad."

"Oh Mum, face it. There's nothing to defend. We're talking about a man who buys his wife the car *he* wants for her birthday, for God's sake!"

"No! He didn't!" Alex chuckled. "How delicious. What is it?"

"What?"

"The car, silly."

"God, I don't know. Some old banger of a Jaguar. Lou never gets to drive it, needless to say."

They were still laughing when Will came through the back door closely followed by Patrick and Eric. Olivia looked again. No, that was Eric coming in first. People often asked her if she found it easier to tell the boys apart, being an identical twin herself. The question always puzzled her. Why would she? Alex threw her arms about the boys. They hugged back, so tightly she broke away, laughing. "Goodness me, how you've grown. You're taller than Uncle Will now!"

Eric smiled over at Will, shy. Patrick said "When did you arrive? We would've waited in if we'd known you were coming today."

"Spur of the moment thing. You know me, Eric." The mistake thudded into a tense silence that filled the room. Nice one, Alex. Patrick stepped back. "Patrick, darling, I'm sorry. You've both grown so much, I can't keep up with you." She laughed nervously.

The twins stared at their muddy trainers, their necks red.

Will spoke up: "How are you, Alex? You look fantastic."

He held his arms wide and she embraced him.

"Will, darling! My, you get more handsome every time I see you. How are you?"

"Great thanks, yeah." Will nodded and smiled. "You're looking really well. Have you been away?"

"Lanzarote. Sailing with friends of Carl's."

Olivia rolled her eyes. Will took the hint.

"Need any help with the tea?" he said. "Or shall I get from under your feet?"

"You can never be in the way, darling!" Alex turned her smile on her sons. "So, you two, what do gorgeous fifteen-year-olds get up to in these parts? Are you going to fill me in on your love lives?"

"God, Mum." Patrick reddened again.

Olivia pointed the bread knife at him. "You remember this, Pat, the next time you're missing her."

"Auntie Liv!"

"Does he miss me? Really? Do you, Patrick? What about you, Eric?"

"Sometimes," the twins said together. They stared at the floor.

"Bless! Look boys, why don't you go and get cleaned up ready for dinner, and later on I'll take you for a spin in my new car. Did you see it outside? The Jaguar?" She winked at Olivia. "That should give me something to talk to your Uncle Mark about, shouldn't it?"

Will and the boys left them to it. They shoved and laughed and left a trail of wet mud across the quarry tiles. Martha tutted.

Alex heaved a sigh as she watched them go. "Lord, I miss them so much."

Olivia was surprised by her mum's reply. It was acid. "You know where they are, Alexandra. All you have to do is say the word and you could have them with you. They'd love to spend more time with you, you know that. They miss their mother."

"Don't, Mum, I know. It's just ... all so very ..." She shrugged. "... complicated."

Martha pushed her hair from her eyes. She got some plates out and banged them down on the table.

"Not half as complicated as it is for those poor boys. They don't deserve -"

"It's not so bad, Mum. The boys are happy enough," Olivia said. She glanced at Alex. "They can't miss what they've never had."

Alex smoothed her skirt. "So you think Eloise has bullied Mark into having this baby?"

Olivia tasted the simmering sauce. "This is about ready. Do you want to give everyone a shout? My brood's in the snug watching TV. Or at least, that's where I left them."

Martha laid a last fork on the table. "I'll fetch them. They'll need to get washed up."

"Thanks."

Alex waited for her to leave the room. "So, do you think Mark doesn't want the baby?"

"I know so."

"But why?"

"Why do you think? He's a bastard."

"Oh, Liv!" She giggled. "When do they arrive? I can't wait to see her."

"Tomorrow afternoon, I think. Honestly, Alex, she's absolutely glowing. She's so full of herself right now. She looks beautiful."

"That's the genes, darling." Alex took a slice of tomato from the salad bowl and popped it in her mouth.

"Naturally." Olivia stirred the sauce. "I just wish she wouldn't let him walk all over her like he does. She never sparkles when she's with him. Not like she does with us. He sucks the life out of her. I can't bear it, sometimes."

Alex stroked her shoulder. "Poor Livvy. It must be hard for you to share her. I can't imagine what possessed her to fall for a man like that. Apart from his looks, of course."

"And don't forget his money."

Alex poked her in the ribs.

Mark looked down on the beach. These holidays came around way too fast. They were never away from Martha's house. They spent all the school holidays here. During the summer, Eloise would install herself with Olivia and the children. He and William came up as often as work allowed. He rarely took Eloise abroad, except for that trip to Florida with the kids, and the occasional weekend in Copenhagen or Barcelona or wherever.

How small the beach was from up here. How insignificant. He gazed across at the house on its cliff top. He shielded his eyes from the low winter sun that glinted in its many windows and bounced off the white facade. It too seemed tiny. Too small to contain all that life and activity. All that trouble. The wind gusted, making him step back. He pulled up his coat collar. He craved the sense of isolation he felt up here on the north cliff. Just sea, sky and him. And yet he needed the hectic lifestyle over at the house, despite the surfeit of family. He loved being with William and the children every day. He loved going to the pub with William each evening. It was like the old days. His main problem with Rowan's Well was the Brooke women. Even Eloise, when she was here in the bosom of her family.

Worse this time, Alex was home on a rare visit. Mark didn't know her well, but he found the stories of her Wonderful London Life increasingly tiresome. The clubbing, the theatre ("darling!"), the restaurants, the men. She was a selfish bitch. He'd seen the hurt in her boys' faces as they listened to how she got along far better without them. Of course, she never put it like that. She said she missed them "terribly, awfully

119

darlings". She tried to buy their affection with expensive gifts. But Eric and Patrick understood only too well where they ranked in their mother's life. They most likely always had understood. He had, with his own mother.

It was cold. He thrust his hands deep into his coat pockets. He didn't want to go back yet. This solitude was seductive. He gazed at the grey horizon. The twins were lucky they had their grandmother. She was there for them when Alex abandoned them so spectacularly. She'd been there for them ever since. He'd take a competent, loving grandmother over a self-obsessed, superficial mother any day. Martha had her good points, despite her constant meddling in his marriage. He kicked the gravel at his feet. Perhaps that was a little unfair. She was well-intentioned. And he enjoyed a bit of mothering as much as the next man. He belonged to a loving family. He couldn't get over that, even after so many years. True, he could take the family only in small doses, but he enjoyed it. He loved the sense of history and shared humour. All those stories, repeated to laughter and interruptions, corrections and disputes. Stories of when Eloise filled the box on her tricycle with thousands of worms. Or when Patrick fell and nearly put his eye out on a pea stick. Or when Martha bit the buttock of a visiting dignitary at the village fete when she was three. Of how great uncle Hubert forgot to come back from the war. Of the ghost of the crying baby said to haunt Rowan's Well. Even the story of the boys' inauspicious births in a Rowan's Well toilet had become the stuff of family legend. He'd never experienced anything like this before he met first the Coopers and then the Brookes. He had no family history of his own. He wiped his nose on the back of his hand. Standing here, braced against the wind off the ocean, his eyes, as well as his nose, were beginning to stream.

A movement in the cove caught his eye. It was Cass, his red setter, no more than a streak of orange from this height, dashing into the waves. The boys were with her. They were hurling driftwood into the sea for her to fetch. He smiled at their antics. Across the sandy expanse of the little bay, there was another smudge of red moving towards the sea. Eloise, or Olivia? It was hard to tell them apart at this distance since Olivia had hacked off all that hair. But the walk gave her away. There was no mistaking Olivia's purposeful stride. She walked like a man. What a pitiful waste of a beautiful body that woman was.

He turned north along the cliff path. He needed to clear his head. Why was Olivia getting involved? It was between Eloise and him. It was none of her damned business. William should keep her under control. Shit. He remembered William, distraught, trying to get between them while Olivia shouted abuse. "You cold bastard! You don't deserve her!" All he'd done was point out the pretentiousness of naming a child after a seventh-century monk. Especially one who already had the family pile named after him. He didn't want to choose names. The baby had been forced on him. How else was he supposed to behave? Olivia wanted him jumping for joy, passing round cigars. He strode on. Eloise had blackmailed him. She'd manipulated him. He should have held out, said no. Christ, he should have talked to her. He should have explained. But he'd been too afraid. He saw that now. The gravel path disappeared rapidly under his feet. She wouldn't have understood. How could she, when he didn't understand it himself? All he knew was the idea of her becoming a mother made him sick with dread. He was losing his

Eloise. And he feared what would replace her. It was mad, but he couldn't help it.

Where were the children during the row? He hoped they hadn't heard. What had he said to their mother? He couldn't remember. Thank God Eloise had been out at the time. He was an idiot. He always let that woman wind him up. He should know better. Yes, she should keep her nose out, but he should have ignored her. She was trying to start something. And he'd let her.

The collision pulled him up sharp. He'd walked full-tilt into a small guy in khaki. Mark grabbed him as he teetered on the cliff edge, unbalanced by a hefty backpack.

"Fuck!" He'd nearly gone over the edge. "Sorry, mate. You ok? Sorry, I wasn't looking where I was going."

The man pulled back, alarmed. He loosened his grip. The man was slight. Swathed in binoculars, camera, map bag, and the top-heavy rucksack. His frightened face was framed by a khaki hood which drained it of colour.

"No! No, really - my fault - entirely. Stood in the way. Not looking out for - didn't think - apologies."

He raised the binoculars to indicate he'd been looking through them rather than at the path. His body was wrapped in an anorak several sizes too big for him. He wouldn't have been out of place standing with a notebook at the end of a railway platform.

"Well, as long as you're all right …"

The little man didn't move, so he felt obliged to make small talk. The least he could do after nearly knocking him flying off a very high cliff.

"Birdwatching?"

"That's right. Plenty of activity this time of year."

"Yes, I see. Well, if you're sure you're all right? I'll be getting back. Bye, now."

"Bye." The man raised his hand in a half-hearted wave.

Mark turned and strode back towards the cove. What a day. Almighty bust-up with sister-in-law followed by near homicide of total stranger. He laughed. The look on that poor bloke's face! Wait until William heard. He rounded the headland. The cove came back into view. And so did Olivia. He stopped and watched her. She was standing at the water's edge looking out to sea. Still seething probably. He would have to apologise. They'd go through that same old tired routine of pretending to kiss and make up. It was all bollocks but it would restore peace. He started on his way again. Something caught his eye. He'd never noticed before: from up here the cove looked like a giant gaping mouth. It was as if the people on the beach, Olivia and Eric and Patrick, were crumbs caught in its throat and it was about to gulp them down with a mouthful of ocean. And the jetty. The jetty was the tongue, lying in wait, ready to savour them.

He shivered. He was suddenly keen to be back in company.

Seven Months Before
Chapter 13

Dread. Invasive quiet enclosed him. Suffocating. Sounds of his own body. Rhythmic footfalls and rasping breath. He must be out of condition. Should get back to the gym. The lane was narrow, winding, high-hedged. No pavement. And it was quiet. He hadn't seen a car since he left - where? He knew these roads. There was something wrong. They were never busy, but there should be some traffic. Farmers. Tourists? He plodded on.

The still air was oppressive. Not the familiar calm of a late summer afternoon. No warmth. He'd been walking for a long time now, but he was cold. He was wearing a T shirt, so he hadn't been cold when he set out from - where was it? He was afraid now, but he kept walking. No cars. No birdsong. No noise from the river? Quiet. Just footsteps and breathing.

What was he doing? He never walked these lanes. He always drove. That was why the hedges seemed so tall. Glowering on either side of him. In Martha's Range Rover he could see over them to the sea. When had he last walked this road? When did he start this walk? The realization hit him. He'd been walking forever. No beginning and maybe no end. His chest tightened.

The road inclined, slightly at first but soon more steeply. This was all wrong. The road followed the river down the winding gorge right on to their beach. How could it be climbing? But it did, more and more steeply until he was scrambling on all fours up an almost sheer face of tarmac. Now the road cracked and shifted under him, creating rough steps. He was clambering up a high and uneven staircase of broken tarmac. His breath burned in his throat. The hedgerows darkened. Drew together above him. He scrabbled for the next rugged step. Blackness enclosed him. The air pressed him. The stillness squeezed him. He caught his breath -

He sat up, heart pounding, blood pulsing at his temples, head fit to explode. The fear was still with him. He fought to get his breath. He was dying. He thumped the mattress. Get a grip. This was just another panic attack. Calm down. Slow your breathing. Concentrate. In, then out. In, then out. That worked. He could breathe. The fear subsided. He was safe. In bed. He listened. Eloise was breathing softly next to him. He felt the warmth of her thigh against his.

He reached out to touch her and made contact with that hard ugly growth where her flat silken belly should be. He snatched his hand away. Shrank from her. She was still pregnant. Nothing had changed. His throat closed up again. He stared into the dark. Fought to quell his fear a second time. Gradually his breathing became less laboured. He allowed himself to think. Pregnant. An ugly word for an unknowable state. Pregnant. What did it mean? How was he supposed to get his head round this? Sweat prickled between his shoulder blades. His stomach churned and cramped. Hell. The doctor said he should discuss his anxiety with Eloise. He hadn't. The doctor said he would feel better if he did. But he couldn't. How could he tell her? She was so excited. So happy. He couldn't spoil it for her. It had probably never occurred to her he wasn't as thrilled as she was. Or maybe it had crossed her mind once, at the start of the pregnancy. She'd whispered in the early hours: "Are you pleased? Are you happy?" He hadn't answered. Feigned sleep, cowardly bastard that he was. She never asked again.

This was what she'd wanted all along. He rolled away from her, to the edge of the bed. The springs creaked. He'd waited for her to ask again, so he could be honest and tell her how he felt. *You're a damn liar, Strachan.* He would never tell her. He couldn't risk losing her. He rolled onto his back. Hot tears trickled into his ears. She used to say he was her world. She'd given up her studies to look after him. They were happy. Or so he'd thought. But he was not enough for her. She wanted more. She wanted this baby. She would be a mother. He would lose her love.

Pain shot through his lower jaw. He winced. He was grinding his teeth again. He didn't want things to be different. He'd never wanted a child. She'd threatened him. She'd trapped him. He needed everything to go back as it had been. Just the two of them. But this child was coming, unstoppable as an express train, and he was tied to the tracks. He pressed his face into the pillow. This was going to destroy him.

He wasn't stupid. He knew he needed help. He'd lost weight. Wasn't sleeping. And now his work was suffering. He'd missed an important meeting about the deal with Smith-Hurst. It had simply slipped his mind. They lost time as a result. That couldn't be allowed to happen again.

And Eloise was getting more distressed. She kept asking what was wrong. She really didn't have a clue. But he couldn't tell her.

"Please, Mark. If you can't talk to me, you've got to talk to someone. I'm sure you're depressed. No babe, I'm serious. You need help. Have you told Will how you're feeling?"

An opportunity arose the following Saturday when William dropped off Olivia and the children to go shopping with Eloise.

"Got anything on this afternoon?"

William exchanged looks with Olivia. "I was going to paint the garage windows."

Olivia heaved a dramatic sigh. "If you're staying, say so. Then we can take our car. It'll save swapping all the child seats over."

Eloise overdid the fake cheer: "Do stay, Will. Keep him out of mischief."

Olivia tutted like a crabby old woman. He cupped her face in his hands and landed a light kiss on the end of her nose. The children laughed. "You are a wonderful woman, Olivia Brooke. Don't let anyone tell you different." He clapped his hands. "Good, that's settled then. Happy to help out where we can, aren't we, my friend?"

He whipped Annie and Tessa into a frenzy of giggles. He caught one, then the other and tickled them until they screamed. Not to be left out, Hugo launched himself over the back of the sofa with a tickle counter-attack.

"Shoes off the furniture. That's enough! Time to go."

The children were always quick to obey their mum. She was too controlling with them. It wasn't William's style. He was all live and let live.

After they'd gone, William wandered round the living room. He looked at the messages on the phone pad. He picked up the Daily Mail, pulled a face and dropped it. He flicked through the post behind the mantelpiece clock.

"You want to get those paid, mate." He flopped onto the sofa. "What are you waiting for? Stick the kettle on."

Mark picked up a cushion and threw it at him on his way to the kitchen. He came back with a plate of chocolate Hobnobs balanced on one of the mugs.

William reached for a biscuit. "Nice one. Shall we watch the rugby?"

"Nah." Somehow, he had to steer the conversation round to the baby. William carried on about the rugby and the football. Fucking oblivious. In the end he could think of no subtle way to start. "I can't have this baby."

William was dipping a Hobnob into his tea. "What? What d'you mean?"

It all came tumbling out. How he'd never wanted children. How Eloise suddenly decided she wanted a baby. How she threatened to leave him if he refused. How he'd started getting the panic attacks again.

William's Hobnob fell into the mug. "Does Eloise know about this? Have you talked to her?"

"How can I? How can I tell her? She'll leave me. I'll lose her."

"Mark, look at me. Think. Tell me why you don't want this baby."

How could he explain to this man who had it all? William wouldn't understand. He'd never been able to tell him about how it felt to have no loving family. No foundation while growing up. How could William ever understand how important he'd been in Mark's life? How he'd become the underpinning on which Mark could finally build. How he and Eloise, and their families, had become his bedrock. How could he explain the horror of having all that threatened? That fragile footing was breaking up beneath him. It wasn't strong enough to bear the weight of a family of his own. His wife was turning into a mother. The baby would become the centre of her world. Where would that leave him?

He couldn't say any of this.

But he had to try.

"We were happy - She loved me. She wanted me - But now she wants something else. I'm not enough for her. She wants a baby - she doesn't want me. She'll leave me, like -"

He couldn't hold back. He broke down.

"Hey. Mark, it's ok. You're not trapped. You've got choices."

"Choices?"

"Yeah. You can - you could leave if it's so bad. Get away?"

"Leave her? She's my life. I thought it was just us, me and Eloise, you know?"

William looked baffled. What was the point? Of course he didn't understand. How could he? He was surrounded by love. Had been all his life. And rightly so. He loved his kids. Loved being a dad. He thrived on it. This was pointless. He stared at the carpet, an ocean gulf separating him from his best friend. William could never understand how he was feeling, because he was accepted and loved wherever he went, not challenged at every turn.

William leaned forward and said quietly: "She'll leave you like - what? Like who?"

"Nothing. Doesn't matter."

He was a fool. He shouldn't be surprised his life was going wrong. How could he ever have hoped to be normal and happy and loved?

Enough. He wiped his eyes. "Fancy a pint?"

Four Months Before
Chapter 14

Another summer at Rowan's Well. Will opened the front door and breathed in the sea air. The sky was an intense blue. Only the occasional white cloud scudded across the sun. He left the house with Olivia and their tribe. Mark and Eloise followed on with their dog, Cass, and the new baby. Martha, with her latest man and Alex's boys, came last of all.

Will was always thrilled to see their private beach. The entire cove, tiny and almost enclosed by its great guarding cliff, was theirs. In the ten years since he married into the Brooke family, he'd never stopped being amazed at the idea of owning a piece of the coastline. Half the village in the neighbouring bay belonged to them too. It all went with the big house. But it was the cove he loved.

They were to spend the day on the beach. They brought sandwiches and drinks. They'd gather at the Ship Inn as soon as it opened at teatime for a proper meal. They spent these beach days sunbathing, paddling, building sandcastles and collecting driftwood, rock-pooling, fossil hunting, fishing. There were few visitors, other than the occasional walker who strayed from the coastal path. The beach was well known for its treacherous tides. So, while plenty of people frequented the pub of an evening, the family usually had the sands to themselves.

The bay formed a three-quarter circle. The cliff to the north curled round like a protective arm, creating a natural harbour. The locals called it Rowan's Haven. Bit of a misnomer as the sea within it was ferocious at times, especially in winter. The wind could whip straight off the North Sea. It pushed through the gap between the cliff and the southerly headland. Trapped in the cove, it would tear round, enraging the water with its centrifugal force.

Will filled his lungs with the salty air. A wooded gorge sliced through the cliffs at the back of the sands to carry the River Crowe onto the beach and thence out to sea. The pub had been built in this dip by intrepid and presumably thirsty fishermen centuries before. Next to the pub was a small boathouse, once also a fishermen's haunt, with a ramp down to the beach. In more recent times the river channel had become too deep and fast-flowing to make access to and from the cove by boat a viable business proposition. The last fisherman to work out of here had moved to Crowton back in the fifties.

The sandstone headland on the south side was crumbling. In a belated attempt to prevent similar erosion to the cliff on which the big house stood, its Victorian owners had built a stone breakwater across the mouth of the cove. Originally, it was made from boulders taken from the headland. More recently, it had been patched up with concrete. Now, it was ugly and grey. It reached out from the headland towards the north cliff, forming the other arm of the harbour. The headland had eroded more since the jetty was built. There was a gap of maybe ten feet between the landward end of it and the rocks of the headland. The sea came in through this gap, marooning the jetty at high tide. For much of the day you had to wade across.

Its concrete surface was always wet and covered in green slime. Years ago, Martha had the breach concreted over to form a little causeway. She put a metal hand rail across the gap and up some steps to the jetty. Of course the children were forbidden to go anywhere near it, on their own.

The River Crowe had been diverted from its course when they built the breakwater. Now, it clipped the end of the jetty on its way out to sea. The water there was always deep and agitated. As Will was to notice this particular day.

Looking at the jetty, he thought about that Christmas holiday a few years back. They must have been out of their tiny minds. Whose idea had it been? He couldn't remember. Mark's probably. Nutter. It had been a wild, windy night and the girls had gone to bed. They were pissed. They decided it would be interesting to investigate the jetty at high tide in a storm. Crazy. You'd think they'd have had enough of freezing water in pitch darkness to last them a lifetime. This night, however, that experience only boosted their faith in their own indestructibility. So off they went with a torch and a couple of beers. How they made it across the causeway he would never know. But things got really hairy when they reached the end of the jetty. They'd seen something on TV where a guy walked to the end of a pier, hammered by massive waves. He didn't flinch. Kept walking. When he got to the end he stood, arms outstretched, defying the sea. Mark thought it was done with trick photography, because the bloke would surely have been swept away. That night, the two of them drunk and all alone, he decided to put his theory to the test. He dared Will to stand right at the end and hold out his arms. The waves were crashing clean over the jetty. The noise of the storm was incredible. And worse, Will sensed the massive presence of the cliff looming over him in the dark. He was scared to death. He told him to piss off. So Mark took up his own challenge. Unsteadily, he assumed the crucifix position. He disappeared from Will's torch beam with the next breaker. Will flung himself on his belly. The waves lashed him. He inched forward shouting to Mark. He didn't respond. It seemed to take forever. At last, he held the torch over the edge to light the black surging water. A hand grasped his. Somehow he helped Mark scrabble up the wall to safety. He'd been swept over the beachward side, which was relatively sheltered, thank God. He managed to grab hold of an old iron mooring ring. If he'd gone over the seaward side, he'd have been dashed back against the wall. Or dragged out to sea.

Will squinted into the sun. It was hard to imagine, on this bright summer's day, the sea as wild as it had been that night. They never told anyone about that one. Way too embarrassing.

High tide was due around four o'clock so for now they could spread out on the wet sands. He helped Martha and Tim, the new boyfriend, pitch camp. The Brookes never did anything by halves. He put up the tatty old wind break, and Annie and Tessa's new beach tent. While they established base, Olivia and Eloise took the children off to play French cricket. When he'd done, he looked about for Mark. He was skulking at the back of the beach, picking over loose stones. Looking for fossils. Eloise had the baby, so this was probably his best chance to catch him on his own.

Mark stood up as he approached. "Don't start, all right? I'm not in the mood."

"Start what?" The previous night they'd indulged in a few beers. Mark had gone all weird about the baby

134

again. Rowan's arrival had changed nothing, it seemed. If anything, he was in even more of a state. It was like he felt no attachment at all to the kid. He'd tried to reassure him it was early days. He told him these were natural emotions, temporary. But were they? He thought he should try again. "How are you feeling today?"

"Fine. How are *you* feeling today?"

"I'm good, thanks, yeah. Found anything interesting?"

"Nope." Mark stooped, obviously hoping this would end the conversation.

"Shall we walk a bit? Round the headland while the tide's low?"

"You're a persistent wanker." But he smiled and fell into step beside him. "Hang on a sec. I'll bring the dog." He whistled to the red setter. She was playing with the children. "Cass, come on girl!"

The dog dropped the ball and ran up the beach to join him, followed by disappointed cries from the kids.

"Back soon!" The dog jumped up, licked his face and covered him in sand. Will was relieved to hear him chuckle as he tickled Cass behind the ears, and threw his head back to avoid her slobbery tongue. They walked towards the jetty, following the curve of the cliff. The dog trotted ahead.

"About last night." Will said. "I thought you'd maybe got past some of that stuff."

"Here we go." But Will let the silence grow as they walked on. Eventually Mark said: "I'm sorry I mentioned it, all right? I shouldn't have. Can we forget it?"

"If you like."

"You're not going to let this go, are you?"

"What did I say?"

135

"You know bloody well. Ok, so tell me. What's your solution? What should I do?"

Will's feet sank into the soft sand at every step. "I'm not sure, mate. Ride it out, I guess. Give yourself some time."

Mark stopped. He gazed out to the horizon, not bothering to shield his eyes from the noon sun's glare. "You reckon?"

"I think it'll pass soon enough. You haven't had chance to bond properly yet, that's all."

"I wish that's all it was, William." The wind whipped around them. Will struggled to hear him. His voice was almost a whisper: "I hate feeling this way. Not being able to enjoy it all with Eloise. I'm spoiling it for her. I hate what it's doing to me, what I'm turning into, but I can't help it. It's going to … it's not right."

Will shivered. A sudden sense of dread gripped him. Like a premonition of catastrophe. "Come on. Let's keep walking."

They followed Cass, who knew the way from countless similar walks, across the boulders, past the jetty and round the little headland.

This beach was much smaller than their cove. It was always covered by the high tide. A pebble beach, it was excellent for skimming. Without a word they bent to select their stones. They took turns to skim the flattest pebbles across the rough surface of the incoming waves. They moved gradually up the beach, silently competing. Cass bounded into the water again and again. Dumb dog never learned she couldn't retrieve the stones.

Finally Mark straightened his back and stretched. "We'll get cut off if we don't go now."

Will knew he didn't want to go back to the family, didn't want to face his wife or see his baby. The

136

way he was feeling right now, he would have preferred to follow the coast path south off this little beach and keep on walking. What if he did do that one day?

The breaking waves made conversation impossible as they picked their way back through the boulders and rock pools. The tide would soon cover the rocks they were scrabbling over, with a spectacular show of crashing foam and sea spray. He loved these few minutes every day when the force of the North Sea met with the coast. It was exhilarating. It had the power to fill him with joy. Today, though, his anxiety for Mark blended with the spine-tingling vulnerability and peril he often felt walking on areas only fleetingly exposed and soon to be reclaimed by the sea. He was as powerless to help him as he was to hold back the tide.

They rounded the headland. Cass ran on, barking. She'd spotted Eloise out on the jetty and was running to greet her. Everything happened so fast, it was over in a moment. Cass bounded across the flooded causeway. She jumped up the steps and onto the jetty. She made contact with the concrete surface only briefly as she skidded on the wet slime and flopped over the seaward side into the waves. They stopped in their tracks, hardly believing what they'd seen. Any moment, a seal-like head would bob up through the waves and she would swim to safety.

She didn't come up.

Eloise's agonised cry, muffled by the roar of the sea, prodded them into action. They struck out, stumbling over the last of the boulders. When they reached the causeway the water was only about knee deep, but the sea broiled about their legs, tugging them, throwing them off balance. How had Eloise managed to get across with Rowan?

She ran to meet them. She was crying. She pulled Mark's arm. "I can't see her. Where is she? Can you see her?"

She cradled the baby's head in her hand, shielding it from the spray. Mark stood perfectly still. He peered into the water. Will raised his hand against the glare coming off the sea. He scanned the waves for any sign of the dog. He couldn't see her.

"Mark? Should we go in?"

Mark stared down at the swirling waves. "No. She's gone. That undertow's got her."

Will followed his gaze to the confusion of twisting, breaking waves at the base of the jetty. Mark seemed fascinated by it.

Eloise was tugging the straps of the papoose. The baby was crying now too. She yelled at them: "She's drowning! Do something! I'll go in, if you won't. Take him!"

She thrust the baby at Mark. He recoiled. She stepped back. Mark reached out to her.

"Babe, it's too late. She's drowned."

She stepped back again. Hugged the child to her chest. "Will. Take him back, please."

Will took the little one from her. She walked past him and made her way across the deepening channel. Olivia was waiting for her on the other side. She must have seen the dog go over. He hoped she hadn't seen the rest.

"Mark? Are you coming?" He turned his back on the sea to protect the baby from wind and spray, but he stayed at Mark's side.

Mark stared into the waves. "She knows, doesn't she?" Then he said, with undisguised disgust: "Take it away."

For that moment, Will hated him. He turned and left him.

Chapter 15

That night an old dream returned. More vivid than ever. Mark was wrapped in darkness. Nausea. Cold sweat. There was something with him in the dark. He turned round. Could see nothing. But it was there. He knew. He was in imminent, terrible danger. He was about to die in the dark and he didn't know how. Or why. He opened his mouth to cry out. His voice was stopped by something cold and wet. Pressing on his face. It stank of rotten meat. It was sticky. He was going to throw up… He used to wake at this point, and in his dream he knew it. This time he didn't wake. He remained, terrified, suffocating, in the impenetrable blackness. He tried to fling away the thing that covered his face. He grabbed it and squeezed. Bones crushed under the soft wet fur. He screamed.

He lay awake long after everyone had gone back to bed. He listened to Eloise's gentle breathing beside him. He wanted to wake her again so he wouldn't have to be alone in the dark. Remembering…

He was nine. He had to do something to get his mum's attention. He thought about getting into a fight at school so they would phone her at work. Make her come and pick him up. He thought about stealing. Shoplifting, maybe. He thought about running away. A fight would be easy, but he might get hurt and he didn't fancy that. Stealing wouldn't work. He often took change from her purse and she never even noticed. Or maybe she did and didn't care. The more he thought about running away, the surer he was she would be happy if he disappeared. She'd think: "Problem solved!" The dog killing wasn't one of his ideas. It just sort of happened.

It was about a month after Jackson kicked his teeth in. He still had those stumpy caps, and he was still getting those electric-shock pains. The dentist said that would stop once he had the permanent crowns done. His mum kept going on at him about the fight. About the expense, the time she had to take off work, the embarrassment. Blah blah. On and on. His dad, as per usual, couldn't care less. When he came home on the fight night, he'd glanced up from his Daily Express. He laughed and said something about wanting to see the other bloke. And that was it. He never mentioned it again.

So now Mark was on his way to school, his mouth tight shut over his broken teeth. His precious satchel was slung carefully across his body so no one could snatch it. He liked wearing it this way because he could smell the leather strap crossing just below his chin. He loved the smell of leather. He walked up Bluebell Close. Later in the day he would never chance this, but he knew he was safe until Jackson's mum left for work at eight thirty. That moron wouldn't dare do anything with his mum around. She was a bruiser.

Wrong. At the bend in the passage, Jackson was waiting for him. The confrontation was on him before he had time to think. He turned and ran, but Jackson was quicker. The bastard rugby-tackled him. They hit the tarmac. Jackson bit him in the small of his back. He wriggled round to face him. Jackson knelt over him. Straddled his body.

"Hope you haven't got rabies," Mark said. Jackson's fat arse was squeezing the life out of him.

"You little shit." Jackson grabbed him by the throat.

"Nigel! Get here *right* now!"

His mum sounded really mad. Jackson leaped up as if Mark had bitten his balls.

"Bloody cowardy bastard!" he shouted after him. His voice was wobbly. He got to his knees and straightened his satchel. It'd better not be damaged. There were some scuffs across the tan-coloured flap. Bastard. He picked gravel out of the grazes in his palms. His back hurt. Had he drawn blood? He would check in the bogs mirror when he got to school. What if he did have rabies? Would he have to have all those injections with a giant needle in his belly like on the telly adverts? Maybe he shouldn't tell anyone about this. He'd get a drink of water in the bog at school. That was a good test for rabies. If he was afraid of the water, he'd know. It'd be curtains.

He rubbed his gritty palms on his trousers. He saw he had company. The Jacksons' Yorkshire terrier was trotting up the passage towards him. Fitz was all right. Mark liked him. He'd walked him every day for a week last Easter while Jackson was away on the Lake District field trip. Mrs Jackson had asked him to. Like all the other grownups he knew, she thought every boy who beat Mark up was his friend. It was weird. Anyway, Jackson probably didn't have any other friends for her to ask. Every day he'd taken Fitz to Marigold Park. He walked him round the playground, then across the football field to the ornamental gardens. They sat together on the grass, watching insects and fish in the pond. He never let him off his lead, because of the busy main road next to the park. And anyway,

142

Fitz wasn't really the kind of dog you could play ball with. He was too small. Too dainty. But he was cute and clever. Especially the way he cocked his head to one side when he was listening. He was a good listener.

So here was Fitz, come to say hello.

"Hiya, Fitzy." He tickled his ears. "You shouldn't be out. Let's take you home."

But he didn't want to knock on the Jacksons' door. He could hear the fat git getting a right bollocking off his mum. Anyway, why should he take Jackson's dog back? What'd Jackson ever done for him, except break his teeth and spoil his satchel? Jackson could bloody well piss off. But he couldn't just leave Fitz on his own. He might get lost or run over. The dog pranced about him. He wanted to play. He had no choice. He would have to take Fitz with him. He could put him in his satchel and smuggle him into school. But that wouldn't work. He wasn't small enough. Plus, he would never stay still and quiet all day. And what if he peed in his bag? He pictured his mum sticking her hand in his satchel for his lunch box and pulling out a handful of dog poo. Good one.

But it wouldn't work. He would just have to skip off school today to look after Fitz. He thought again about his plans to get his mum's attention. Maybe this was a good one. Playing truant. The school would phone her at work. She'd be mad as a bag of ants. She'd come all the way home. She'd think he was there. But he'd be gone. Then she'd be sorry. She would call the police. They'd send out search parties like on "The Adventures of Tom Sawyer". They'd find him eventually. Wrap him in blankets. Give him hot chocolate. With cream and a flake. Then they would have a go at his mum and dad for being bad parents. And the police would keep an eye on them after that in case they stepped out of line again. It'd be great. He scrambled to his feet.

"Come on, Fitzy. We'll hide out in The Wood."

The Wood was not as exciting or as daring as Tom Sawyer's caves. But it was handy. It wasn't far from the passage. With a bit of luck no one would see them sneak in. There were back garden fences on three sides of the Wood. Well Lane ran down the other side. If they sat in the bushes in the middle of the trees no one would see them.

The Wood was scary. There were loads of stories about strange noises in there, and people seeing things out of the corner of their eyes. And of disappearing children. It was dark and damp. He entered the greenish shade with Fitz in his arms. It was like walking into the Mines of Moria. He hugged the dog close to his chest and made his way to the clump of bushes at the centre. He went round the back of them, out of sight of the road. Here, the ground dipped to a hollow. A pool had formed over the last few rainy days. He sat cross-legged near the edge of the water. The little dog settled into his lap.

Soon he felt hungry. What time was it? He opened his satchel and pulled out his lunch box. It might be dinner time by now. He prised off the lid. It was the usual potted meat sandwiches wrapped in greaseproof paper. Boring. But there was also a p-p-p-Penguin biscuit so it wasn't all bad. He shared the food with Fitz. He thought it was dinner time too.

"Hey, I've just thought, Fitzy. This is all my plans put together." He counted off on his fingers. "One: I've run away. Two: I've stolen you. Three: I'm playing truant. School will have to phone my mum now. That's bloody brilliant, that is."

When they'd finished eating, he put the biscuit wrapper and the greaseproof paper back in the lunch box. He turned to place his satchel behind him on dryer ground. He felt a twinge in his back where Jackson had bitten him. Damn. He'd forgotten about the rabies.

He might be infected. If the police didn't find him he might die a horrible death. Like on the telly. The only symptoms he knew were foaming at the mouth and writhing around in a mad rage, like the weirdo in the advert. And everyone knew people with rabies were afraid of water. He glanced at the dark pool. Looking at it didn't bother him, but he didn't fancy drinking any of it. It was muddy. There was a nasty farty smell rising from it. And then it came to him. Of course! If Jackson had rabies he must have caught it off his dog. Fitz looked up at him in that cute cocky-head way.

"You don't look like you've got rabies."

But the only way to be sure was to see if the dog was afraid of water. He lifted the terrier out of his lap and placed him on the soggy ground facing the pool. Fitz sniffed at the water and turned back to him.

" Drink it, Fitzy. Good boy." He put on that silly high-pitched voice people always used with pets and babies. "Go on. Just try it."

He pushed the dog gently towards the water, but Fitz really didn't want any. He wriggled from his grasp and ran a few feet away, out of reach. Mark got up and brushed the backside of his trousers. He had a wet patch from sitting too long on the damp ground.

"Come here, Fitz." He patted his thighs.

Fitz stood his ground, cocking his head to one side, watching him. Then he must have decided everything was ok because he trotted back to him. The dog trusted him. That made him feel proud. He scooped

145

him up. Gave him a big hug. Fitz licked his face. His little pink tongue was tickly.

"Get off! You're not snogging me!" He laughed. "Listen Fitz, we've got to concentrate. We've got to be serious, so no more messing about. This a proper test, right?"

He knelt on the ground by the pool. He held the dog firmly but gently. He didn't want to frighten him again.

"You need to drink the water, Fitzy. For me. To save my life, see?"

He turned the dog to face the water and placed him on the ground. He held on to him. Fitz squirmed and struggled. He was ready for him this time and held on tight. He pressed down on the dog's shoulders so he couldn't stand up.

"Drink, Fitzy. Drink up, there's a good boy."

The dog scrabbled in the mud. He tried to push away from the pool, but Mark wouldn't let him go. Not even when mud sprayed into his eyes and his mouth. He spat out the gritty dirt. It tasted like dead bluebottles. But he daren't let go of the dog to wipe his eyes. He tried to blink them clean. They began to sting.

"Come on, Fitz, you stupid dog. What's the matter with you? Just bloody drink."

He felt that hot, thumpy feeling rising in his throat. The one he got when his mum and dad went out at night. His nose began to run. Did Fitz have rabies? Is that why he wouldn't drink? But if Fitz had rabies, so did he. What should he do? He couldn't think. The thumpy throat feeling was getting too strong. He strengthened his grip on the dog and pushed him into the water. He pressed down as hard as he could.

"Drink! Please drink. Please, please …"

The dog struggled and bucked in his hands. He pushed all his weight onto Fitz's shoulders and neck.

"Just a little sip. Just a sip. Just a sip." He pushed down harder each time he said "sip".

The dog wasn't fighting anymore. He'd gone limp. He pulled his hands away as if he'd touched something hot. The dog lay face down in the pool. The top of its head stuck out of the water. Its pretty little ears were all flat and wet and muddy. It didn't move.

He scrambled away. He hugged his knees close to his chest and rocked himself. He watched for any sign of movement. He wouldn't move, though. He was dead. Mark felt shivery. Was he starting with the rabies? There was mud all down his front, his arms, his legs. His mum would kill him. He shivered more violently. Before he had time to turn his head to one side, he was sick into his lap. He lay on his side. Curled into a tight ball. He cried for a long time.

He must have fallen asleep because he woke up feeling sticky and dirty. The smell of sick nearly made him throw up again. He let his eyes skim over the dog. It hadn't moved. He stood up and went nearer the pool. The little body seemed much tinier now its fur was wet and clogged up with mud. He'd done a bad thing. A very bad thing. The worst thing. He was a bad person. He'd suspected this for some time. It explained why his so-called friends picked on him. Why the teachers ignored him. Why his dad never played with him. Why his mum was always angry with him. This was the reason. It made sense. Bad things happen to bad people. Bad people do bad things. He dug his fingernails into his clenched palms. He was not going to cry again. He deserved to feel bad. He should get used to it. He pushed back his shoulders. For a moment he felt like the soldier on the beginning of "Branded". Defeated, but still proud. But that feeling passed. It was like metal shutters coming down to block off his imagination. He was just a nine-year-old boy who'd killed his best friend.

He stood for a long time, looking down at Fitz. Not really seeing him. He heard a car drive past on Well Lane and dropped to his knees. He couldn't stay here forever. He didn't want to be found by a search party now. The thought of anyone seeing him like this, seeing Fitz like that, made him feel sick again. He picked up the dead dog. The little head flopped back as he turned the body over to look at his face. The eyes were open. Fixed and cloudy. He tried not to look at them. He held the dog at arm's length. It was stupid, but he was afraid of it. He turned to the bushes. He found a little gap in the branches. He thrust the dog into the space and let go. He snatched his hands back. He didn't know if the body dropped to the ground or if it was caught in the branches. Hanging there. He didn't dare look, so there was nothing more he could do. He rubbed his hands on his trousers. He was about to turn and run when he remembered. He cleared his throat.

"Our father who aren't in heaven hollowed be thy name thy kingdom come thy will be done in earth as it is in heaven. Give us today our daily bread and lead a snot into temptation but forgive us our trespasses as we forgive them that trespass against us. For thine is the kingdom the pure and the glory for ever and ever amen."

Was it the right prayer for a funeral? It was the only one he knew. "Rest in peace, Fitzy. I'm sorry."

Mark screwed his eyes tight shut. He couldn't remember how he'd got himself home that day or if his mother found out about his truancy. What he knew for sure was this had been the day he discovered who he was. And he didn't like it. He looked at the clock: 03.00. He should try to get some sleep. He closed his eyes. Thought of Fitz and Cass. He thought of the baby. He rolled over, and tried to stop thinking.

The Day Before
Chapter 16

The summer ended. It gave way to a wet, windy autumn in Bolton, during which Mark became ever more distant with Eloise. He worked crazily long hours. He booked into a hotel near his office for a whole week in October so he could concentrate on an important negotiation. He went to Brussels three times over some land deal. He hated Brussels. She was relieved when Christmas came and they were all back with her mum at Rowan's Well.

She woke to the sound of laughter. She rolled over to Mark. He wasn't there. She sat up. Rowan hadn't cried. He always woke her, crying for his morning feed. She leaped out of bed and ran next door. She hated him being in a separate room. The cot was empty. He was gone. Oh God, where was he? Out on the landing, she heard the laughter again. She opened the door to the girls' room. Mark was sitting on Tessa's little bed, his feet up, a pillow at his back, Rowan on his knee. Annie, Tessa and Hugo were pressing in trying to make them laugh. Hugo shouted: "Tickle attack!" and all three dived on Mark. He laughed, gently fending them off, shielding the baby. He saw her watching.

"Help! Get 'em off me!" They attacked with renewed energy. Rowan cried in alarm. "Ok, ok. We're getting a bit rough for baby Rowan. Shall we let Auntie Lou give him his breakfast?"

The children backed off long enough to let him pass Rowan to her, then he disappeared under flailing legs and arms.

"Don't get them too excited, babe. Someone'll end up getting hurt."

She heard a muffled "Ok". Mark's hand emerged with a thumbs-up before descending on Annie's back, tickling furiously. Annie let out a shriek. Eloise left them to it.

She held Rowan close and went downstairs. She tried to dismiss from her mind that first thought when she saw he was gone.

There was a lot of squealing and thundering feet upstairs. Eventually, Mark joined her in the kitchen. His hair was sticking up, his face flushed.

"I don't need to ask who came off worst. Open?" She shovelled another spoonful of mashed banana into Rowan's mouth. "Have you heard Will and Liv moving about yet?"

"I think they're lying low." Mark poured himself some coffee. "Sleep all right?" He kissed the top of her head and sat down across the table from her.

"Fine. Until about fifteen minutes ago." She stirred the baby food.

"The kids heard Rowan crying so they came and got me. I thought I'd keep them all occupied a while. Give you chance for a lie in."

Typical. She couldn't help laughing. Rowan chimed in, making her laugh all the more. "Funny little man. Yes, you are!"

"Anyway, they'll be down in a sec. They're ready for breakfast." He slurped his coffee and girned at Rowan, setting him off into trills of laughter. "What are we giving them?"

"I think there's cereal. Or we could do toast? Or porridge?"

"Porridge sounds good, doesn't it, Fatty?"

"Don't call him that, Mark."

"Why not? He doesn't understand, do you, Chubby? D'you want me to finish feeding him while you get breakfast for the hordes?"

"Are you sure? You don't mind?" Had he ever fed Rowan?

"For you, anything."

He took the bowl from her and pulled the highchair round. "Here we go, Fella. Just you and me. Let's show Eloise what we can do." He scooped up a spoonful of mush, and circled it in the air like a plane before bringing it in to land in Rowan's gaping mouth. He must have been watching her.

There was a rumble from the stairs. The door burst open and the children tumbled in, shoving and shouting.

"Hey, quiet down! You'll wake your mum and dad." She went over to the Aga. "Do you all want porridge?"

Tessa shook her head.

"Tessa doesn't want porridge, Auntie Lou. She says it tastes like sick." Annie was official spokesperson for her little sister.

"Yes, but that's only when your dad makes it. Auntie Lou makes lovely porridge. Especially if you put loads of honey on it. Yummy!" Mark rubbed his stomach, rolled his eyes, licked his lips.

"Mark, give over." She laughed along with the children. Rowan banged on the high-chair tray and kicked his legs. The children sat at the table to watch him being fed.

"You keep missing his mouth, Uncle Mark."

"I don't. He keeps missing the spoon."

"Try not to get it *all* over him, babe. Wipe his mouth with the bib."

"I knew that." Mark winked at the kids. "How many sleeps 'til Christmas now, Tess?" She counted her fingers, her face serious. "Help her out, you two."

"Five!"

"That's right. Clever girl." Tessa beamed. Mark scraped the last spoonful from the bowl. "And what's Father Christmas bringing you, Annie?"

"Me two front teeth." Annie grinned, showing off her gap.

"That's my girl." Mark put down the bowl. "All gone, Buster."

Rowan began to cry.

"He wants some mummy milk," Annie said, looking over at her.

"I think you might be right, sweetie. Mark, can you finish this off while I feed him?"

"Sure. Anyone for a bowl of sick?"

The children squealed and pulled faces.

"Bet I could eat a bowl of actual sick," Hugo said.

"Yeah, but could you eat a bowl of *dog* sick?" Mark switched off the hotplate.

"Blaargh!" Hugo mimed throwing up on Annie. She shoved him away.

"Mark, they'll not eat at all if you carry on like that."

The twins shuffled in, tousled and groggy. They were so handsome, the pair of them, even in this state. Rowan was definitely looking a lot like them these days, despite having Mark's thick dark hair. "Sorry, boys. Did this noisy lot wake you?"

"Smelled porridge. Any left?" Patrick scraped back a chair and sat down. Tessa held up her arms. He lifted her on to his knee.

Eric took some orange juice from the fridge and drank from the carton. "Shall I do some toast?" He wiped his mouth on the back of his hand.

"Good idea. Toast, and lots of it," Mark said. "Now, where are my helpers?" The children jumped up. "I need bowls. I need spoons. I need glasses. I need juice. I need sugar. I need honey. I need jam. I need Marmite. I need runny snot."

"Yuck!" Hugo pretended to vomit again, egged on by Patrick.

"Ok. Forget the Marmite."

Livvy's tribe sprang into action. They rummaged in the fridge and cupboards, standing on chairs to reach the high ones. Patrick lifted Tessa to get to the top shelves. Mark switched on the radio. Mr Blobby was on. A cheer went up. She watched as they all marched around the table led by Mark, singing along to the chorus. When the song finished, Mark flopped down next to her, out of breath. He blew his fringe from his eyes.

"Come the revolution, that Noel Edmonds is first up against the wall. Now, where were we? Oh yeah. Porridge."

He got up and filled the bowls, singing softly, "Blobby, oh Mr Blobby, If only you could make us understand."

She laughed. She stroked Rowan's hot cheek as he fed. Maybe things were going to get better.

The Day
Chapter 17

The December wind bit hard. It whipped off the sea. Raced round the cove. Olivia had wanted to stay indoors. She was on rather a roll with the novel. But she'd been outvoted. The family was already scattered across the sands. The Brookes took being outdoorsy to extremes sometimes. She paddled at the edge of the sea. She burrowed her toes into the cold sand. It felt positively warm compared with the freezing water. She surveyed the beach, trying to frame a usable sentence to describe this weather. *The wind was like a savage ghost tearing into the scars of the cliffs in search of lost souls.* Yes. Gothic. Over the top? Maybe. It went with the shipwreck theme, though. She hadn't brought her notebook, as usual. She would have to remember it. She knew she wouldn't. She'd rolled her trousers up and was carrying her trainers. She'd read that paddling in cold water stimulated the circulation, as long as you didn't do it for too long. She breathed deeply. There was Mum, in her tatty wooden deckchair, clutching a paperback and talking animatedly with Tim. He was gesticulating toward the house. She still hadn't got to the bottom of that one. Mum insisted Tim was the grandson of an old friend, but there'd been an awkward moment on the landing a couple of nights back when he seemed to have lost his way. It wouldn't be the first time. She looked for the children. She could relax. Patrick and Eric were with them. They were practically young men now. They took good care of their little cousins. Will and Mark were deep in conversation as usual, as they wandered over to join the kids. What did the two of them always find to talk about? When they reached the rocks they parted. Will picked his way to the children at the rock pools. Mark diverged onto the jetty. He turned in her direction, grabbing the handrail to steady himself across the causeway. He was holding the baby. What a bloody idiot. The wind was too cold for Rowan out there. And who in their right mind would wade through that water in the middle of winter? She looked down at her blueing feet and bent to pull on her trainers. She winced as the sand scraped her skin.

Lou joined her. They linked arms. Lou kicked at the waves with her wellies.

"How can you stand it this cold, Livvy? You'll get chilblains."

"Haven't so far." She nodded at the jetty. "They'll both sleep tonight after a blow out there."

"What the hell's he doing? Mark! Mark! What are you doing? It's too cold!"

Mark didn't react. Maybe he couldn't hear her.

"Fucking hell!" She stomped off round the curve of the beach to retrieve Rowan. Olivia followed her, running to keep up.

Mum waved. Tim was losing his battle with the ancient deckchair. It had no intention of folding to his superior strength. Scraps of their conversation drifted to her on the wind as they strode by.

" … such a sweetie, darling … language, Tiger. Girls! Darlings! We're heading home. Make sure the boys come back with you, yes?"

Olivia waved back. "Ok. We won't be long. Not with this wind." Facing round, she collided with Lou. She'd stopped dead. "Hey! Careful! Lou?" She followed her gaze to the jetty. She saw Mark dive into the water on the far side. She saw Will wade, incredibly fast and surefooted, across the causeway. He dived in after Mark. She blinked.

Lou groaned like she'd been punched in the belly. She ran into the sea towards the jetty. The tide was coming in. The water was deep. Olivia lunged, grabbed her coat, fell on top of her. They wallowed in the biting surf. The salt tasted like bloodied noses.

"What are you doing? You'll freeze." She shouted over the clamour of the waves.

"He dropped him." Lou said it quietly, almost inaudibly. But then her voice rose to a scream. "He dropped the baby. He dropped Rowan!"

Olivia held her tight. What? That couldn't be. Everything outside them was suddenly distant, silent, slowed down. Like a dream. No one on the jetty. She peered over her shoulder, her wet hair lashing, poking her eyes. Tim was running, slipping on the dry sand, his legs pumping too fast for the speed he seemed to go. Comical, somehow. She saw her Mum standing, still and erect. The look on her face spurred her to action.

"Get up. Come on!"

She hauled Lou to her feet and half-carried her, still screaming, to the shore. Martha ran to meet them. "I've got her. Go, go!"

Olivia ran. She saw the children hesitate at the edge of the causeway. "Stop!" Her three obeyed at once. But the twins leaped across in quick heedless strides. One of them - Patrick? - disappeared over the far edge of the jetty, like Mark and Will. God. Oh God. Her breath burned as she ran over the wet sand. Tim reached the jetty just ahead of her. He pushed Hugo aside and stepped into the sucking water. The girls threw themselves into her open arms, crying. She hugged them. Looked over their heads at Hugo.

"Mum, Uncle Mark dropped Rowan in the sea," he said.

His little face echoed his grandmother's. He opened his mouth to cry. No sound came out. His look of abject terror horrified her. Later, it would be this she remembered. She would blot out the pictures of Lou rocking back and forth, pulling her hair. She would erase the image of Will shaking, crying, smeared in blood. But Hugo's face when he told her what he saw was etched on her mind for ever.

For now, she summoned briskness. "Back to the beach, all of you. The tide's nearly in. Run to Gran. She's over there, see?" She pushed the girls toward the sands. Hugo hung back. "Hugo, take them to Gran. Don't argue. I need you to do this."

He hesitated, then walked forward and grasped his little sisters' hands. She watched them go. With a sickening mixture of relief and mounting horror, she turned to the jetty.

"Give me your hand!"

Tim and Eric were on their knees leaning over the seaward edge. The waves swelled and crashed over them. They'd be swept into the sea. She made out two heads bobbing in the hurling water close to the jetty. Will and Patrick were struggling to hold on to Mark. They seemed to wait for the next strong wave to lift him up the sheer wall. The three of them disappeared under the swell. They emerged moments later, coughing and gasping. They were being pulled under by the cross currents. What was he doing? Mark was trying to fight them off. She heard Eric shout a warning. A massive wave loomed behind them. It swallowed them. Crashed over the jetty. She closed her eyes.

When she opened them, they were still there. Tim and Eric were drenched but safe. The others bobbed helplessly, too close to the rough concrete wall. Mark's head sagged. He went under, but Will and Patrick had hold of him. They dragged him up. Blood appeared on his face. It washed away when he sank again. This time, as they hauled him upward, another surging wave lifted them high enough for Tim to grab the back of his collar. Eric hooked an armpit. They heaved up the dead weight. They dropped him to the floor. He lay face down on the concrete. He couldn't be dead? They turned back for Will and Patrick.

Patrick reached up to them. He looked so small. How was this happening? Eric grabbed his hand. It looked like Will pushed from behind. Patrick popped out of the sea on the next surge. Like a baby born from a sudden contraction. She heard herself laugh. Put a hand to her mouth. He landed on the hard concrete, coughing, sobbing. She tried to pull off her jacket, but it was soaked and heavy. Damn. She stepped into the water. It was colder than she'd thought. She gripped the handrail. The tide tried to suck her feet from under her.

"Give me your hand!" Tim yelled over the waves' roar. "Come *on*, Will!"

But Will moved away. He was swimming away. "Couldn't see him. 'Nother look."

"It's too late! Will, come back!"

But he'd already dived under. He came up again further from the jetty. He twisted about in the water. Searching. He dived once more.

"Fuck." Tim hesitated on the edge. Looked like he was screwing up courage. She heard shouts from the beach.

Later, after the police had finished their interviews and the family could talk together, she found out what happened next. Hugo had run up to the pub to raise the alarm. He'd always been a level-headed child, but she was amazed, and so proud, that he'd kept his composure when he needed it most. He'd certainly saved his father's life. As she heard it, some men who'd arrived at the boathouse to do repairs ran down the sand, shouldering between them an inflatable dinghy. At the water's edge, two of them jumped into the boat and took up the oars.

"Over here!" Tim waved frantically.

Next thing, while she was wrapping Patrick in her sodden fleece, two men waded across the causeway. One was John Peart from the Ship. The water was up to their hips. They went to Tim.

"Where's the kiddie?"

"In the water."

The one that wasn't John kicked off his boots. He was a fisherman based out of Crowton. Mick. She knew him from the pub.

"Where did he go in?"

"Here." Tim pointed at his feet.

Mick dived. The dinghy appeared round the end of the jetty. The two men in it were scanning the sea all about them. Will surfaced just within their reach. Thank God. Hold on, love. They leaned out. Pulled him close to the rubber side. They scooped him up like he weighed nothing. She guessed they were used to handling the writhing weight of a full net. They turned the dinghy. Disappeared back towards the beach. Will was safe. She hugged Patrick tight. He was shivering terribly. Mick was still in the water. He dived under the surface.

When he reappeared, John shouted: "That's it, Mick. No more."

He waved and struck out with strong strokes for the beach. He clearly preferred to spend longer in the icy water than chance getting smashed against the jetty.

She heard sirens. She looked back to the beach. It was filling with blue lights and uniforms. Still, Mark did not move.

Wrapped in blankets, Will sat in the doorway of an ambulance. He watched the muted activity around him. He was having difficulty understanding he was alive and safe. He'd survived. He was battered and raw, and possibly rendered deaf, so quiet was it here compared to the roar and thunder of those waves. But he was alive. He began to shake. He mustn't think about the sea. Not now. He must hold himself together. He needed to be sharp. He looked about him.

There was plenty of movement, but an ominous lack of urgency. Three ambulances were gathered in the little pub car park, as well as police cars and the coastguard's van. There were dark uniforms everywhere, gathered in groups. The crackle of police radios filled the air, distracting from the mocking roar of the waves that was, he realised now, discernible even here behind the pub. He ducked instinctively. A yellow helicopter swooped and clattered overhead, low enough to stir the fine layer of sand which perpetually covered the tarmac. He had the strangest feeling he wasn't supposed to be here. This nightmare couldn't be happening to him. It was as if he was sitting on the sidelines of the drama. He was there to observe, but on no account to participate. This was a comforting delusion. He held it close as he watched Olivia, Martha and Eloise, supported by two policewomen, get into a car. They were driven off up the track to the house. He looked across the car park at Mark. He found he was afraid to meet his eye. Mark, too, was bundled in blankets. He was shuddering violently. Will needn't have worried. Mark wouldn't look at him. As Will watched, he pushed away an ambulanceman who'd been dabbing a wound on his face. He strode after the women. Two policemen fell into step on either side of him, but they didn't try to stop him.

A paramedic came over. "Keep your head still, mate. Let me clean up this cut for you. It could do with stitches. We'd better get you to A&E."

"No."

"This needs seeing to. And you were in the water a long time. You need checking over, mate."

"No." He brushed the man's hand away. "Have you finished? I need to get back to my family."

The paramedic stepped back and looked him over. "Albert? Over here. This gent's refusing hospital. What d'you reckon?"

His colleague shrugged. "Same as the other guy. And the boys. He's *compos* so just get him to sign. Then we're covered."

"What about the boys? Are they ok?"

"Yeah, they should be all right. We're concerned about the risks from exposure. He was in the water a good while, yeah? And the other one: he's showing signs of shock. There are no parents, that right? Are you the guardian?"

"No, their grandmother is. But let me talk to them. They'll listen to me. They need to go with you."

"Sounds like a plan. They're over here. Are you all right to walk?"

He stood and was surprised when his knees buckled. But the men were ready for it. They supported him under each elbow.

"You need to get out of those wet things pretty damn quick, mate, ok?"

He wandered from room to room. That strange subdued activity had crept up the hill from the car park and seeped into the house. The boys had gone to hospital with Tim. He found Olivia and Martha in the living room with Eloise. They were holding her, rocking her. Or was she rocking herself? He couldn't tell. Mark sat on the sofa opposite them. Shoulders slumped. Staring at the floor. He had a red gash across his right cheek. It was beginning to bruise up. He was still shivering though he'd changed into dry clothes. A policeman sat next to him. Watching him. The Christmas tree stood in the corner. Mocking them. Olivia moved to get up, but he signalled her to stay with Eloise. She nodded and tried to smile. She'd aged ten years since they left the house that morning. Was it only that morning? He smiled back at her. How did he look to her? He wanted to bury his head in her neck and cry. But he had to stay strong. He blew her a little kiss on one finger. Who had the children? He went through to the kitchen. A couple of women from the village, Thora and - was it Phyllis? - were making drinks and sandwiches. They tried to give him some tea. When he refused they shooed him upstairs.

"You need to get into something dry, love. Go on. The children are up there with Maggie and John."

He looked into the girls' room. They sat cross-legged in a duvet bivouac. They were munching jam butties, though most of Tessa's jam was round her mouth. Tears threatened again. His little daughters. So

163

trusting. So soft and weak. How could he? What had he been thinking? Maggie Peart, the pub landlady, a great favourite with the kids, was reading 'Each Peach Pear Plum'. The girls looked up. They waved at him, oddly quiet. They seemed content to stay in their den, so he left them with Maggie. He went into the next room. As soon as he opened the door, Hugo was on him, clinging to him, crying into his belly. Will hugged him, stroked his unruly straw-coloured hair. He fought back the tears.

"Shh. It's ok, love. It'll be all right. Shh."

John stepped forward. He'd led the men with the dinghy. "Come on, son. Let your dad get out of those wet clothes. Then you can talk properly. Hugo's got something he needs to tell you." Will nodded. "Come and have a bite to eat while you're waiting for your dad."

There was a tray of sandwiches and orange juice on the bed. He handed his boy over. "Thanks, John."

He went to his own room. Closed the door. It was happening again. How could this happen again? Everything was strange. Nothing was right. Olivia had left the children to the care of relative strangers. Mark, usually in the thick of everything, sat limp and lifeless. And Eloise... The house was full of people he didn't know. Their cosy, dependable reality had broken. In an instant. His family. All broken. He sat heavily on the bed. There were fresh clothes laid out, with a warm hot water bottle lying on top of them. It was creepy. How did they know where he kept his stuff? Disaster had hit like a bolt of lightning. No warning. Yet the villagers seemed to have been rehearsing for it. They had a preparation, a response for everything. It was weird. He suddenly felt trapped. At their mercy. Like that poor bastard in the 'Wicker Man'. Christ, if only things were that simple. He picked up the rubber bottle and put it in his lap. Hugo needed to tell him something. He knew what it was. He didn't want to hear it. He slumped forward, compressing the hot water bottle. Sobs racked him. But he couldn't indulge himself. Not yet. He sat up. Drew a wet, sandy sleeve across his eyes. He must get changed.

"Get a grip. They need you."

He took the clean clothes into the bathroom. He set the shower as hot as he could stand it.

A few minutes later he was back with Hugo. He was warm at last and stronger for it.

"John, I want to thank you. I think you guys saved my life." He held out his hand.

John took it. "This is a hell of a thing, Will."

"Yeah." He glanced at Hugo. "Could you give us a minute, please?"

"Yes, of course. I'll go and check on Mark."

John closed the door behind him. Hugo tried to whisper but couldn't sustain it: "Dad, I need to tell you. It's really important. I didn't tell John, cos - I don't know - it might be a secret."

His heart lurched. Was it going to be a secret? Could he do that to Hugo? Could he - *should* he? - hope to control this, even now? He swallowed, trying to ensure his voice came out calm and steady. "What is it, lad?"

Mark stared at the carpet. He didn't see it. He saw the sea. The agitated waves at the end of the jetty. He'd killed his son. Incredible. Impossible. He'd killed his baby son. Mark Strachan. Loving husband. Doting uncle. Respected solicitor. Killer. Ridiculous. It couldn't be true. But he knew it was. He'd got what he wanted. He'd made it happen. Murderer. He said it. In his head. Over and over. Murderer. It was a seductive word. If he kept saying it, he wouldn't have to think about - Rowan. In the water. They still hadn't found him. He made himself stay seated. They didn't need him down there, running about on the beach. He glanced at the clock on the mantelpiece. The police officer looked up too. When would they start asking questions? It had been ages. They hadn't found him. They might yet, but he doubted it. He looked at Eloise and recoiled. She was staring at him with raw rage. He looked at the carpet again. He longed to go to her, to comfort her. To beg her forgiveness. Share her grief. But that was impossible now. He'd destroyed everything. This wasn't how he'd imagined his life would end. The woman he adored hating him. He should have stayed in bed. He shouldn't have taken the baby from Eloise. He should have stuck with William. He shouldn't have unzipped his coat. He shouldn't have... He shouldn't have. What the hell had got into him? For Christ's sake, what had he been thinking? Nothing he could do or say now could put things right. Nothing. So he must say nothing. Say nothing, Murderer.

"I saw it, Dad."

Will seized his opportunity. "Yes, we know, love. Uncle Mark dropped baby Rowan. It was a terrible accident -"

"No. He did it on purpose, Dad. He didn't slip or anything. He just let go of him. Like this."

Hugo stood back. He held out his arms at full stretch in front of him, palms turned in. Then he turned them down to the floor and spread his fingers wide. He looked Will straight in the eye. The hairs on the back of his neck stood up. He stared at Hugo. Not only had his boy seen what happened, he'd understood the cold deliberation behind it. He'd seen it too. What should he do now? What should he say? He had to say something. Hugo misinterpreted his hesitation.

"I'm sorry, Dad. Shouldn't I have said it? I didn't know what to do. Don't be angry. Please, Daddy." He started to cry again.

"Come here." Will pulled him onto his knee and held him. "Don't cry. You've been really brave. I'm so proud of you. It's just I don't - I don't know what to do either. I don't want to believe it -"

"It's true, Dad. I'm not lying, honest." Hugo's sobbing voice was muffled, his face pressed to Will's chest.

"Hey, I know that. I believe you. It's - I wish it *wasn't* true. D'you understand?" Hugo nodded. "Don't worry, love, because I saw it, too. I saw what happened. I'll deal with it. You don't need to speak to anyone else about this. Not even Mum, ok?"

"Ok." Hugo tilted his face to Will's. "So is it a secret, then?"

He blushed. "I'm not sure yet, love. Uncle Mark's in a lot of trouble. I need to think."

"If we tell, he'll go to prison, won't he?"

"I think so. Yes."

"Poor Auntie Lou." Hugo's face crumpled again.

Will rocked him. He was soon asleep. Done in. He lay him on the bed and pulled the duvet over him. He stood a moment gazing down at him. How did kids manage to simply tune out like that? How he wished he could do the same right now. But he couldn't put it off any longer. He must speak with Mark. And then - Christ knows.

He left Hugo and looked in on the girls. They were listening with rapt attention to 'Winnie the Pooh'. They didn't even notice him peering round the door. He caught Maggie's eye. She nodded slightly. He withdrew. Thank God for good neighbours. Downstairs, he stopped at the living room door and looked in. No one had moved. Olivia and Martha were still at Eloise's side, arms about her. Mark sat opposite, still staring at the floor. The police officer watched him. How was he going to speak to Mark without the bobby eavesdropping? He stepped into the room. It felt like he was stepping off a cliff. Three faces turned to him. Eloise and Mark seemed oblivious to his presence. He sat down next to Mark. There was a knock at the front door. He started up again.

"I'll get it, sir." The policeman stayed him with a hand and went quietly from the room.

Liv gave him a blanched, but warming smile. With renewed courage, he gathered his wits to start the hardest conversation of his life. He took a deep breath. The policeman returned, followed by two plain-clothed officers. This was bad. He stood up.

"Mr Cooper? I'm Detective Inspector Rowe. I'm sorry to intrude, but we need to speak to Mr Strachan. Perhaps there's another room we could use?" His glance slid to the women.

"Why? What's going on?" Olivia stood up, looking from him to Mark and back again.

Mark rose. He pushed his shoulders back. "You can do it here, Inspector."

"If you're sure?" The policeman glanced at Eloise again.

Mark nodded.

"Mark Strachan. I am arresting you on suspicion of the murder of Rowan Strachan earlier today. You do

168

not have to say anything, but anything you do say may be written down and used in evidence. Do you understand?"

Mark nodded.

"What? What the hell does that mean? Mark, tell them they've got it wrong. Will, tell them." Olivia shook Will's arm.

He pulled her to him. "Let them do their job, love."

The officer stepped toward Mark. "We need you to come with us now, please."

Mark looked at Eloise. She appeared not to have understood or even heard the exchange. Her head rested listlessly on her mother's shoulder. He looked at Will. Afterwards, Will would marvel at how he'd managed to survive that moment. It felt like all the oxygen had been sucked from the air when Mark looked into his eyes that last time.

He didn't say goodbye. He said: "Look after her."

The police led him away.

No one moved. Martha held Eloise close. Olivia gripped his arm. She stared at him. He clung to her. How could this be happening? What had they done to deserve this?

"Did you know?" Olivia asked.

She sounded accusing. How to answer her? He'd failed to speak up. And he'd failed to protect Mark. He'd run out of time. He should have come forward straightaway. But how could he, when he didn't understand? When none of it made sense? It was all mad.

"Will? Answer me. Did you know?"

"No... Yes... I don't know. I saw him. So did Hugo."

169

Olivia shook off his arm and ran from the room. He let her go. Helplessness and exhaustion overwhelmed him.

"What did you see?"

Her voice chilled him. Eloise looked at him through damp strands of hair. Her eyes and nose were red. Christ, this wasn't fair. Why did he have to be the one to tell her? But who else was there? Who else did she have now? He knelt before her. Took her hands in his.

"Do you understand what just happened, Lou?" He tried to keep his voice steady. He glanced at Martha for moral support.

She brushed the hair from Eloise's face. "Darling? You know Mark has gone with the police?"

Eloise nodded, her honey eyes dull, but fixed on Will. He squeezed her hands. He tried to smile, but the tears he'd held back so far were unstoppable now. He pressed on. The sooner she knew, the sooner she could come to terms with it. Like hell.

"I saw him lift Rowan out from his coat. He held him up. Like he was having a good look at him, you know? I thought he was talking to him." His voice gave way, but he struggled on. "Then he held him out over the water. I'm so sorry, sweetheart. I shouted. I tried to get there. I tried. But it was too late. I couldn't get to him. He dropped him. He just - dropped him."

Will lay his head on her lap. He gave way to his confusion and grief. She stroked his hair until he regained control.

When he raised his head, she wasn't crying. She seemed preoccupied. He looked at Martha. She shrugged, frowning.

"Do you understand what I told you, Lou?" He stroked her cheek.

170

She nodded. "Yes. I understand. He killed Rowan. My baby is dead. Mark killed him. Yes. Thank you, Will. Thank you for trying to save him. Actually, I'm quite tired now. I think I'll go for a lie down." She squeezed his hand and let it fall. "Mum, will you come up with me?"

"Of course, darling." Martha was crying now. She too squeezed his hand. She followed Eloise from the room.

He was alone. He went to the big sash windows overlooking the sea. How could he do it? How could his best friend, the man he knew better than anyone, have killed a defenceless child? His own son? He couldn't take it in. He must speak with Mark. He had to find out what really happened. Because this couldn't be it. He'd tried to talk with him before they were brought up from the beach. He'd got no sense out of him. He'd just cried. It must have been an accident. He couldn't have meant to do it. He'd seen it. He knew what it looked like, but he must be mistaken. He saw Mark holding Rowan. Reaching out. Letting go. It was deliberate. Mark had found a way out. He'd killed his baby. Will felt dizzy and sick. He sat down heavily on the window seat. Stared out to sea. Mark had killed his baby. Murdered him. Tiny little mite, in that water? He'd had no chance. Mark had given him no chance. How did the stupid fucking bastard think this was going to solve anything?

He clasped his hands behind his head and squeezed his elbows together. He stayed like that for a long time.

He was roused by a gentle tap at the open door. It was Maggie.

"Will? Can I come in?" She stepped inside. "Sorry to disturb you, love. Only the policeman outside knocked to say there are some press people on their way up. He said to draw the curtains for now, and he'll deal with them."

"Maggie -" He cleared his throat. "Sorry. D'you think you could...?" He couldn't say more. He gestured to the Christmas presents under the tree.

"Oh, Will. Yes, of course I'll see to them. Don't you worry about it." She hesitated, her eyes on the tree. "So, shall I draw the curtains?"

He stood to let her get to the windows. She swept the red velvet drapes closed, plunging the room into semi-darkness, but not before Will saw a group of reporters and TV cameramen emerge, jostling, from the cliff path to spill onto the lawn. Maggie saw them too. She hurried from the room.

He went to sit on a sofa, but stopped himself before he made contact with the seat. This was where Mark had sat. Goosebumps prickled his skin. He sat on the sofa opposite, half-expecting Mark to materialise before him. He leaned back into the plump velour, breathing in the scent of tea roses that followed Martha always. His eyelids grew heavy. Exhaustion was kicking in, on top of the shock. He wanted to sleep forever. He wondered how Olivia was coping with the kids. He slid into oblivion.

PART THREE

2003: Ten Years After
August
Chapter 18

Will sat on the warm sand, going over his conversation with Mark's probation officer.

"The ten-year tariff on his sentence runs out in a few months," Ian Selby had said. "But he still refuses to talk about his crime, and that's where I hope you come in. If he won't address his offending behaviour," - offending behaviour? Christ! - "he won't be released on licence. Simple as that."

He watched the sand slide through his fingers. Did he care?

Their lives had been torn apart in the weeks after Rowan died. The day it happened, those reporters couldn't wait to tell him, cameras poised, about the birdwatcher on the north cliff. Spying on them. Seeing it all. He'd lashed out. Lost control. He'd wanted to hurt that birdwatcher so badly. The scumbag reporter was just convenient. Or was it Mark he'd wanted to hurt, even then? The reporter had got his revenge. "Monster's Best Mate!" Not his finest hour.

That Christmas didn't happen. He could still hear Liv's stifled sobs as she took down the tree. The kids had watched, bewildered. Later, she'd carefully packed away all the presents. They were in the attic, here at the Well, yet. He hugged his knees. They'd gone home to Bolton, but the press followed. Every time they set foot outside the house, cameras and microphones were pushed in their faces. Reporters had even pestered the kids at school.

They'd all been made to suffer for what Mark Strachan did.

He rested his chin on his knees. Mark probably knew nothing of this. That last day in court was the last time he saw him. Mark had pleaded silently with him, eyes full of what he'd refused to recognize as grief. Until today. What Mark said, as Will left him this afternoon: maybe he *had* done it to himself as well as them? Had he turned his back on Mark when he needed him most? He'd been his closest, his only friend. He should have seen it coming.

The incoming tide surged over his feet. He jumped up. Now he had a wet arse, on top of everything else. He walked along the water line toward the jetty, kicking the newly-wet pebbles. He stooped to pick up a likely-looking skimmer. The water pushed gently up the beach, lapping his boots. Quieter now than then. He touched his forehead. The scar through his eyebrow would always remind him of the ocean's force that day.

That day. He didn't want to think about it. Didn't want to be reminded of his part in it. His lack of judgement. His piss-poor character judgement. Was Mark a monster, like the papers had said? Or was he merely a misguided, fucked-up fool, made a killer by an irrational impulse? But he must have always been capable of murder. He'd been his best friend and not known it. He kicked the sand. He should have seen it coming. If only he had. If only. He shook his head. Pointless.

He scanned the cove. The scene of such horror and pain. And yet he loved this place. He'd been here every year since it happened. Compelled. But it was a mistake to come here again after last year. Alex and

Eric would never want to come back. He and Olivia had sworn they would never return. They were going to sell up. But when it came to it, Liv couldn't let go. Not yet. He gazed at the jetty. Why did they have to go on picking at the scab? What could they gain from going over Rowan's death? However silently, however unacknowledged, every day they stayed here, they relived it.

He turned his back on the sea and headed up to the house. He wished he hadn't gone to see Mark now. He hadn't prepared himself. Hadn't reckoned on feeling so angry all over again. And Olivia would know. She would sense it. Hell, she would probably smell the place on him. He'd been an idiot not to tell her. What had he been thinking? She would be angry. And hurt. He walked up the side of the pub. He started to prepare his defence.

They'd all turned forty last month. His birthday was on the first of July, then Mark's on the twelfth, and Olivia and Eloise, on the twenty seventh. There hadn't been much of a celebration. Eloise had remained in London. She'd refused to join them. It hurt Olivia more than she would admit. It wasn't the fortieth they'd once envisioned, but it had set him thinking. Remembering.

Birthdays had always been important to them. It was like they shared one, the four of them. And they first met the twins on their twentieth birthday. They'd been celebrating in the student union bar. He smiled as he walked up the cliff path toward the house. He remembered how he hadn't seen it straight off that they were identical. Eloise was striking. Her copper hair, cut in a short smooth bob, caught the light as she reached for her cocktail at the bar. She had a ridiculously long fringe. It covered her eye. Like the girls in The Human

League. She was gorgeous. Slim and curvy. And she knew it. She wore a skimpy black dress. It had a plunging neckline, revealing white delicate-looking flesh. The dress was so short it barely covered her arse. He grinned now, looking back. Those coquettish flicks of her crossed legs had been aimed at James and Pete who were plying the girls with drinks. Mark soon put a stop to that. With their mates, he was often awkward and offhand. But put him with a pretty girl, and he really turned on the charm.

From their seats in a dark corner of the crowded bar, Mark watched Eloise's flirtation, openly drooling. He yelled over the jukebox:

"Look at those two. Jesus! D'you think they're twins? Never seen them in here before. What's Pete playing at? He's way out of his league there. Come on. Let's introduce ourselves."

He strode over to the bar with his usual arrogance. Pete must have thought the girls knew him, because he stood back to make room for him. Will stayed where he was in the corner, his elbows resting on the beer-sodden table. He'd finally noticed Olivia. She perched on a bar stool next to Eloise. She wore a long, flowing frock. It seemed to billow and float even as she sat there. It was many shades of green. She didn't cross her legs, he noticed. She seemed to be barefoot. Her toenails were painted green. He watched her pick up the pint of Guinness James placed before her. She took a long pull from it. Wiped the foam from her mouth with the back of her hand. God, he thought he loved her already. Her hair was long and curly, the same rich red as her sister's. Her skin was pale, rendered paler by the deep greens of her dress. Just like Rossetti's Lizzie. He'd spent many happy hours, as a teenager, studying those paintings in Manchester Art

178

Gallery. He'd dreamed of fair maids and damsels in distress who lived only to be seduced by him. In his dreams, they were always quick learners. Now, here was his dream girl, come to life.

He approached the house, lost on this tide of reminiscence. It wasn't the thought of the row lying ahead that left him dry-mouthed, but the memory of scraping back his chair and walking over to the bar, jelly-kneed...

"Ah, my man!" Mark flung an arm around him, blocking out Pete and James, nudging them further down the bar. "Ladies, may I introduce William? William, this is Eloise. And *this* is Olivia." He flourished his free arm, like an eighteenth-century explorer presenting some rare treasure to the Royal Society. He must have been thinking of the Pre-Raphaelites plastered all over Will's bedroom walls. He'd seen the resemblance, too. Will smiled. Olivia whispered in Eloise's ear. They both laughed. That was hard. He thought he heard her say: "Tosspot". Yet, even in his humiliation, he noticed her lips. Beautifully formed and perfectly pink. He backed away, but she turned a radiant smile on him. She said: "Not you."

He opened the front door. That night had been the most important of his life. He'd fallen for Olivia on the spot. They'd rarely spent a night apart in the twenty years since.

They soon got rid of the other lads. They moved back to the table in the corner, and now it seemed intimate and cosy, all lit up by the fiery lights in the girls' hair. He hadn't wanted that night to end. He could have sat there for ever with these three people. He sensed, even then, they would become his family, the centre of his life. They joked about getting together again on their fortieth birthdays.

"We'll meet here. In this bar," Mark said to Eloise. "I'll wear a red rose in my lapel, so you'll recognise me." He scooped up her hand and kissed it with theatrical passion.

"You won't need the rose, darling. You'll be the only man in here with grey hair and polyester trousers."

"And you'll not have all this, then." Olivia laughed and ruffled Will's hair. It was the first time she touched him.

"Will you like me bald? Could I carry it off?" He squashed his hair flat and pushed his face into hers, apeing toothlessness. She kissed him. They laughed at the outrageous idea they could ever be as old as forty. They were so happy. So full of themselves. So bloody young.

That was why he'd gone to the prison, he would try to explain. Twenty years is a big deal.

He hooked his coat over the banister post, and caught his reflection in the hall mirror. He ran a hand through his thick, windblown hair, remembering the shock this afternoon of Mark's bald pate. He went through to the living room. All was quiet. The house felt empty. They must have gone to Scarborough. Liv had said they might. She'd given the girls some of the money their grandmother left them. She said they needed to learn how to handle cash and how to budget. So they were hitting the shops. This was the kind of female logic he could never get his head round. He was best off out of it. He flopped onto the sofa and put his

180

head in his hands. What the hell was he going to do about Mark?

Chapter 19

Mark sat on his metal-framed bed, hardly aware of how he got there. Mr Carter popped his head round the open door. He raised his voice over the clatter of dinner trays on the landing.

"How did it go, Strachan? Did he turn up all right?" Mark looked at him, barely recognising the grindingly familiar ruddy face and sandy moustache. The prison officer's confident tone wavered. "Is he going to come again?" Mark stared at him. Carter held his gaze. "All right, Strachan. Looks like you need some time to think. Come and see me during association, will you?"

This was not a request. "Yes, Mr Carter."

Carter stepped inside the cell and lowered his voice. "I'm after a quiet shift here, Strachan. I'm not going to have to be worrying about you, am I?"

Mark fixed his gaze on the grey wall opposite, the one with his photos of the family. "No, sir. I'm fine. Just need a minute. Like you say."

"Ok. Well, don't forget to look in at the office later." He paused at the door. "Have you eaten? Dinner's nearly over. You'd better look sharp."

"Yes, sir." Mark made no move. The officer opened his mouth to speak again, then drummed his hand on the door frame and went out.

The photos were tatty and faded, mounted on a cork notice board that had room for many more. There was one of William and Olivia, wrapped up warm, cheek to cheek, hair flying in the wind, beaming into the camera, rosy-faced. He'd taken that one. In the cove. Another was a school photograph of William's three, lined up in age order. Hugo, Annie, Tessa. Like Russian dolls. All big grins, especially Annie with that gap in her teeth. It was a recent one because Tessa only started at the school nursery that autumn. Recent? What was he thinking? She must be twelve, thirteen now? How did they look, all grown up? The girls would be pretty. Beautiful, probably. How did Hugo sound with a man's voice? The next picture was Patrick and Eric with their mum. It had been snapped outside the front door at Rowan's Well, the last time Alex was home. The last time he knew of, anyway. The boys towered above their mother, their arms about her. She smiled up at Pat. The twins were looking over her head at each other. They were up to something. They usually were. Moments after that photo was taken they'd scooped her up between them and run across the grass with her, threatening to chuck her over the cliff. She'd shrieked and laughed and pleaded for mercy. They'd slipped in some mud and collapsed in a heap. The last photo was his most treasured. It was of himself with Eloise and Rowan, soon after the birth. They were still in hospital. Who had taken it? Martha? Or William, maybe. Eloise was in bed. Tired and dishevelled, but beautiful. Always beautiful. She was looking down at the little bundle in her arms. He was perched on the bed next to her, his arm about her, gazing as adoringly at her as she looked at the baby. They were like a happy family. How he'd wished over the years, prayed even, that the Eloise in the picture would raise her eyes to the camera and smile out at him. Just one smile.

Faded, dog-eared images. They helped keep the memories vivid.

He'd hoped to ask William for more photos. Up-to-date ones to add to this stolen collection. He'd fantasised about a notice board full of pictures, as some of the others had. Tokens of love, longing and enforced separation. But that wouldn't happen now. He'd hoped to ask about the family, to be told stories of the kids' escapades now they were grown. He would even have welcomed William's previously dull tales of faculty intrigue. The idea of fresh news had sustained him since he heard William wanted to visit. Most of all, he'd hoped to screw up the courage to ask about Eloise. He realised now he'd broken the golden rule of prison life. Never get your hopes up. He'd wondered why William wanted to see him after all this time. Maybe he had news, or he pitied him or missed him. Maybe he forgave him. All these had been possible until a few minutes ago. That William hated him still, he had not permitted as an option. He heaved a deep sigh and felt that tearing sensation in his chest. He started coughing. He sat as still as he could, and clutched his side. He would have to make do with these few snapshots, snatched from the fridge at Rowan's Well and stuffed in his pocket, on the day he killed his son. He pushed his shoulders back. They had kept him going thus far. There was no reason why they couldn't continue to do so. Except the game plan was different now. This was no longer an endurance test. He had endured enough. He wanted out, and he intended to get it.

He called at the wing office to reassure Mr Carter he wasn't about to top himself.

"Can I go to the chapel for the rest of association?"

Mr Carter exchanged looks with Evans, the new wing officer.

"Not like you, Strachan? Haven't got you down as a god botherer. Are you sure everything's ok? You can talk in here if you want to. You know that."

Mark glanced at the new guy. He didn't trust him. He'd heard he didn't show respect.

"Course, yeah. I don't want to talk though, thanks. Want to think. And it's a bit difficult out there." He jerked his head at the door as the makings of a row echoed around the landings.

"Check that out, Jack, will you?" Evans left the office. Carter picked up the phone. "Phil? John." He must have been told to hold, because he put his hand over the receiver and said: "Didn't go well, then?" He shook his head. Carter scrutinised him. "Pity, that." His attention was recalled to the phone. "Got anyone free to see Strachan down to the chapel if he waits at the gate? Yep… will do." He replaced the receiver. "You've got forty five minutes. It's all we can manage today. But you know you can make appointments for the chapel? There's a list on the wing notice board. Have a look on your way to the gate. Mr Babbage'll meet you there."

He listened to the clang of the key turning in the lock. He looked about the room. It smelled good. Like furniture polish. It was a meeting room as well as for worship by all denominations. He didn't attend meetings and, as Mr Carter so rightly pointed out, he was no god botherer. He'd never been in here before. But that was going to change. He sat down on a bench at the back of the room, facing the wooden lectern and altar table. It was blissfully quiet down here. Why hadn't he thought of this before?

First, he had to consider if William's visit had changed anything. Of course it had. He'd hoped for regular visits from him, buoying him up, giving him

185

confidence to go ahead. But now he knew that wasn't going to happen. He was on his own, still. Did that really change anything? He was on his own whatever happened. It would have been much easier with William's support, but he could get along without him.

He leaned forward resting his elbows on his knees, his face in his hands. It was too much to think about. He felt panic rising, and with it, a sense of nostalgia. This wasn't the claustrophobia that plagued his life in prison, but the old-style panic of his life outside. The panic that came with decision-making and action. He rubbed his face, and tried not to remember some of those decisions and actions. His breath scraped out of his delicate lungs in short retching bursts. He was alone. He'd hoped he wouldn't have to be alone anymore. But enough of the self-pity. This was all his own doing. Anyway, things were different now. He'd learned from his mistakes. He had grown.

He looked at the plain brass cross on the table. Best to break down the process into chunks and take it step by step. That would work. His breathing eased a little. So what was the first step? To choose who he would go to. That was easy. Carter knew him. Had known him all the years he'd been here. He'd accepted, and even seemed to understand, Mark's refusal to cooperate with the parole system. He'd respected his need for detachment and distance. He'd never rattled his cage, unlike other screws. Carter was his man. And tomorrow would be his opportunity. He was down on the wing cleaning rota for the morning stint. He'd volunteered for cleaning duties when he came back to the landing, softened by nearly a month on the hospital wing. It was the only way to escape the unremitting boredom of being locked in his cell for hours at a time. Cleaning always took place during bang up. The wage he earned, a couple of quid a week, came in handy for buying his coffee and toiletries, as well as the wind-up radio he was saving for from the catalogue. He would collar Mr Carter tomorrow during cleaning. He'd have his undivided attention. If he was lucky he might even get a free cup of coffee out of him.

Decided on his first step, he relaxed a little. He got up and wandered round the room. He glanced at his watch. Mr Babbage would be back for him soon. He stopped in front of the altar table, enjoying his last moments of peace and quiet. He thought again about his meeting with William. He should have known there would still be resentment and bitterness. How could it be otherwise? He should have let William take the lead. He should have kept his mouth shut. If William came again, he would do it differently. But he wouldn't come again. He'd blown it. He touched the smooth cool surface of the cross. Might there yet be a chance to retrieve the situation? Might there be a slim chance he could still persuade William back into his life? It was possible, wasn't it? Worth a try?

When the prison officer opened the chapel door, Mark turned to him with a smile.

October
Chapter 20

Weeks passed. Will couldn't get Mark out of his head. He watched his students file out of the class room. Rachel Peterson, looking pale and tired, hung back. She fiddled with a tassel on her shoulder bag. He pretended to write some notes. Finally, she wandered over to his desk, and asked for an extension on the Richard II essay. How was she falling behind so soon into the term? He'd hoped she had learned from the mess she got into in her first year. But right now he was too weary to argue. He gave her another week, and let her go. He would sit her down after the next class and do the pep talk.

He picked up his tatty copy of 'Romeo and Juliet'. They'd been reading through the death of Mercutio. He gathered up his notes and dragged his feet down the corridor to his office. He turned the corner. David Worthing was hanging about outside his door. Hell. The boy was looking the other way so he dodged back round the corner and ran down the stairs. He couldn't face one of David's earnest dissections of Shakespeare right now. He rummaged in his pocket for car keys. Yes, he had them. He hurried out of the building through the smokers sheltering from the rain, exchanging vague hellos as he went. He had to get away. He couldn't think. He couldn't breathe. Clutching his course notes to his chest to keep them dry, he ran to the car. Without a plan, he headed down the bypass to the country park. He pulled up facing the duck pond, and switched off the engine.

He stared out at the water.

Friendship. The girls in the faculty office, laughing and gossiping. His colleagues meeting after work for drinks. His own kids, never in the house these days, always out with their friends. And even here, by the pond, two old guys sat on a bench, not talking much but enjoying each other's company, seemingly oblivious to the drizzle. He looked at the books on the passenger seat. Romeo and Mercutio.

Who did he have? He didn't count Olivia. That was different. Besides, since she found out about his visit to the prison, things had been difficult between them. He wanted friends he could go for a drink or to the gym with. Mark had ruined all that for him. He was known among colleagues to be 'family-orientated'.

There had been, for a while after Mark was gone, the get-togethers with Greg and James from university. Those meetings were always painful. So much left unsaid. Until the day Greg apparently could stand it no longer. They were in the pub round the corner from Greg's huge and thriving garden centre. The little bird of a boy had surprised them all with his success in business. He never talked money but they knew he was well into the millions.

"Tell me, Will. What would it take for you to see that scumbag for what he is?"

"It's my round, yeah?"

"He's a psychopath, Will. You can't defend a psychopath."

"He was mixed up. Confused. He was ill."

"Fuck's sake." James muttered this. He wasn't one for confrontation. "I'll get them in." He sloped off.

"And what about Luca? Was he ill then? Was he confused then? He was just plain angry, Will. He was angry with him and he punished him. Simple as."

"No."

"Where was he that night? Eh? You don't know, do you? You didn't then and you don't now. You *know* it was him."

"No."

"He drinks. Luca. Did you know that? His wife left him last year. Took the kids. Did you hear about that? You've never been in touch with him, have you? Why is that?"

James came back with the drinks. "Leave it, Greg. Will didn't do anything."

"No, I know, but I want him to see -"

"What's the point? It's done. Salut."

That was the last time he met with Greg. They'd exchanged cards at Christmas for a while until Greg wrote telling him Luca had died. Cirrhosis of the liver. Greg had enclosed with the letter a photocopy of the original newspaper report. It was dated about a week after that séance.

"Hit and Run Crushes Career

Police are appealing for witnesses to an incident which took place late last Thursday evening in the centre of Broomhill. Rising rugby league star, Luca Kocaj, 19, an undergraduate dentistry student at Sheffield University, was crossing Glossop Road at 10.55pm when a car struck him and sped away from the scene. One witness, leaving a nearby pub, says: "It came fast out of nowhere. It looked like he saw it coming because he sort of dived onto the pavement. Still hit him though. Nasty." The car, a light blue Ford Escort, was stolen an hour earlier from a petrol station forecourt in Crosspool. It was found burned out on London Road on Friday morning. Police would like anyone who might have seen this car at any time on Thursday or Friday to contact them. Mr Kocaj sustained fractures to his pelvis, hip and thigh and remains in a serious but stable condition in hospital. A spokesman for the Kocaj family says: "Luca loved his rugby and had a promising career ahead of him. We've been told not only will he never play again, he'll be lucky if he doesn't have to rely on crutches to walk again. If anyone knows who did this terrible thing, please talk to the police." The police have so far refused to comment on the claim of one eye witness that the driver appeared to be wearing some sort of balaclava covering his face. Investigations continue."

He didn't know why Greg sent it. He was hurting, he supposed. They hadn't communicated since.

He'd trusted Mark. Mark betrayed him. He destroyed the family. He left Will to pick up the pieces.

Visiting him had been a bad move.

The windscreen steamed up. He turned on the heater and opened the window a crack. Since the visit, he'd been really low. It wasn't like him. Even after Rowan died, he hadn't got depressed. He'd been upbeat. He'd tried to energise the family. He'd refused to allow them to go under. Except for Eloise. She'd been beyond help. He let his head fall back against the seat rest. Recently, his mind was racing all the time. Maybe he was going mad? He couldn't talk to Liv. She wouldn't discuss Mark. She wanted to pretend he didn't exist. He sighed. It was all so fucking confusing.

He watched the glass gradually clearing to reveal the two old codgers. One nudged the other and pointed to the water. His companion nodded and said something. They might be life-long friends. Friends since boyhood. The kind of friends he'd assumed he and Mark would always be. And there it was again. That sickening flare of anger that had plagued him since the prison visit.

His stomach rumbled. Shit: his one o'clock class would be waiting for him. The Great American Novel. He started the engine. Sod Mark. Let him rot. For now, he must focus on William Faulkner and how to expose the man's genius to a group of unreceptive and poorly-read first years. It was like throwing pearls to swine. It was what they paid him for.

The letter came the following morning.

"Dear William,

I am writing to thank you for coming to see me. I know it was very hard for you. It was good to see you. You are looking really well.

I know and I understand the visit was difficult - painful for you, and I wanted you to know I am grateful that you came anyway.

What I said before you left? I should not have said that. I have no right. And I did not mean to offend you or increase your pain. I have no right to compare what I go through with what you all suffer. My pain is self-inflicted and so should be borne in silence. And would be, I promise you, if you ever felt able to visit me again.

Now I screw up my courage to dare to send you all - all of you - my love. Please do not be angry with me for this when there is already so much to hold against me.

All the best, William. Take care of yourself, my friend.

Mark."

There was a postscript. Unlike the rest of the letter, executed in Mark's meticulously neat hand, this looked like it had been scribbled hurriedly.

"P.S. Do you remember how we used to talk all through the night? I think about those days a lot. Those memories have seen me through some dark times. So thank you.

Take care, M."

"Bastard." Will crushed the letter and threw it across the room. Annie looked up from her Argos catalogue, a spoonful of cornflakes half way to her mouth. "Sorry, love. Some bad news, that's all."

Annie's eyes widened. "About Uncle Mark?"

"How did you know?"

She started flicking through the catalogue. "I , er… I heard you and Mum talking the other day. And, um… I recognised his writing. On the address." She nodded at the discarded envelope on the table.

"Recognised the writing? How?"

Annie had been only six when Mark was sent down. He was never discussed in the family. Not until recently, anyway. Will had always hoped the girls had forgotten him. He didn't like to think of them recalling that day. It was bad enough Hugo had to carry that burden. But now, here was Annie, remembering his handwriting, for Christ's sake.

"He taught me to write my name and address. Don't you remember?" As usual these days, she spoke to him like he was the village idiot. "At Rowan's Well? That Christmas when he gave Cass to Auntie Lou, remember? God, Dad, you're hopeless."

He stared at her, open-mouthed. She picked up her breakfast pots and wandered through to the kitchen.

It was true. Mark did teach Annie to write. And he got Hugo riding his bike without stabilisers. And he put together Tessa's Princess Pony Fairytale Palace, all one hundred and twenty three pieces of it, one Christmas when Will had been too hungover to do it himself.

Annie stood at the door. Hesitant. "Is Uncle Mark ok?"

"Yes, he's fine, sweetheart. Don't worry. He sends his love."

Why the hell did he say that? Too late. She beamed at him and disappeared again. He listened to her blasting music and clattering about until she called:

"I'm going, Dad. I've got my key. I've got hockey after school, so I'll be late in. Bye!" She slammed the back door behind her.

He went to the window to watch her go. He stood there long after she turned the corner. His eyes weren't seeing. His mind was crowded with images. Memories he'd locked away for ten years. Good memories of when the kids were small. They'd been one big family. Right up to Eloise getting pregnant. The kids loved their Uncle Mark, and he loved them back. Spoiled them. Olivia was always on his case for some excess or other. Trips to the pictures and the zoo. Giant teddy bears. A Barbie electric car they had no room for. New bikes. Always the latest United strips. Just before Tessa came along, Mark and Eloise had whisked Hugo and Annie off to Disneyworld in Florida for a whole week. That had been blissful. Olivia had soon managed to swallow her pride that time.

He shook his head. He needed to get on if he was going to clear out the garage before his lunch-time tutorial. He turned back to the room. There, on the floor, was the scrunched up letter. Shit. He picked it up. He sat at the table and smoothed the letter out. It was cheap blue writing paper ripped from a pad, written on in blue biro that had leaked a little and soaked through to the other side.

"Bastard."

He was being manipulated. Mark had always been good at that. In a strange way, it was part of his charm. Being in his power. Giving in to him. It was always easy not to make decisions when Mark was around. He used to tell himself he was just going with the flow, but he saw now he had been surrendering. How could a relationship like that have been the foundation for such a strong friendship? He read the letter again. He wanted more than anything to have that friendship back in his life.

Before he could change his mind, he went into the hall and looked up the probation officer's number. An answer phone kicked in: "You've reached Ian Selby. I'm not in the office right now. Please leave your contact details and I'll get back to you."

Will stretched round the kitchen door to squint at the clock on the cooker. It was only eight thirty. He left a message asking Selby to phone him, nothing urgent, and replaced the receiver feeling he'd done something he would come to regret.

He was in the garage when he heard the phone. He listened. He could let it ring. The situation was still retrievable. He didn't have to pursue this. But what if it wasn't Selby? It might be one of the kids. Hugo had started university a few weeks before. It could be him. He wiped his grimy hands on his jeans and ran inside the house.

"Hello," he said, a little out of breath.

"Hi, William? Ian Selby. Returning your call."

His stomach lurched as if he'd driven over a humped-back bridge. "Yeah, hello, Ian. Thanks for getting back to me. I… I got a letter from Mark this morning, and - well, I'm thinking I might give it another go. Visiting him, I mean. Only -"

"That's great news, William."

"Only I need to discuss it with my wife first."

"Yes, of course. Naturally. Can I say, though? Not wanting to influence you either way, you understand. We've seen a considerable change in Mark since you visited."

"Oh?"

"He's become quite angry and argumentative with the staff."

"Oh, God."

Selby laughed. "No, this is potentially a very good sign. It could mean he's beginning to engage, finally. With his emotions. With his situation. As I told you when we met, he was subdued before. Switched off, if you like. Now, he seems to be waking up. It's maybe a first step to addressing his offending behaviour. And, of course, eventually being released."

"Ok." Will wasn't convinced. It irritated him how Selby referred to what Mark did like that. As if he'd merely got down from the table without asking permission, for God's sake.

Selby seemed unaware of the offence he'd caused, however. "Yesterday, he surprised us all. He requested counselling sessions with the prison chaplain." Counselling? Mark 'Row Your Own Boat' Strachan? "So, you see, it's all looking good."

Will pictured him rubbing his hands with glee.

All he had to do now was convince Olivia it would be a good thing for him to see Mark again. Difficult, when he was having a hard time convincing himself. He was being completely selfish, of course. But he had to see him again. There were no altruistic or noble reasons. He wasn't fooling himself that seeing Mark would bring about any resolution to their grief and hurt. Nor would it help bring Eloise home. In fact, if she ever got wind of this, it would push her farther from them. He didn't even believe that renewing their friendship would assist Mark's rehabilitation. To be honest, the best thing for all concerned, except possibly Mark himself, would be for him to end his days in prison.

But he couldn't change how he felt. God knows, he'd tried. He missed Mark. He had to see him.

Chapter 21

Mark stood up. He had to lean on the table for support. Damn. This was not a good start. William wouldn't meet his eye. He held out his hand. William looked at it. He took it. First hurdle.

"Shall we sit?" They sat. "It's great to see you, William. Thanks for coming."

"I got your letter." Resentment was clear in his voice.

"I'm sorry. I shouldn't have sent it. I didn't want to leave things as they were. After the last time. You know."

"Yeah."

William looked older. He hadn't noticed last time. His face seemed to have lost definition. It was like looking at the man he used to know, the young William, through a fine gauze veil. It had been a hell of a long time.

His plan was to leave most of the talking to William this time, but he was making it hard work. "So how are you? How was the journey? You've come over from Bolton this time, I guess? Did you drive?"

William slouched in his seat. Inflated his cheeks. Hugo used to look like that when he was told to tidy his room. Mark put a hand to his mouth to conceal his smile.

"Yeah. M62's a nightmare."

"The rush hour?"

"Yeah. Set out about half eight." He glanced at his watch. "Still, that's not bad. It's taken me a couple of hours." He drew a hand through his hair. "It takes longer than that to get through all the security here."

"Really? I had no idea. What d'you have to do?"

"There's the paperwork. But you did some of that." Mark nodded. "Then the searches. Then it's mostly waiting around. Not sure why."

"Right." What to say next? On no account must he say what was on the tip of his tongue. *Please William. Tell me about Eloise.* "Have you taken the day off work?" Was he still lecturing? Dare he ask?

"I've juggled some meetings and I'm teaching this evening anyway, so…"

"Ah." He would risk it. "Still at the Institute?"

"Yeah. Well, back there, actually, via a stint at Manchester University." Mark nodded, hoping this would encourage him. "Came back as Head of Humanities."

"Impressive."

"You think? It's not what it's cracked up to be. It's all about funding now. They're going for university status. It's all politics. I have to fight for the time to keep hold of a little teaching. It's not what I went into higher education for."

"More money, though?"

"Yeah, there is that. And I get an office to myself, mostly." He smiled at last. The old, goofy smile. He sat up straighter, took his hands from his pockets and placed them on the table. He started to drum his fingers softly, while he looked about the room.

Mark smiled. "Does that still get on Olivia's nerves?" It was out before he could stop himself. William stiffened. Shit. "Sorry - sorry."

William glared at him with open hostility. Please, not again. He said: "I don't know if this is going to work out." Mark dared not reply. The silence lengthened until suddenly William gave the table several sharp raps. It made him jump. "Right, Mark. Cards on the table time."

He sat up straighter himself. "Ok."

"If I *am* going to be visiting," Yes! "We need some ground rules."

"Makes sense."

William took a folded piece of paper from his pocket. "I've written them down."

"That's a good idea."

He cleared his throat and read from his list. "One. I won't discuss any member of the Brooke family, except for my kids." Mark bit his lip. "Two. I won't discuss - the reason you're in here." Mark felt himself flush. Damn. "Look, Mark. You've got to see it from my point of view. Olivia's dead against me coming here at all. It's - well, it's caused big problems between us. And that's my choice. My problem. But this," he held up the piece of paper. "This is what I agreed with her. This is what I promised her. The first part, anyway." Mark didn't trust his voice to stay steady. "So, is that clear?"

He coughed. Still bloody painful. "Can I not even ask if they are all … keeping well?"

"No." Oh God. William must have seen his alarm. "I mean, no, you can't even ask me."

"That's hard, William. That's very hard for me." His voice came out as a cracked whisper.

"I know. But that's the deal."

"What about the boys? Are they out of bounds too?"

"Yes." But then he seemed to relent a little. "They're fine, both of them. Patrick's a police sergeant now, and Eric - well, Eric's still Eric."

"Thank you. You don't know how much that means to me. I've been so cut off. I think about them every day... Every day. What about the second part?"

"What?"

"Point two: you won't discuss the reason I'm here. Is that for Olivia as well?"

William looked away. "No, that's me. I can't go there, ok?"

"I don't blame you. Neither can I."

He looked at the paper in William's hand. The people at the next table were laughing together at some photos. William screwed up the paper and put it back in his pocket. "That reminds me. I've brought some photos to show you. Just of my three, like."

He reached into his jacket and pulled out a Kodak wallet.

One of the screws stepped forward. "May I look that over, sir?"

William handed him the photos. The screw backed away to examine them.

"Shit. I didn't think. I saw some of the visitors were handing in parcels and stuff to pass on. But photographs?"

"Don't worry. They'll give them back in a mo. They're checking for drugs. Not slipped any in there, have you?"

"How remiss of me. Have to see what I can arrange for next time." Mark laughed. Was the tension lifting? "They're just some pictures of the kids, that's all."

"That's all? Jesus, William, you have no fucking idea." He grabbed his hand and squeezed it. Too impulsive. William blushed and pulled away.

The screw returned the wallet. "Thank you, sir. In future would you hand any items in at reception. We'll return them to you, if you wish, during the visit."

"Yes, of course. I'm sorry, I didn't realise."

"No harm done, sir." The screw backed off.

"They seem ok, the staff?"

He held out his hand for the wallet. "May I?"

"Sure. Knock yourself out."

Will sat back while Mark examined each photo in minute detail. He occasionally asked a question. "Where was this taken?" "That's never Hugo?" "Have they got their own horse?" "Still in the same house, then?" Now and again, he beamed at Will and commented. "They're a credit to you." "They're stunners, both of them." "He looks taller than you now." Eventually, he squeezed the top of his nose with thumb and forefinger, and bent his head. Will leaned forward to put a hand on his shoulder.

"I'm sorry, Mark. I shouldn't have left it so long."

He looked up. It all passed between them then. The roar of the waves. The paralysing cold. That unforgiving concrete wall. The not finding. Mark leaned forward. His voice was tense and angry.

"Don't you apologise, William. You've done nothing wrong. I brought all this on myself." He glanced around the visiting hall. "I deserve this." His black eyes glinted. There was something animal about them that Will had never seen before. As he watched, fascinated, they dulled and became ordinary once more. "I have one photo of them, from when they were little.

A school photo of the three of them together. D'you remember it?"

"They had two or three done together, I think, before Hugo moved on to high school."

"This was Tessa's first school photo. It's faded now, but I love it."

"Do you want some of these? I can't let you have them all. Liv would notice. But she won't miss a few."

"Are you sure? That would be incredible. Really, you don't know what this means to me. Thank you."

His naked gratitude was embarrassing. Will sorted through the photographs and laid out ten. "These do you?"

Mark's big smile looked sinister, it was so out of proportion with his emaciated face. "William, I want to kiss you."

"Piss off."

They laughed. Then stopped short.

"Time now, ladies and gentlemen."

Unlike last time, when he couldn't wait to put as much ground as possible between them, now Will couldn't bear to leave him in this god-awful place. He didn't want to go. He stood up. "You'll be all right, then?"

"Expect I'll manage." Mark stood also, with an effort he tried to disguise. They waited until the other visitors started to move to the exit. Then Mark said, the words tumbling out: "Can I ask you? Is - ? Will you come again?"

Will knew this wasn't what he'd meant to ask. "Sure. If you want me to. But we need to keep to the ground rules, yeah?"

Mark held out his hand. "Yes, absolutely. Thanks, William."

He shook it. "You take care of yourself, mate. I'll be in touch."

With a lump in his throat, he turned away. He heard Mark call: "Safe journey". He raised a hand in acknowledgement. He couldn't look back. He knew Mark was watching him walk away.

Chapter 22

"Now I try it, I think maybe it wasn't such a bright idea to write down my thoughts. But, as you said, if I find it hard to talk face to face with you, it might be - less hard to write to you instead. It's a start at least.

They've always wanted me to talk. To explain, I suppose. But what could I say? There is no explanation for what I did. Or at least not one that would satisfy them. I killed my own child in a pathetic attempt to save myself. It's as simple as that. There's nothing complicated about it. I wanted rid of him, so I disposed of him. Nothing I could say, then or now, could possibly explain that. And nothing can excuse it. I live with it every day. That's my proper punishment.

My biggest regret, apart from what I did, is that I never spoke to my wife again. The last conversation I ever had with her was about mundane everyday stuff on the way down to the beach that morning. I don't know if I had decided at that point to do it - I think the idea was hovering somewhere in my head. Maybe it first occurred to me when the dog drowned, now I come to think of it? - but I certainly didn't consider the possibility of estrangement from her. Yes - I do know how ridiculous that sounds. I wanted to remove the child so that my relationship with my wife could continue as it had been before he was born. I never for a moment thought about how she would react to his death. To my killing him. But as soon as I had done it, I knew right away I had spoiled everything - forever. There was no going back and no going forward. So I stayed still. I spoke to no-one. Not to my family, nor the police, nor the doctors. I had nothing to say to them.

I don't know how much you know of my case. My wife divorced me."

Philip Dutton sat back, took off his glasses and dangled them. Once again he found himself doubting his ability to help this man. In thirty years of pastoral work, first in his own quietly affluent parish, then in hospitals and finally in the prison service, he had never come across a person quite so enigmatic. What was it Strachan wanted from him? This man, intelligent, educated, finally, after serving ten years of his life sentence, wanted to face his crime, to 'address his offending behaviour' in the hideous jargon. And yet he refused point blank to see a specialist counsellor or a psychologist. Recently he'd been spending long hours in the prison chapel, head bent, hands clasped, for all the world as if he was praying. And yet he insisted, to him at least, that he had no faith. He'd made appointments, many of them, to see him in his office and was always punctual, never missed. But he would sit in preoccupied silence, hardly responding to gentle questions and cues. The officers on his wing reported that he'd become angry and difficult to manage after years of calm and compliant behaviour. They were reluctant to leave Dutton alone with such a volatile prisoner. But he had never yet experienced aggression from Strachan. Just a sense of deep sadness and loneliness.

He repositioned his glasses and picked up the sheet of neatly-written paper. Obviously certain elements, certain words, leaped out at one: referring to the killing as an attempt to save himself; his clear insight now into his lack of insight then, and his equally lucid reasoning for why he maintained his silence. All this pointed to an individual who was intelligent, self-aware and, frankly, already well on in some kind of therapeutic process. But then there was that thin veneer of bravado about his words. Was that for his reader's benefit or his own? Was he even aware of it? He pushed his glasses up his nose. Why on earth was the man insisting on seeking help from such a limited resource? He'd been open with Strachan from the start about his own relative lack of counselling experience compared with other professionals at his disposal. But Strachan had politely and obstinately insisted he was the one he wanted to work with. When pressed, he would say he felt comfortable with him, that he felt they'd built up a rapport. This had been enough to satisfy the governor. But Dutton knew that no such relationship existed between them. And worse, he felt the last thing this man wanted was to make a meaningful connection with him.

He slid the paper into a folder on his otherwise empty desk. Strachan was waiting outside for his appointment and he had little clue where to start with him.

"Come in, please." He tried to convey welcome, warmth and authority in his voice. What was it about this man that made him feel constantly wrong-footed?

The door opened. Strachan walked in. He was tall and thin. Severe ill health had left its imprint on his worn face, but it was clear he had once been a fine looking man: something about the line of his nose and the shape of his chin. He held himself like a man defeated, wary and diffident, but sometimes Dutton caught a spark of fight about him, the way he would sit up suddenly, and push his shoulders back and his chin up. Then his eyes would fire up and it could be hard to hold his intense gaze. He had to admit he was intimidated by this prisoner. And yet he wanted to help him. He sensed the struggle going on inside him. He didn't know the nature of this conflict, but his instincts told him the man needed someone at his side to get through it. And that someone was, apparently, him.

He stood. "Morning, Mark. Please take a seat." He walked round his desk to join him in the easy chairs by the window. "How are you today?"

This would elicit a polite and monosyllabic "Fine thanks. And you?" He must work on that opener. It seemed to be setting the tone for these sessions, somehow closing down communication before it had begun. But, of course, today was different. He had the letter to work with. He sat back in his chair, trying to adopt a relaxed posture, aware that Strachan had noticed this. He felt himself blush. Damn the man. How did he manage to make him feel uncomfortable in his own space, just by sitting there?

"I got your letter. Thank you for taking the time to write it. I thought perhaps this morning we could look at some of the issues contained in it, if that's all right with you?" Strachan made no response, merely looked at him over hands loosely clasped in front of his mouth. He pressed on. "First, though, I thought we might reflect on how you felt writing those thoughts down. Mm?"

There was a short pause before Strachan said, without emotion: "It was painful, obviously. Mr Carter said I should talk to you about the courses I need to do if I'm going to apply for release on licence." This threw him. He'd envisaged this conversation coming up somewhere further along in their sessions. "And he said something about a therapeutic community?"

"Yes. Yes, indeed." This was in line with his own thinking, if somewhat premature. "Did Mr Carter explain what these are?" Strachan shook his head slightly, now holding his forefingers in a steeple and tapping his nose.

"A therapeutic community is usually a special wing in a prison - though it can be a completely separate unit within a prison's grounds - where the prisoners have all asked for the chance to work on their offending behaviours in an intensive fashion. There are opportunities for group therapy as well as one-to-one counselling and the focus is very much on rehabilitation into the community." Strachan continued to gaze at him silently. He ploughed on. "As you can imagine, demand for such places is high, so only those prisoners who show strong evidence of their ability to benefit are considered." He hoped Strachan might come in with a question or a comment, but no. Why did he end up doing all the talking with this man? "It's not easy to get a transfer to a therapeutic community, Mark. And we've a way to go before you might be allowed to apply."

"So, what do I need to do?"

"Well, I believe you would need to have undertaken several courses aimed at addressing your offending behaviour." That phrase again. He cringed inwardly. "Before you can get on the courses you need to show you've acknowledged your crime and that you're working towards understanding the reasons for it." Strachan nodded. "The good news is that, since last week, I think you've made great strides in this by writing that letter."

"Good." Strachan was suddenly brisk. He stood up, as if he was closing a business deal. He was once a solicitor, Dutton recalled. "So what are the courses and when do I start them?"

"Hold on there. Slow down. I had hoped we could talk a little about what you wrote?"

Strachan sat down, visibly deflated. "That. Yes."

"Look, I'll be frank with you, Mark. I find you a little puzzling. You say you want counselling to help you come to terms with - what you did." He felt embarrassed at the bluntness of his approach, but he had to do something to get things moving with this man. "But so far you seem to have found it difficult to engage with the process." No response, just that steady gaze. "Then you appeared to embrace it by writing this letter, as I suggested. But now, again, I sense resistance from you. What do you suppose I'm to make of this?"

"I'm not sure, Mr Dutton. It's very hard to break a habit I've had for ten years now."

"Please call me Philip. Yes, I appreciate what you say. But you must understand. In order for me to support your application to attend courses, I'll need some more concrete evidence of your progress. You have a review coming up, am I right?"

"On the twentieth."

"Not long, then. I suggest at that meeting you express your wish to attend training and eventually to transfer to a therapeutic community. And if you'll cooperate with me, I'll be happy to support your applications."

"Sounds fair." Monosyllables still. Was he taking the mickey? But then he said: "My friend, William, has started visiting me." Dutton hardly dared breathe. "He's

210

more than a friend. Brother-in-law. Ex brother-in-law, I suppose, now. He said he'd come again next week." He was well aware Strachan had received not one social visit during his entire sentence prior to these recent ones. He also knew the officers on the wing put his changed behaviour down to that first visit from this friend. He remained silent. Let Strachan do some work, make some connections.

Eventually Strachan said: "Can I write you another letter?"

November
Chapter 23

Rain battered the windscreen. It had gone dark. Will could barely see to drive there was so much spray from the road. That bloody wiper was still not making contact with the glass properly. He'd fiddled with it several times already. He would have to book it in at the garage. Let the buggers sort it out under the warranty. He squinted, dodging about to maintain a clear view of the road ahead. Not the safest way to drive on the most exposed motorway in England. He saw a streak of blue sky before him. Looked like the squall might be passing over.

Which was more than he could say for the atmosphere at home right now.

"I don't understand, Will," Olivia had said. "Why do you want to see him?"

He'd tried to explain. Again. "What he did was - it was the worst thing possible. I know that. But he's served ten years, Liv. It's broken him. I wish you could see him." She drew in a sharp breath at this, but he'd persevered: "He's suffered too, is all I'm saying. Isn't it time he was given a chance?"

"A chance?" Her face was red and twisted. "Did he give Rowan a chance? Or Eloise? So he's suffering. So what? I'm glad. I am, Will. I'm glad he's suffering. I hope he rots in there." She'd glared at him, but he could see her tears close to spilling.

"Liv, please don't do this." He reached out to hug her, but she put up her hands and stepped back from him. "Please don't be angry. Try to understand."

She stared at him, her eyes full of rage and hurt. Then she walked out of the room. A couple of minutes later, he heard the front door slam. He didn't blame her for being angry. In her shoes, he would probably feel the same. Mark Strachan had destroyed her family.

He switched on the de-mister. Why was he doing this? Schlepping across the Pennines, disrupting his work, distressing his wife? Olivia should have more claim on his loyalty than Mark. And she did. Of course she did. But there had to come a time when Mark could expect to live his life as a normal person once more. What would be the point in punishing him endlessly? He was no threat to anyone. He could never again do what he did that day in the cove. His life was being wasted in prison. If only Olivia could see this.

But, of course, she'd hated him long before he went to prison. She'd never really trusted him from the first day they met. It was a long time before Will had come to understand this mistrust. This tension between them. Mark had always fancied Olivia. He never tried to hide it from him. He said it was only natural and healthy to be attracted to both twins. Often, when he was drunk, he'd try to get Will to admit he fancied Eloise, too. He'd seen Mark's interest in Olivia intensify after she started having the kids. That was a bit weird, but on the whole he wasn't worried and certainly not threatened by it. He knew Olivia wasn't interested. He also knew Mark wouldn't go behind his back.

So when he saw the two of them kissing at that barbeque he suddenly understood. It was years ago now. He'd looked up from the vegetable kebabs. Saw them through the kitchen window. They were in each other's arms. She was running a hand through his hair. It was blatant. He shivered now as he recalled how his blood had seemed to run cold. It was clear as daylight to him, then. He was astounded he hadn't seen it before.

He'd waited days, weeks, for her to tell him about it. He'd hoped she would be mad as hell at Mark's presumption. But they made love that night, and she said nothing. Weeks, then months, passed. And then he'd left it too long. So he let it go. He decided to get on with life. He knew they both loved him, whatever their feelings for each other. He kept a closer eye on them after that, though. And he did make it clear to Mark he wouldn't put up with him lusting after Olivia anymore. But he never challenged him about it. Strange that, looking back. Maybe it was because he couldn't shake loose that nagging memory of Mark coming back into the garden, tripping on the steps, clearly a bit drunk. Whereas Olivia - Olivia had been sober. She was pregnant with Tessa at the time. She knew exactly what she was doing when she kissed Mark. He squeezed the steering wheel. She would never forgive him for her own infidelity.

So did she deserve his loyalty more than Mark? After what he'd done, of course she did. But Mark had no one. He couldn't abandon him now. Olivia would come round. She couldn't stay angry for ever. Deep down, he knew she could. She had good reason to hate Mark now. Nothing could change that.

By the time he reached Swainsea Prison, on the outskirts of York, the weather had cleared to reveal a beautiful autumn day. He got out of the car. Buttoned up his coat against the keen breeze. He reached into the back seat for the books, and walked toward the austere red-brick building.

After the usual searches and delays, he was shown into the visiting hall. The other visitors were mainly young women, track-suited and pony-tailed. Some clutched toddlers by the hand. He exchanged pleasantries with one or two he recognised from his last trip. He'd already picked up on the camaraderie amongst the visitors as they waited to see their loved ones. They were lumbered with the same burden. They were making the best of it. These girls probably understood more about how he was feeling right now than his own wife. How depressing was that?

The sight of Mark, looking much better than when they last met, cheered him. Ian Selby had said, over the phone, that he was engaging more in prison life. Using the gym. Enrolling in some classes. It was clearly doing him good.

Mark rose to take his hand. "Hello, William. It's great to see you. Thanks for coming."

"Said I would." Will smiled. "You're looking well, mate."

"I'm feeling a lot better than I was. I think I'm on the mend now. Sit down."

He gestured expansively to the plastic chair as if he was in his own living room. A picture flashed in Will's mind of the cosy little cottage on the moors. Eloise had sold it soon after Mark's incarceration. They sat across from one another. Smiling like idiots.

"God, it's good to see you, William. You have no idea how much this means to me."

"It's good to see you too. So that makes us quits, yeah?"

Mark laughed. "All right. What's in the bag?"

He placed it on the table between them. "Books. Ian said you were after reading matter, so I thought -"

"Great." He rummaged through the contents. Pulled out five paperbacks. "They're all French writers?"

"It's a course I've been putting together. It's just been validated. 'Realism And The Nineteenth-Century French Novel'. Thought I could try it out on you. Give us something to talk about."

"Why? Does it feel like we're particularly short of topics to discuss?" Mark flicked through 'Madame Bovary'.

"No. I just thought -"

"Sorry, William. This is a great idea. Thank you. Can I keep hold of these? I've read this already, you know." He held up the Flaubert.

"You'll have to read it more than once to do the essays, mate."

"Essays?" He burst into laughter. "That's brilliant. Thank you! When do I start?"

"How long will it take you to read them all?"

"On eighteen-hour bang up?" He laughed again. "Not long."

"Ok. I'll bring an essay question for you next time, yeah? How about we start with the Flaubert seeing as you're already familiar with it?"

"Ok, kimu-" He checked himself. He looked at the other novels. "Balzac. Never read him. Zola, ditto. George Sand. A woman, right? But this one I've never heard of. Stendhal?"

"'The Red and the Black'. That's the most interesting of the five, I think. Not necessarily an easy read, mind you. Let's see what you make of them."

Mark put the books back in the bag and placed it on the floor at his side. He beamed. "Thanks, William."

"Do you do much reading?"

"Shit, yes. I'd go mad if I couldn't read. All that time locked in your cell. You have to keep your mind occupied, you know?" He nodded. He had absolutely no clue what it must be like. Mark continued: "I spend what time I can in the library."

"Any good?"

"Adequate, I suppose. The librarian's helpful. She'll order stuff in from the public library if you ask her. If she can get hold of it."

"Anything you want, books-wise, I'm your man."

"Roger that."

They watched a small boy, just a toddler, shy, reluctant, urged on by his mum, walk around the edge of a table to stand before a father he clearly didn't know. The prisoner scooped him up and placed him on his knee. He jogged him up and down as if he was on a horse. The child's delighted laughter filled the room. It cut through the ever-present air of tension. Visitors, prisoners and officers exchanged glances and smiles.

"It must be tough on the families," Mark said, his eyes on the little lad.

"It is."

Mark winced. "Shit. I'm sorry, William." He coughed. "So, how's this invasion been received outside?"

"What, Iraq? Depends what papers you read. But there's been loads of demos and protests. We've been on a couple of the marches. Only in Manchester and Bolton, like."

"Good for you. On the next one, think of me. I'll be there in spirit."

"Fair enough."

"This whole place is obsessed with it. The TV rooms are packed out for the News. Standing room only."

217

"Really? How many TV rooms have you got?"

Was this the right time to ask? Mark had been practising how he'd phrase the question for weeks. Now it came to it, his nerve was failing him. But visiting would soon be over. He had to take a chance.

"Can I ask you something, William? I know I have to be careful. Can I ask how 'everyone' is, and then you tell me about whoever you feel you want to?" He paused before the word 'everyone'. He said it like it was a name. He looked at William with what he hoped was irresistible pleading.

"This is daft, in't it? But I've got to stick to it. I'm sorry, Mark. I promised."

"I know. And I respect that. I don't want you to break any confidences. It's just I need to know. About ... you know ... 'everyone'." William didn't reply. He tried a different tack: "How about if I ask: is everyone safe and well?"

William's reaction was frightening. He seemed to go pale. He stared at the table and Mark realized he was welling up.

"There is something you should know." Suddenly Mark didn't want to hear. "It's not what you think." William reached across and laid a hand on his arm. "No. It's Martha."

He couldn't hold back his sigh of relief. "Go on."

"She - we lost her. She died. Last year."

"Christ."

"Yeah."

"How? She's ... indestructible."

"Yeah. She was, wasn't she?" William drew in a breath. He was hurting. He'd always been close to their mother-in-law. "It was an accident. A stupid accident."

He had to prompt him. "Yes?"

"It was in the summer. We were all up there at - Martha's. Me, Liv and the girls. Hugo was camping with some mates in Wales. But Alex was there with us. And Eric. Patrick was away. He lives in Carlisle now. I think I told you he's in the police?" He nodded. "It was during the night. She must have gone downstairs for a cup of tea or something. We don't know. We never will now. She fell on the stairs. Top to bottom, we think."

"Jesus."

"We heard the noise, of course. Got to her straightaway. But she was already dead." The pain was clear in his eyes. "There was nothing we could do. She was lying all twisted. It was horrible. It was obvious her neck was broken." Mark said nothing. What could he say? "It was bad, Mark. Really bad. Liv and Alex were right there. They saw it all. I couldn't protect them from it. And the kids - Christ." He passed a hand over his face as if to erase the memory. "Annie and Tess. You know how they worshipped their Gran. I don't know how I would've coped if Eric hadn't been there. He was a revelation. Really strong, like." William sighed. "I needed you that night, mate. I'm telling you." This was almost a whisper.

"I'm sorry. I'm so sorry, William."

"So. It's been a tough year for us. But it's right you should know. I know you two didn't always get on, but for her part, she cared a lot about you, Mark. She worried about you after -"

"Don't!" This came out louder than he intended. He looked down, as people at the other tables stared over at them. "Sorry. I didn't mean to shout."

They sat quietly. How must it have been for William, that night? He would have tried to resuscitate Martha. He would have been desperate to shield his loved ones from the horror of her death. What the hell was the point of his own existence if he couldn't be there when his family needed him?

William seemed to recall how they'd got on to this subject. "But apart from that, 'everyone'," he stressed the word as Mark had, "'Everyone' is well. Not happy, but well. Living in London." His absurd joy was extinguished the moment it was born. William hadn't finished. "She's with a new bloke." Mark tried to control his quivering lip. A tear rolled down his cheek. He brushed it away. "Mark?"

He held up a hand. "I'm ok. I'm glad. She deserves a chance to be happy." He coughed. "Is he all right? Does he treat her well?"

"He's a nice guy. Older than her. Accountant."

"Are they married?" William nodded. Mark's voice almost gave out now: "Children?" William shook his head. "Thanks. I won't ask anymore. I promise."

William broke the silence that grew between them. "Oh, before I forget. The girls sent you this. I told them you'd enjoyed those photos, so."

He pulled an envelope from his pocket. Mark glanced at the screws, but William said: "Don't worry. It's passed inspection."

"To Uncle Mark" was written across the envelope in large black print. He opened it carefully. Inside was a pink homemade card with a photo of Hugo, Annie and Tessa pasted on the front. It was a professional portrait. Recent. They were a handsome family.

"I see the Brooke genes won through in the end." He was going to cry. Hold it together. He opened the card. Inside it read: "Dear Uncle Mark, do you like the portrait? We hope you are feeling better after the pneumonia. Lots of love n stuff." It was signed by Annie and Tessa. Now the tears spilled. He couldn't stop them.

"Yeah, they get *me* that way sometimes, too," William said.

December
Chapter 24

Mark was on the beach with Eloise and Rowan. The sun blazed. They sat on a rug spread over the sand. It was a beautiful, still day. But something wasn't right. There was something he couldn't see. Lurking just out of sight. Threatening them. He watched Eloise bounce the baby on her knee. She spoke to the child, sang to him maybe, but he heard no voice. All was silent. Except for a low rumbling. Distant like summer thunder. He watched his wife with their child. Seeing the two of them together grated on his nerves. He wanted to slap Eloise. To bring her to her senses. To make her look at him. Why was she so wrapped up in this little creature?

He watched. The image of mother and child darkened. It blurred into that purple mist that billowed through his every thought. He was being pulled from them. Wrenched from them. And it hurt. He needed them close. He didn't want to lose them. But he knew he already had. This was only a dream. He fought against waking, to stay with his family a few moments more.

Once again he was with them on the beach. He knew it was the cove, though it looked nothing like it. Why did he feel so angry? They shouldn't make him feel this way. What would happen if he lost control? The rumble of thunder grew until it became a roar. He saw, too late, it wasn't thunder but the sea. Unleashed.

Coming at them, full of rushing rage. The giant wave smashed into them.

It was still dark, but he got out of bed and went to his table. He switched on the torch and sat down. The pen and paper were there, ready. He began to write.

"I suppose you will need to know what I felt after I killed him. Numb, mostly. I don't think I understood what I had done - the seriousness, the finality of it. Rowan was not a person to me, then - not a living breathing human being. Not my son. But I tried to save his life. Of course, I took his life. I understand that. But, to me, it's important that I tried to save him.

Because the numbness came later. That's right. He was real the moment he hit the water.

It was such a tiny splash. The wind was in my eyes and my ears - tearing at me. I opened my mouth to shout for help, but the wind forced the words back down my throat. It gagged me. I saw him go down like a stone. But he bobbed up again. His coat was inflated with trapped air. It acted like a life-jacket, and dragged him back to the surface. There was still hope.

I couldn't see his face, and I am thankful for that now. In my memory, he's simply a purple balloon. No tiny hands or tiny feet screwed up and turning blue. No little face frozen in bewilderment and pain. I don't see these things. Only the purple.

He came up, and there was a chance for me to save him. Save myself. As I dived in I saw a wave smash over the purple shape. It was slammed against the concrete. I crashed into the water. The cold took my breath away. I too was thrown against the wall. I remember hitting my head and thinking -

quite lucidly, considering the impact - if it's done this to me, the baby can't have survived. But even while I was thinking that, I was striking out away from the jetty, struggling against that damned undertow. I had to get him. I had to bring him back for Eloise. For me.

They said I was in the water for minutes only, but it felt much longer. I was thrown back against the wall at least twice more. I knew it was crazy. I couldn't see. The water forced itself under my eyelids, up my nose, into my mouth. Choking me - trying to kill me. But I kept telling myself - I can do it, I can save him. This was my baby, my little son, out there, helpless and lost.

I tried to dive under again, but someone grabbed me and held my head above the water. William. God, and Patrick. When I pushed away from them they held me tight. I lashed out. My fist made contact with William's face. Then everything went grey. I could taste the bitter salt and I could just about hear William over the noise of the waves shouting my name. But I couldn't see. I tried to shake them off, but they held on to me. I remember feeling surprised by Patrick's strength. He was only sixteen, but he had become a grown man. I hadn't even noticed. It was pointless feeling pride in him though, because he was not my son. It was then I knew I had lost my boy. So I gave in."

Dutton pinched the bridge of his nose, dislodging his glasses. He was tired. It had been a long day. He glanced out of the high window at the darkening rainy sky. He should get moving. The Friday night traffic would be building up. The longer he delayed setting off, the longer it would take to get home. Still, he was in no hurry. Since Bella died he'd been working longer hours. Finding reasons, excuses really, to stay on late. It was ironic. Most of the officers couldn't wait to see the back of the prison at the end of each shift. But even this place was better than the chippy supper and the lonely bottle of cheap red wine that awaited him later tonight.

He looked down at the letter before him. Painful as it was, his own loneliness must be nothing compared with the gaping black hole this man had wilfully ripped through the centre of his own life and now had to find a way to live with every day. He shuddered.

This time, Mark was in the chapel. Only it wasn't the same. It looked familiar. All white. And it smelled of that furniture polish. But it was different somehow. He couldn't put his finger on it. He paced the room. Back and forth. No, this wasn't the chapel, after all. He wasn't even in the prison. He couldn't tell how he knew. He simply felt - not locked in. He wandered around the featureless room, touching the cold plaster walls. Listening for clues. Where was he? All was silent. He turned, and saw a man. The stranger was himself. He shrank back. The figure on the other side of the room flinched with him. He raised a hand to his gaping mouth. So did his other self. Just as the terror was almost too much to bear, realisation hit him. It was a mirror! What a fool! Confident once more, he strode forward. He reached out to touch the cool smooth glass.

He felt the clammy flesh of the other palm against his...

He sat up in bed, sweating and breathless. He whirled round. Peered into the darkness. Was that his mirror-self crouching in the corner? A resounding metallic clang made him jump. He heard an angry shout: "Keep

225

the fucking noise down!" Masterson, three cells along, needed his beauty sleep. He flopped onto the thin pillow and pulled the blanket up to his chin. He was shivering. Jesus, where had that one come from? He hadn't thought about all that for the longest time. Not since he was a child. His mind drifted toward sleep once more. And he remembered...

The mirror was like a tear drop. Mrs P thought it looked like a pear drop. But she ate too many sweets. It was definitely a long, stretched tear drop. There was no frame around it. It was just a tear drop. It hung on the dark, swirly-patterned wall of the dining room. It was called the dining room, and there was a big shiny table that smelled of Mr Sheen, but nobody ever dined in here. It was a criminal waste of space, according to Mrs P. Mark and his parents ate all their meals in the breakfast room or, more often, in front of the telly in the lounge. Nobody ever came in here except Mrs P, who was the cleaning lady, and Mark. And the boy in the mirror.

He was losing himself again. He could feel the slipping. He didn't remember when exactly he'd discovered the strange boy. It must have been a long time ago because at first he had to climb on a chair to see into the mirror. He was seven now so he could see his reflection in the polished glass without even standing on tiptoe. He'd found the further away from the mirror he stood, the more he could see of himself. But to lose himself he only needed to see his face, so he was standing quite close. As close as he dared. He didn't like this bit. The slipping feeling as he stared into his own eyes. The dizziness as if he'd been twirling in circles. And then to see the stranger standing where *he* had been a moment before. He got a hot, tickly feeling

226

deep down in his belly. This was something big. Special. Something only he knew about. It was almost as good as being invisible. It was Magic.

But his excitement and pride in this special power were spoiled every time by his nagging doubt. Where do *I* go when the slip happens? He thought he knew the answer. He went nowhere. He was nowhere. He was nothing. That was too scary to think about. It wasn't Mark who was that boy in the mirror. He was still here, in this body. On this side of the glass. Thinking this, now. The reflected boy - that was who everyone thought was Mark. But look. He was a stranger. That wasn't Mark's face. It didn't seem familiar, now. It did a second ago, but the flip had happened, as it always did if he stood here long enough, looking into his mirror eyes, letting his brain relax.

One moment he was me and now he isn't. His hair is the same colour as mine. His eyes are the same. And he is wearing the same school uniform as me. He still smiles like me. He still stares like me. He frowns like me too. But I don't like that. He looks angry now.

He was suddenly aware of being alone in the house, this strange boy staring out of the mirror at him. Threatening.

"Stop it now. I don't like it," he said in a loud, brave-sounding voice.

He squeezed his eyes shut and darted sideways to the door. Out of view of the mirror. He dreaded opening his eyes to find that boy still looking back at him. He ran to the lounge and put the telly on loud. He didn't know - he didn't want to know - who he had left behind in the mirror.

Mark kept his eyes tight shut and pulled the blanket over his face.

Chapter 25

"I'm dreaming a lot, lately."

Strachan seemed different today: edgy and distracted. He kept rubbing his thighs and glancing about the room. He was certainly nowhere near as composed as he usually presented. Dutton had a feeling this might be the day they finally started to work together.

"Dreaming?"

Strachan stared at his knees. "Yes."

That was both brief and unhelpful. He was going to have to take the initiative. "You seem a little anxious today, Mark. Is this because of these dreams, do you think?"

"I think so, yes."

"Do you want to talk about the dreams?" Strachan didn't answer, just gazed down at his lap. "Mark?" He looked up. "Do you want to talk about your dreams?" He shrugged. "Increased and vivid dreaming is very common in people who are participating in a therapeutic process. It's to be expected. In fact, I'd go as far as to say it's a very good sign." He dipped his head to make eye contact, but Strachan wouldn't look at him. "Can you tell me what you dreamed last night?"

Strachan shifted in his seat. "I keep having nightmares. Wake up sweating. Last night I think I woke up screaming." He glanced up, and away again. Then he seemed to make up his mind, and sat up straighter. He looked at Dutton fully for the first time since entering the room. "I thought I would dream about what happened. About what I did. I thought I would dream about Rowan." He lowered his voice: "God knows, he's all I think about when I'm awake."

"But you don't?"

"No. Well, yes I do, but no more than usual. Nothing new, you know?" Dutton nodded. "I keep dreaming about … about me. Is that normal?"

"There's no normal or abnormal in this, Mark. Everyone's unique. Each person has his own individual journey to travel. Tell me more about your dream, if you feel able."

Strachan drew in a deep breath, held it a moment and let it out slowly through his nose. "I keep dreaming of me. Only it's not me now, it's me when I was little. Only, in a way, it's not." He rubbed the side of his face. "It's all so fucking mixed up." His voice was strained.

"Take your time."

He leaned forward. "Like last night, I had this dream. And it was me now, the adult me. In here, in prison … only not. Anyway, that wasn't the important bit. But what happened … what happened wasn't from now, wasn't about me now. It was something that happened to me as a child, when I was really small. Something I hadn't thought about for a long time."

This was more like it. He must be careful not to push him. "Do you want to talk about that?"

Strachan sat back and folded his arms. "To be honest, no, I don't. It wouldn't make any sense to you, anyway. I just want to know why." He punched his fist into his thigh. Dutton winced. "Why am I remembering all this stuff? It's got nothing to do with what I did, why I'm here." Strachan glared at him, his eyes black and passionate, demanding an answer.

"All I can say is, we can only work with what you're prepared to bring to these sessions. I haven't got the answers: you have. I can help you work everything through. I can be your companion on this journey, if you will. But ultimately, all the answers lie within you."

Strachan laughed. "Have you any idea how fucking ridiculous you sound?"

It was the first time he had encountered anything like hostility from this man. "In what way?" he said, as evenly as he could.

Strachan shrugged. "Doesn't matter." He paused. "This talking thing isn't working for me. Writing the letters feels better. D'you mind if I do that again?"

"Very well. On one condition."

Strachan smiled. "Go on."

"You promise - now, before we finish today - that you'll *talk* about whatever you write, at the next session."

"You've got me sussed, haven't you?"

"Do you promise?"

"I do."

He held out his hand. Strachan shook it.

The letter, when it appeared in his pigeon-hole the following week, was not what he had expected. It seemed to be a short story. He read, fascinated.

"The Boy was a loner. He had no friends and every single day at school was torture. He was constantly afraid. He woke on school days already in a cold sweat. He quivered with fear as he dressed in the uniform that made him feel nauseous, struggling to fasten his shirt cuffs with moist and shaking hands. Frequently, he was unable to eat his breakfast cereal, much to his mother's irritation. When he dragged himself upstairs to clean his teeth, he would spend ages in the toilet, his bowels emptying uncontrollably. Then he would stand on tiptoe to open the window to try to disperse the smell - he dreaded an interrogation from his mother. He need not have worried however - she never noticed.

He would sit on his bed, his beloved satchel balanced on his bare knees. He drew comfort from his satchel - he loved the smooth warm feel of it - he loved the rich deep smell of it - he loved its light tan shades. He felt as protective of and as strongly loyal to his leather satchel as other boys seemed toward their pet dogs. He perched with his sandaled feet dangling lifelessly, hopelessly, staring straight ahead, frowning with concentration, as he rehearsed the walk to school, the route providing the best cover - the most driveways to run down - the biggest bushes to crouch behind. He had only three choices of route to school and tried to vary them so that They would not always be lying in wait.

His mother's impatient shriek up the stairs - 'Get down here now. I'll be late for work' - always made him jump. He would shoulder his satchel and dawdle downstairs, leaning against the wall, not because he knew this irritated his mum, though it did, but because his legs refused to work for him. It was an act of strong will to plant one foot in front of the other, his thigh muscles tightening and cramping in revolt - to leave the house was madness, his muscles protested. He would enter the kitchen without a glance or word in his mum's direction, which seemed to suit her fine. He would pick up his Tupperware lunch, shove it into the bulging satchel and leave through the back door, his legs barely holding him up.

Five days a week the Boy was this afraid - afraid of the teachers, and of the large, unprotected school spaces, but most of all afraid of Them. Children can smell weakness. From his first day at school, starting half way through the reception year, when he was coaxed, crying and reluctant, into that classroom where friendships and alliances were already forged, he was marked out. When Tyrone Pendlebury cornered him in the wendy house and punched him hard in the belly, he did not retaliate or even react - only stood rooted to the spot by surprise and horror. And his fate was sealed - he was easy prey.

Always he had to think one step ahead of Them. For instance, the schoolyard at playtime was bad. He would avoid the fringes from where he could be snatched unnoticed. He would try to stay close to the teacher on duty, without getting on their nerves. But inevitably he would be shooed away, told to go and play, get some exercise. And then They would pounce. His so-called friends would descend - 'That's right Johnny. Take him with you to play football'- and frogmarch him to the edge of the yard, their arms, relaxed and chummy round his shoulders, disguising his own arm jerked up painfully behind his back under his jacket. They would march him round the corner and push him up against the wall. There were four of them. Connor, Andy, Johnny and Jez. And the weird thing was they *were* his friends sometimes. They worked on projects with him in class - sat at the same table. He even went to Andy's house for tea sometimes, invited by his interested and sociable mother. Singly they were ok, he could handle them, but not when they were in a group, not when they were in this mood. In this mood they were dangerous - terrifying.

Johnny pushed him hard against the rough brick wall of Classroom 5. His head flicked back with the force of the shove and bashed against the unforgiving surface. He felt tears start to his eyes. This was bad, he must not show weakness. Weakness drove them crazy, like those hyenas on 'The World About Us' who tore the antelope apart when they smelled its blood, and it was still alive. He blinked the tears back, tasting them salty in his mouth. He must stay calm, because he had to talk his way out. This was bad, all four of them. They would egg each other on. He must convince them that nothing was happening, that he was not scared, that they were just hanging around chatting together and that was all. He could do this with only two of them and maybe with three, but he had never yet had to do it with all four. Connor stepped forward, and Johnny dropped back with a big grin on his face. Shit, this was really bad. He could have handled Johnny. Connor lunged his face right up to the Boy's, blotting out the light and somehow making everything sound quieter. The shouts and laughter coming from the yard were muffled and far away.

'I'm gonna marmalize you,' threatened Connor through gritted teeth, his face almost touching the Boy's, glaring into his eyes.

'Marmalize, that's not a word. What does it mean?' the Boy garbled, playing for time.

'It's how they make marmalade, stupid,' said Connor, taking a step back.

The Boy stood up straight to occupy some of the space left vacant - gaining ground, like in trench warfare.

'How's that then, how *do* they make marmalade?' he asked, putting on his interested look. Connor always liked to show off his knowledge.

'Like this.'

Connor kicked him hard on the shin. Caught off-guard, he stifled a yelp, but he could not stop the tears this time. This was going bad.

'Hey Andy.' He tried to keep the tearful waver out of his voice. 'Your mum phoned last night. She wants me round for tea tomorrow, that right?'

'Er, yeah.'

Andy began shuffling, looking at his feet and backing off gradually, maybe thinking about what his mum would say if she got to hear about this.

'Going round for tee-ee. Going round for tee-ee.' The other three started to jeer good-naturedly, prancing about. Jez mimed drinking-tea actions, making slurping noises and holding out his little finger all dainty.

'Piss off,' laughed Andy, shoulder barging Jez, but not hard.

And that was that. They were finished with him - for now anyway. The bell went and they ran back round the corner, Andy calling over his shoulder, 'Come on, Mark!'

He heaved a sigh of relief and trotted obediently after them."

Dutton took off his glasses. Was this an elaborate attempt to distract him, to avoid the real issues? He read it over, and saw there was more to it. This man was a challenge. Probably too much of a challenge, if he was honest. But he wanted to help him. Perhaps the story contained an important key. He scanned the pages. It was fascinating how Strachan seemed to disown the events by telling the story in the third person. He had tried to protect, or at least disguise, his identity almost to the very end there. And the mother - yes, the mother...

He opened his diary. For the first time, he looked forward to their next encounter. Here was progress.

Chapter 26

Olivia stirred in the milk. Steam rose, moistening the tip of her nose. The smell filled the kitchen, warm and reassuring. Cauliflower cheese. Comfort food. She always made this after an argument. It was easy, required no thought and everyone would eat it. They'd been having it a lot lately. She stirred the slowly thickening sauce. Will had changed. All this shit about Mark Strachan had changed him. He'd been happy once. When they first met, he'd been carefree and funny.

Her hand tightened around the fork and she stirred faster. Sauce splashed onto her teeshirt. She lifted the stray globules with her finger and put them in her mouth. Making cheese sauce always reminded her of the first meal she made with Will, in the shabby kitchen of that appalling flat she and Eloise had rented briefly. The room had been tiny and cramped, with a small dining table squeezed in. It smelled perpetually like the inside of an old biscuit tin. That day, Lou and Mark had gone shopping or something, so they had the kitchen to themselves. They were drinking coffee, gazing deep into each other's eyes. They'd spent the afternoon making energetic love. She smiled. All sex at that age was energetic. She'd torn herself away from those lovely green eyes to go to the cooker.

"What are you doing?" Will followed her and squeezed her bum.

"Making cauliflower cheese."

He withdrew his hand. "Oh. You're having your tea, then?"

She laughed. "I was thinking you might want some, too."

"Oh. Right. Well, no thanks. I'd better be going." He moved to the door. "Thanks anyway, like. But I've got to get back for … for tea."

"Will? You can have tea here. I just said, you dope."

"No, I can't. I've got to … I'll see you later." He bolted from the room.

She remembered how she'd carried on stirring the sauce, not understanding why he'd gone. She recalled the warm sting of tears.

Then, as suddenly as he'd gone away, he was back.

"Sorry, Liv." He slipped his arms around her waist, and hugged her from behind. She continued to stir, head down, hiding her tears. "Is there enough for me?"

She wiped her eyes quickly. "I said so, didn't I?"

"Shall I grate the cheese?" He sat down at the table. After that, they worked in tense silence until the meal was ready. They ate, but she dared not look at him. Something important had just happened.

"Olivia?" She put down her fork. "I'm sorry about that. I didn't mean to offend you. It's just … it's just cooking's a big thing in my family, like." He rubbed his forehead. "It means … a lot. It's special. My mum and dad … they do it together. It's what they do." She couldn't resist a smile. Finally, he spat it out. "It's serious. It's a big commitment. I panicked. A bit."

She knew enough not to laugh. "Ok. I understand, I think. You're saying it's a bit like … having sex? But more important?"

"Now you're taking the piss." He laughed. "I know it sounds stupid. But we *are* serious, aren't we? So I thought: where's the harm?" She threw the damp tea towel at him. He caught it. He grabbed her hand, entwining his fingers with hers. "I am serious about us. D'you feel the same way?" She nodded, a thrill of anticipation shooting through her. Then he said it. "I love you." That was the first time. He hadn't waited for her to reciprocate. Not like other boyfriends. He wasn't needy like that. He had an innate, unassuming self-belief. It was so attractive. She smiled, remembering. He'd said: "I want us to be together forever. Wouldn't that be brilliant?"

"Yes." She had beamed until her cheeks ached.

The sauce was too thick. She'd used too much flour. Wholemeal never made the best sauce, but she couldn't bear to feed her kids the processed stuff. Even now when there was no danger of stunting their growth. She added a little more skimmed milk and stirred vigorously.

She had loved Will so much, then. And he'd loved her. They had been so happy. What had gone wrong between them? The fork handle bit into her skin. Nothing had gone wrong with them. It was Mark. It was his fault. He'd ruined everything. He'd broken Will's spirit all those years ago. Now he thought he could come back and do it all over again. The anger she felt was so thick and hard she thought she might choke on it. She stepped back, staggered almost, from the stove. She sank to her knees, wracked with sobs. It was all ruined. They'd worked so hard to build their life again after Rowan. Now Mark was destroying it all over again. And Will didn't seem to understand. He was letting it happen. How could he bring himself even to be in the same room with that man, let alone spend time with him? She couldn't bear Will to touch her after he'd been with that … animal. But he couldn't, or wouldn't, understand how she felt.

She smelled the sauce burning. With an effort, she got to her feet. She switched off the cooker and walked wearily from the room. Leaving her comfort behind.

Chapter 27

"What did you think of the story?"

Strachan's hands were trembling. Dutton showed him to the easy chairs. "Good morning, Mark. Please, do sit. I found it very interesting."

He gave a brief laugh. "That's one way to describe it, I suppose."

"How would *you* describe it?"

He smiled. "Yep. Fell right into that one." He began to pace the room. "I feel a bit nervous today. Don't know why."

"Perhaps because you've committed to talking about what you wrote?"

"Mm." He continued to pace, though he covered little ground, about the length of a cell, back and forth. "You're not for letting me wriggle off the hook, are you? Ok." He paused in his stride. "No point in prevaricating. Let's get on with it." He came back to his chair.

"Very well. But feel free to walk as we talk, if it helps you." He shook his head and sat. "Where shall we start?"

Strachan's response was quick. "I wrote the story during the creative writing class last week. We had to write something from personal experience but without using the first person." Ah. He'd been too quick to read significance into the story's third person narrative. "It's a good group. We have a laugh. Although if I'd waited

240

for this week's class before giving you the story, I don't think I would have bothered."

"Oh?"

"They ripped it to shreds."

"Ah."

"You know I've enrolled in a few classes? Literacy, numeracy, cookery and this creative writing one. The choice was limited. Obviously, I don't need the literacy and numeracy. I usually end up helping the teacher. And I can already cook. So creative writing's the only one I'm learning anything from. I've got to go through the motions, though. Show willing. Tick all the boxes."

"Is that what you're doing here, Mark?"

"What?"

"Ticking the boxes?"

Strachan looked surprised. He appeared to give it some thought. "No, I don't think so. When we started, maybe I was."

"And now?"

"Now I'm just trying to get my old life back. Simple as that."

He let this statement hang in the air for a few moments. "Is that a realistic goal?"

Strachan rubbed his palms along the polished wooden arms of his chair. "No, it's not. I destroyed my old life. I'm not stupid. I realise that. So what I *should* say is: I'm trying to build a new life for myself."

He nodded. This was the most talking Mark had done in any of their meetings so far. His whole attitude to the sessions seemed to have shifted. Yet still he had managed to avoid discussing what he had written. "All right. Let's get back to the letter, shall we?"

"Yes, of course. Sorry. What do you want to know?"

"Whatever you want to tell me."

Mark smiled again. "No more getting away with it, is that it?" Dutton raised an eyebrow in acknowledgement, but said nothing. "Ok. Here goes." Mark clasped his hands. "We had to write something from personal experience, and I think I said last time I've been thinking a lot about my … my childhood? So this story just sort of appeared. Did you like it? No, I get it. *I'm* supposed to be doing the talking. Ok, so." He paused, his eyes unfocused. "As you saw, I was bullied at school. Primary school, that is. Grammar school was a different story." He leaned forward and looked at him with that dark intensity that made him so uncomfortable. "I still don't know why I keep harking on about those times. I don't see the connection with - And I have tried, God knows."

"I don't doubt you, Mark. But maybe we won't see the significance until you've explored your memories further. There's no easy way through this, I'm afraid." As Mark didn't resume, only looked down at his clenched hands, he decided to take a chance. "The comments about your mother interested me."

The effect on Strachan was immediate. He sat upright. Dutton sensed his hackles rise. "Oh? Why?"

Idiot! This was where his plain lack of experience let him down. He had put his client on the defensive again, and that would get them nowhere. He had to think. Strachan had distanced himself from his childhood experiences by putting them in the safe confines of a story. Perhaps the way forward, for now at least, was to treat them in like manner.

"You don't describe a close relationship in your piece. The mother in the story isn't portrayed in a sympathetic light. Or am I misreading it?"

Mark appeared to relax slightly, though he frowned still. "Yes, I see what you mean. The mother in the story -" He shut his mouth. The blood drained from his lips as he pressed them together. He took a deep breath. "The mother in the story *is* my mother. That's what she was like." He rubbed his nose as if it itched. "And, um … Yeah. That's what she was like." He looked at him, his eyes begging him to interrupt, to rescue him. But he held fast to his resolve. This man must do some work for himself. The air was tense between them. "I was a difficult child, you see."

He was about to say more, but his face appeared to crumple. He raised his hands to cover his eyes. His shoulders began to shake. He cried, openly and for a long time.

He heaved a sigh and stood. "I'm sorry about that, Mr Dutton. I've made a fool of myself."

"Not at all, Mark. Tears can be very healing."

Mark turned to the window, his back to him. He raised himself on his toes to look out. Despite his height, Dutton guessed all he would see was a strip of rain-sodden sky and the upper floors of the high-security wing opposite.

"God, it's drab out there." Mark said, without turning round.

"I've seen better views." Where was this going? Only fifteen minutes remained of their session.

"Can I tell you one more story before we finish?"

In his head, Dutton punched the air. "Yes, of course."

2004: Eleven Years After
February
Chapter 28

He dreamed of purple. The foreboding was stronger than ever. Each time he had the dream, it oppressed him more. He woke with a start. Sweating. Heart pounding. He dared not go back to sleep. He got up, pulled the blanket from the bed and wrapped it about his shoulders. He sat at his table, switched on the torch and began to write.

"I'm going to tell you exactly what happened, God help me.

The baby kept me awake. Eloise had insisted on moving its cot into our room because it had a cough. She was worried it might stop breathing and we wouldn't know. I was angry because I'd been hoping to be intimate with her. This may sound trivial to you, but I hadn't had sex with my wife since at least a month before the birth, and the baby was coming up to five months old. I was frustrated. It was causing friction between us. The day before it happened, all that day I'd been flirting with her, making her giggle and blush. I felt sure we would make love that night. I turned down an invitation to join the others for a meal in Whitby, and I chilled the wine. We would have the house to ourselves. It would be perfect.

But at eight o'clock she was still mithering with the baby, endlessly feeding him. I couldn't stand to watch that, so I went to watch some TV instead. Then I heard banging and scraping upstairs. I went up to find Eloise dragging the cot out of the box room onto the landing. She said the baby was wheezy. I know this sounds crazy now, but at the time I think I actually believed the child was manipulating her. We argued. In the end I gave in and brought the cot into our room. But still she wasn't satisfied. When I suggested an early night she said the baby wasn't ready to settle. And so the evening went on. We were still up when the others got back at eleven. William got the children off to bed, while Olivia held Eloise's - sorry, <u>our</u> baby, Rowan, <u>my</u> baby - for a bit. She managed to soothe him and suggested putting him down in the cot. But Eloise wouldn't. To Olivia's credit, she tried to persuade her not to be so anxious, the baby just had a cold, but she wouldn't listen to reason. Soon William came down, grabbed Olivia and pulled her upstairs, both of them giggling. This compounded my frustration, knowing we would be lying awake, listening to them across the landing.

When we did finally go upstairs, well after one, Eloise wasn't interested. She got irritated. She said she couldn't do it in front of the baby. So I rolled over and tried to get some sleep. But what with the baby coughing and Eloise getting up to feed him, even though he wasn't crying, and that disgusting sucking and slurping, and William and Olivia playing Happy Families, it was impossible.

The next morning - the morning it happened - we were both exhausted. I thought I might lie in, but William's girls burst in at about nine. They were all going down to the beach and could Rowan come, please Uncle Mark? William's girls were the sweetest things. They're young women now, of course. Eloise was already up, sitting in the armchair, feeding it again. She seemed so smug, she made me angry. I got up, chased the girls from the room and dressed warmly. The cove is cold in December.

I'm trying to remember exactly when I decided to do it. Was it then, when I thought how cold it would be down on the beach?

The kitchen was full of bustle and breakfast smells. I sat down at the table full of kids. Olivia placed a plate of fried egg, potato cakes and beans in front of me with a wink and a radiant smile. Since the pregnancy, I'd been fighting off some inappropriate fantasies about my sister-in-law. I was excited by the touch of her breast against my arm as she leaned over me. This was completely unintentional on her part, I'm sure. She didn't like me, never had. Especially not since I - But that's nothing to do with this. She was only being nice to me in the hope I wouldn't give her beloved sister a hard time later. Those two were so tight.

After endless eating, bickering, looking for warm enough clothes, and more bloody feeding, we set off across the lawn and down the beach path, leaning into the wind as soon as we left the shelter of the house. I remember Patrick and Eric - my wife's nephews, also twins - kept me entertained en route telling me about two gorgeous girls they'd seen the previous night in Whitby. The boys were kept on a short leash by their grandmother and had been unable to introduce themselves, so now they were plotting to get away later in the day to go looking for them. They thought they were with a group of Australians they'd seen braiding hair in the old Market Place. They made me laugh with their scheming. I felt jealous of them. These young lads, with all their lives ahead of them, had more chance of getting some sex by the end of the day than I, a supposedly happy married man, did. I think it was right then I realized the baby was wrecking my marriage. My marriage was the best thing I'd ever done. I had to save it.

The top of the cliff path is - or used to be, anyway - sheltered by thick gorse bushes, which make the sea sound distant. Harmless. On that day, as we emerged from their protection, the wind hit us hard. It was bitterly cold - a daft idea to go on the beach in such a biting wind. But the Brookes were nothing if not stalwart in the face of adversity, as Martha often reminded us. We marched on down the slope, the wind lashing and choking anyone who attempted to open their mouth to speak. Martha's toyboy was struggling to keep hold of the ludicrous deckchair she always insisted on taking with her. William caught my eye and winked. One of us usually copped for that job. William had his little girls firmly by the hand. They ran and skipped to keep up with him, giggling and spluttering, cheeks even pinker than usual. How I envied him, in that moment, his effortless relationship with his kids. Don't get me wrong - I had a great relationship with his children too, all three of them. I loved them very much. Still do. But they're not my children. I'm not their father. The three boys ran on ahead, William's son, Hugo, struggling to keep pace with his older cousins. God, when I think back to little Hugo as he was then - nine years old, with not a care in the world. When I was that age my life had already gone bad.

The path came out round the back of the Ship Inn. We paused in the shelter of the pub, relieved to be out of the wind. Eloise fussed with the baby, readjusting its hat and mittens. She asked me to carry it down to the beach, zipped up in my coat to keep it warm. I didn't like being that close to it, but I agreed. She reached up, and landed a soft little kiss on my cheek.

That was the last time she ever kissed me.

I walked with William, the baby safely zipped in. It dribbled and wiped snot on my sweater. William laughed. I tried not to think about what might be seeping through its nappy.

On the beach, everyone peeled off in groups. We walked through billowing sand to the cliff face to see what the high tide had loosened. We always enjoyed fossil hunting together. William chatted about this and that. He sympathized on my sleepless night. He had some gossip about Martha's new man. He was the same age as us, apparently, but William seemed to think he was all right. I couldn't see how a man of thirty who found a sixty-year-old grandmother alluring could possibly be all right. William laughed. He offered to carry the baby. It had begun to wriggle, straining against the confines of my waxed jacket. I declined. He started waffling on about Faulkner or Golding or someone. I switched off. I looked out to the jetty. William stooped to grub around in some fallen fragments of stone. I unzipped my coat, exposing the baby. It took a sharp breath. It gripped my sweater. I held it close.

The tide was coming in fast. I suggested we follow the kids down to the rocks. When we reached the causeway, I dropped behind and called to William that I'd catch him up. He raised a hand without turning or stopping, to show he'd heard. I turned to the jetty. The causeway was already submerged and I had to steady myself across the slippery concrete. Thirty three paces to the end of the jetty. The wind was pressing all around me. At the time, I had the strangest idea it was urging me on. Now I think perhaps it was pushing me back.

The horizon blurred. The child clung to me, radiating heat. A faint scent of talcum powder came off its woollen hat. I found the spot where the cross currents were strongest - the spot where my dog Cass had disappeared. Then I gripped the bundle, my hands around his tiny chest. I held him out over the water. My blood screamed in my ears to stop. He looked into my eyes. He kicked his legs. He smiled at me.

I let go.

This is the part that caught me by surprise. When I let go, the world fell away from me. Everything went dark. My chest felt like it was caving in. I scrabbled uselessly in mid air, snatching at nothing. My child was in mortal danger. Every fibre of my body strained to grab him, to snatch him back to safety - to never let him go. My baby was in the freezing sea. I saw the purple of his padded suit emerge momentarily on the broken surface before it was dragged under again.

Then I was in the sea. I was gulping and choking on salt water, trying to catch a glimpse of purple. The cold was savage and crippling, but the pure anguish was worse.

I couldn't find him. I couldn't put it right.

I was pulled from the water and covered with a blanket. But I didn't need it. I was numb. I could feel nothing. The next thing I remember clearly was William standing before me on the beach."

Dutton turned the page. There was a further sheet attached. This had clearly been written at another time: different paper, different pen. He read on, fascinated.

"Have you ever looked down the wrong end of a telescope? When you were a child, perhaps? You can hear people talking and moving about very close to you and yet they appear to be far away. If you do it for any length of time, it's eerie. You're part of the life going on around you - you might even sense the warmth from other bodies– but at the same time you're completely detached. You feel invisible. That's how it was for me immediately afterwards.

I was cold, wet, and hurting. I could hardly believe I was still alive. Yet these were physical sensations, so I must be. I remember wondering what it would feel like to have done something so very wrong. Surely I must feel something? William was shaking me. He had me by the shoulders. He pushed me backwards, his fingers digging in. There were people milling about us, but they seemed distant. Over his shoulder, I saw a boat in the water. A little dinghy. They were still looking. He was shaking me. His face must have been inches from mine but it seemed far away. He was shouting. Or was he crying? He was wet too. His face was streaming. I couldn't tell if it was seawater or tears. And there was blood all down the side of his face.

250

He was talking to me, shouting at me, his face distorted, his lips blue. What was he saying? I couldn't tell. I couldn't hear. God, yes, that's right - I actually couldn't hear. It was like that old black and white film - "Mandy" I think it's called - about the little deaf girl. She runs in front of a truck. The driver slams his brakes on and stops just in time. He leaps out, grabs her by the shoulders, shakes her, shouts at her. But she can't hear. She can only see this contorted angry face. She's terrified. She doesn't understand what she's done wrong.

Only I did. I did understand. I knew what I'd done and it was too late to change it. It was too fucking late.

So I willed myself not to think about it. That seemed safest.

But I had to do something, react in some way. William was waiting for something from me. I decided to cry. That would be acceptable. And expected, probably. I recall how his face seemed to dissolve in my tears. He stopped shaking me. He held me instead. In a big bear hug. I couldn't speak. I couldn't move. I didn't want to. I began to feel warmer. With the warmth came a torrent of grief and anger and self-pity. I clung to him.

A diver glistened black as he rolled over the side of the boat and plopped into the sea."

Dutton pushed the papers away and leaned back in his chair. He said a silent prayer of thanks that he still had a couple of days to try to prepare for their next session. But before then, there was to be an informal review of Strachan's case. Damnation. The timing couldn't be worse. This was the breakthrough the authorities had waited for, the point when Strachan accepted his crime, in the eyes of the system at least, and Dutton knew it would be pounced upon. He was reluctant to show this last writing to the governor, but he was obliged to make monthly progress reports.

Frank Nuffield was the lifer governor responsible for guiding Strachan through the rehabilitation process. He was impressed.

"This is great stuff, Philip. You've worked wonders. I'd have laid odds we wouldn't get this level of acknowledgement out of Strachan any time soon. How did you do it? I find the man impenetrable, myself."

Dutton always shrank before Nuffield's ebullient good humour. On this occasion a sense of shame and betrayal added to his discomfort. "I didn't do it. He did."

"Yeah, yeah." Nuffield waved a dismissive hand. "But you brought him to a point where he felt safe to say it. After more than ten years, that's no mean feat. Don't undersell yourself."

"I suppose." He wished he could have held back about Mark's leap forward. "So, what happens next?"

Nuffield flicked through Mark's file. "Well, he's been after getting onto courses. I think it's time to make that happen. We've a place on our anger management course starting next week. What do you reckon?"

"Yes, I think he'll be keen."

Nuffield held up a finger. "Hold on. I got an email this morning. They've got places on two of their new courses at Hartoft, if we have anyone who fits the bill. Would mean a transfer, obviously."

Dutton shifted in his seat. "I feel that might be too disruptive at this stage. What are the courses?"

Nuffield shuffled some papers on his disorganised desk. "Ah, here it is." He held the sheet close to his face: "Victim empathy and enhanced thinking skills, looks like."

"Do you think Strachan is in need of an ETS course? The victim empathy might be useful, certainly, but ETS?"

"Mm." Nuffield stroked his cheek thoughtfully. "Yes, I know what you mean. But the parole board's going to look for ETS, regardless of background. To their mind, he wouldn't be in here in the first place if he'd applied some thinking skills. No. He's going to have to do ETS, anger management and VE as a minimum before they'll even consider a move to open conditions."

"But a transfer to another Cat B prison? At this stage? It's a sideways move at best. There's not much incentive for him in that. I feel it might prove too unsettling for him."

Nuffield raised an eyebrow and read from his notes. "It's not as if he'd be going to the other end of the country, Philip. It won't be a problem for his visitor - brother in law?" He glanced up. Dutton nodded. "No. It says here he travels from Manchester way, so Leeds should actually be more convenient for him."

Dutton shrugged. "Looks like Leeds it is, then."

"Yes."

"The only thing is, Frank, I'm concerned - will he have opportunity to continue with counselling at Hartoft? He's made such progress."

"To be honest, he's done as much as we require of him at this stage, Philip, as you know. But I suppose if he requests more sessions… I don't know, is the short answer. I'll give them a bell and find out. But I have to say I'm minded to push the move through regardless to take advantage of those free places. It's not often opportunities come up to do two courses at once. This could be a very good thing for Strachan."

Dutton had to agree this could fast-track Strachan's release. But would he cope on the outside if he didn't get chance to learn more about himself through therapy? Dutton doubted it. He was about to say so when he was interrupted by the clang of the alarm bells.

"Hell. That's C Wing again." Nuffield sprang to his feet. "It'll be Reynolds kicking off. Fourth bloody time this week. Look, sorry, Phil, I've got to go to that. We'll finish this another time." And he was gone.

They never did finish their conversation. Strachan received confirmation of the transfer to HMP Hartoft in Leeds two weeks later.

March
Chapter 29

Olivia stretched, and rubbed the small of her back. She reached into the trolley for more bags of fruit. The girl on the checkout persisted with her inane chatter.

"Doing anything nice this afternoon?"

"No."

"Do anything exciting over the weekend?"

"No."

"Lovely out there now, in't it? I wish I was out there."

The girl's high-pitched whine was giving her a headache. Were they trained to be this irritating? She shoved her overloaded trolley out of the store, and swore once again to try that farm shop next week. She squinted into the bright spring sunshine. Her headache swelled. Where had she parked? It would help if she could remember which car she was in. She rummaged in her pocket and pulled out the Punto keys. Looking for red, then. She set off down the car park, straining with the trolley against the sideways slope of the tarmac. She heard someone shout, "Olivia! Hello!", and walked faster. She made it to the car before Julia Fasbender caught up with her.

"Hi, Olivia. How are you? Didn't you hear me? I called you. Head in the clouds as usual?" Julia placed her designer sunglasses on top of her carefully tousled blonde hair.

For reasons Olivia had never tried to understand, Julia seemed to believe she was some kind of ditzy artistic dreamer type. She would compliment her on her retro dress style and bohemian ways. "Retro" Olivia took to mean "frumpy", and "bohemian" was simply an acceptable way of saying "hippy". As far as she could tell from their enforced dinner party acquaintance, the woman had never had a useful thought in her life. She was the trophy wife of a middle-aged academic, who should have known better. Unfortunately for Olivia, their paths had to cross occasionally because their husbands worked together, but that was as far as the association went.

"I'm so glad I bumped into you. I've been meaning to phone." Olivia steeled herself against an invitation to yet another dire college colleague love-in. She was planning her excuse when she was pulled up short by what Julia actually said: "I don't know how you're coping. It must be so hard for you after what that man did. How can Will even bear to speak to him, let alone visit him? I mean, what on earth do they talk about? It makes my skin crawl to think about it. Olivia, are you all right, sweetie?"

Olivia clamped her mouth shut, and swallowed hard. "Then don't." She started chucking her shopping indiscriminately into the boot.

"What? Sorry?"

"Don't think about it, Julia. It's none of your *fucking* business, anyway." She turned on her, her face burning. "Is it?"

"Well, no - I just - I was -"

"No. So keep this," she jabbed her finger at Julia's nose, "out."

Julia stepped back. She raised her hand to her face, and examined her palm as if she expected to find blood there. "Olivia! Please!"

Olivia held her hurt gaze a moment, then turned her back and continued to toss bags into the car. She heard Julia's smart high heels clack away. She remained bent over the shopping, shaking uncontrollably, until she was sure she was gone.

"We need to talk."

Will dropped his briefcase on the hall floor and tossed his car keys onto the phone table.

"Ok." He slipped off his jacket. "Now or …?"

Olivia took in the greying temples and the newly-etched lines around his mouth. "We'll eat first. The girls are out. Tessa's sleeping over at Danielle's. Annie's gone to the cinema with Jack. So we won't be interrupted."

"Ok." Will was obviously waiting for a clue to the topic up for discussion. As if he didn't know.

"Get cleaned up. Tea's ready when you are. Do you want red or white?"

"Does the pope shit in the woods?"

She didn't laugh, just poured the already-breathing bottle of red.

They ate mostly in silence. "What time did they get up this morning?"

"Don't know. I was out."

After a while he tried again. "Did Tess do the washing up after what we said yesterday?"

"Aha."

"I bumped into Jed Spooner this afternoon, at the cash till. He sends his love. Says we should get together some time soon."

257

"Right." She hadn't made eye contact since he got home. She wondered if he'd noticed. Probably not.

When the meal was over, he gathered up the dishes. "You go through. I'll see to these."

"Leave them."

He followed her into the living room and sat down. "Ok. What's the matter, love?"

She'd gone over and over what she would say, and what he might reply. But now it came to it, she felt deflated. No, defeated was how she felt. This had been a long, exhausting battle. Maybe it was all pointless. Maybe she'd lost it right from the start? She was not capable of persuading Will to give up his friend. They had a bond she could not understand. She knew the pragmatic thing to do, the wisest thing if she wanted to save her marriage, was simply to let him get on with it. To look the other way. But how could she? That would mean betraying Eloise, and Rowan. And herself. She took a deep breath.

"I saw Julia Fasbender today."

"Oh yeah? How is she?"

"She knows you've been visiting the prison." She watched for a reaction. "Aren't you going to say anything?" She waited in vain. "You can't talk to me, but you can discuss it with your cronies down the pub? Is that it?" Will held her gaze through narrowed eyes. "How am I supposed to feel, Will, when people I don't even *like* know everything about my business?"

He sat forward. "Look, I'm sorry, Liv. Yes, I have talked to Vince Fasbender about it, but no one else. I've got to talk to someone, for Christ's sake. And you won't listen, so -"

"So it's my fault. Oh, ok. Yes, that makes sense. It's my own fault that my nose is being rubbed in all this - this shit."

258

"No. Christ, Olivia, that's not what I said. You're always twisting what I say."

He stood up and strode to the door.

"Where are you going?"

"I can't keep going over this. I'm sorry you feel how you do, but you know I'm seeing Mark and I'm not going to stop. He needs me. You know that. And I'm sick of apologising all the time. You've got to accept the situation or -" He stopped abruptly.

"Or what?"

Will wouldn't look at her. "I'm going back to the office. There's some stuff I need to catch up on."

She didn't try to stop him. The front door closed with a slam.

Mark walked across the rain-puddled yard, accompanied by Mr O'Leary, a sullen old-school screw who seemed more moody than usual this evening. Mark was invigorated by the fresh air on his face. He breathed in deeply. Air unbreathed by others: what a pathetic luxury.

He looked up at the tall wet-bricked buildings surrounding them. "It's a cold one," he said, to be polite.

"Huh."

O'Leary was not a gifted conversationalist. Mark was glad when they entered the administration block where the chaplain had his office. He hadn't slept again last night, not after the purple dream woke him, and he was feeling tired and anxious. This was going to be a difficult meeting, and not just because it was to be their last. For a while now, Mark had been aware he was pulling back from the chaplain, dodging and sidestepping him. It was strange because until recently he thought the sessions were going well. He'd been able to talk about Eloise, and about Rowan, a little. And he'd started to imagine a possible future for himself. He'd been feeling good about his progress, about attending his classes, doing more work, and, above all, about seeing William. His life in prison had actually been bearable for the past few months. But then he'd got word of this transfer. And the dream had got more insistent, and ... He knocked on the chaplain's door.

He heard the usual cheery "Come in!" and turned the handle. Dutton came round his desk to greet him with outstretched hand.

"Congratulations on your move, Mark. This is a great step forward for you, I think?"

"Yes. Thanks." He took the offered hand and shook it warmly. He'd become fond of this open-hearted man.

"Do sit." They made themselves comfortable in their usual places. "I don't need to tell you, I'm sure, that my only regret is we won't be able to continue our work here." Dutton spread his hands to indicate the room.

He nodded. "I know. I feel the same way."

"You do? This may sound perverse, but I find that gratifying."

He laughed. He held Dutton's gaze. He knew what he should do. He should tell him he hadn't been sleeping. He should tell him about the purple dream. How it made him afraid. But he knew he wouldn't. He couldn't.

"You've helped me a lot, Philip. These past few months have been the best I've had in prison. I feel like I'm actually living again, you know?" He felt himself colour.

"Thank you, Mark. That means a great deal to me." Dutton paused, and said more briskly: "Now I thought we might best spend this final time we have together reviewing our progress over the past months. We can look at some future goals for you to take into counselling sessions at Hartoft. What do you think?"

He didn't answer. Sweat trickled between his shoulder blades. This was his final chance. Take it. Grab it while you can. He mustered all his strength to say, "There *is* something, Philip. Something deeply troubling me. Something dragging me down." But he didn't say that. He said: "Yeah. Sounds like a plan."

She was staring into space, still hearing the door slam, when the phone rang. She ignored it, but it kept ringing and she remembered the girls were out. It might be one of them. She ran to it, suddenly afraid it would stop.

"Hello?"

"Hi, Auntie Liv. How are you?"

"Patrick. Hello, love."

"Liv, what's the matter? Have I called at a bad time?"

She smiled. Patrick was sharp, and sensitive with it. He could read people. That was why she was always on at him to try for CID. And it would get him off the streets, of course. "No, it's fine. I'm fine. Tired, that's all."

"Were you sleeping?"

"No. Just -"

"Auntie Liv, what's up? Tell me. You sound upset."

"I'm just tired, really. It's been a long day. How are you, anyway? How's the delectable Tish?"

"It's Will, isn't it? I knew you weren't happy about all this. How could you be?" Olivia heard him swear under his breath. "He's still visiting him, then?"

She didn't answer. "I knew it. What the hell's he playing at? Can't he see it's upsetting you?"

She couldn't help smiling. He was so protective of her. Proprietorial, almost. She loved him and his brother like they were her own sons. She supposed they were, in a way. They'd been brought up, for better or worse (better, she liked to think) collectively by the Brooke women. They were a joint effort, Martha had always said. Eric was living in London now, spending time with his mum and looking out for Eloise. But Patrick had stayed close, physically and emotionally, to Olivia and Will. He rang at least once a week from his flat in Carlisle. He visited often, especially when there was a square meal on offer. "It's all right, Patrick. Never mind."

"But I do mind. This isn't right. He's got us all sneaking around behind each other's backs as if *we* were the criminals, not -" He sighed. "You've been crying again, haven't you? It's no use saying no. I can tell."

"Patrick, please just -"

"No, I'm not going to leave it. I'm sick of this. I'm shit-scared every time I talk to our Eric or Mum that I'm going to blurt something out, let it slip. I bet it's the same for you when you're on to Eloise - worse, probably. It's not fair. This has gone on long enough. Let me talk to him."

If only it was that simple. If only Patrick could talk to Will and make him see sense. She yearned for his clarity of view, but that was the preserve of the young. "He's not in at the moment, love."

"Later then. Is that ok with you? If I talk to him?"

When she spoke again, she heard an old woman's voice. Ancient. "No." She cleared her throat. "No,

262

Patrick, please don't. I don't think it could help right now. I don't think he would listen."

"Well, what shall we do? I can't leave it like this. He needs telling."

"He won't listen. I've tried talking with him. I have. But it doesn't do any good. It causes arguments and bad feeling. I'm tired of it. Leave it, love, please."

When the session was over and their final brief goodbyes said, Mark asked to be escorted to the chapel. He couldn't face the noise and bustle of the wing right now. It was evening association. Everyone would be out on the landing.

O'Leary let him in with his usual bad grace. "Fifteen minutes, got it?" He slammed and locked the door behind him.

"Wanker." Mark turned to face the cross. Suddenly his heart started racing, the beats irregular. His legs gave way and he sank onto the nearest bench. A lump swelled in his throat. Was he going to throw up? *Get a grip.* What the hell was happening? He must have picked up some kind of bug. His breath came in shallow, desperate pants. He recognised this. Panic attack. But it had come out of nowhere. He'd been virtually free of them since seeing William again. What had triggered this? *Never mind that, fool. Concentrate. You need to breathe, remember? Calm the breaths. Slow them down. In through the nose...* But he couldn't breathe. The cross blurred and slid from view as he slipped to the floor. He was locked in. Only O'Leary knew he was here, and he wasn't coming back for fifteen minutes. Fifteen minutes. He was going to die. He closed his eyes. There was the purple. Waiting for him. He forced them open. With sudden glaring clarity he remembered the last time he'd felt terror like this. It was the last time he'd seen that purple for real. When it cocooned his dying son. His heart was still missing beats. His chest hurt. He was losing control. It was over. He was done. Finally.

He gave in.

Relief swept through him and he went limp. And then the breaths came more easily. He lay still on the cold stone floor. After a while, he knew he wasn't going to die. The disappointment didn't surprise him.

He heard a key clank in the door and struggled to his feet.

April-August
Chapter 30

Easter came, with a chocolate egg from William and his girls. Mark's first gift since he was incarcerated. He didn't eat it. He loved the splash of colour it added to his new digs. He spent hours, probably, gazing at it. Remembering.

He soon settled into the new regime. It was easier than he thought it would be. The other prisoners were neither overtly interested in him nor ignoring him completely. He was soon on nodding terms with most of the men on his landing.

He got stuck in with the courses straightaway. He tried to impress the teaching staff with his diligence. There was nothing remarkable about the sessions. Except the day some women came to the Victim Empathy class. They talked about being victims of crime. It felt weird and confrontational at first as the prisoners sat across the room from the women. He wondered if the course leaders had chosen all women deliberately or whether it was merely a quirk of availability. He sensed the other men felt the same discomfort. But after each woman delivered a short prepared statement, with varying degrees of trepidation, the atmosphere relaxed a little and they were introduced to the prisoners. A woman in her fifties, who'd been burgled, chatted with a young lad doing his third stretch for housebreaking. An older lady explained to another youngster how the theft of her car had meant she couldn't get to her husband in hospital before he died. There was a very young woman among them who reminded him of Eloise. Her auburn hair lit up the room. It turned out she'd been a victim of rape. She sat with Jon, a rapist lifer. Neither of them said much, as far as he could tell, except for Jon's monotonous repetition of "I'm sorry". The poor bloke seemed confused by the whole event. Mark couldn't take his eyes off the girl. Eventually, near the end of the session, she said: "How does sorry help me?" There was no one for Mark - how could there be? - so he sat in with the lady whose husband had died. They ended up chatting about life in prison. He realized he'd forgotten what it was like to make polite, pointless conversation. He enjoyed it. That session had a big impact on the prisoners. Some even shed tears in the safety and confidentiality of the classroom over the following weeks. He listened to the other inmates' anxieties and acts of contrition, and he sympathized. He answered their questions about what he'd done as honestly as he could. But he would never let his guard down enough to share any real emotion. Plenty of time for that in the privacy of his cell.

And in that privacy he still had his dreams of purple.

By the summer he'd completed the courses to the review panel's satisfaction. He was allocated a transfer to open conditions with a view to eventual release on licence. The lifer governor told him he was going to HMP Wrelton, a nearby open prison.

He phoned William.

"Hello?"

Shit. It was Olivia. Shit. He'd been so keen to share his news, he'd forgotten the deal about phoning. Only on Tuesdays or Thursdays, between six and eight.

That was when she went riding. What should he do? *Put the phone down, dickhead.* But it was so good to hear her voice. She sounded so much like…

"Hi, Olivia? This is -"

She hung up.

She stared at the phone, wiping her hand on her skirt. She struggled to bring her thoughts into focus. What had just happened? That was Mark Strachan. On her phone. Wasn't it? It *was* Mark, wasn't it? Suddenly she was unsure. How could it have been? Mark was - gone. It was probably some friend of Annie's, or Tessa's even, who happened to sound like… An image of Mark's face, smiling, loomed before her. She stepped back. She thought she'd forgotten what he looked like. Whenever she thought of him, she never pictured his face. Just his hands. Opening, to let go.

Annie and Tessa thundered down the stairs.

"We're off now. Mum? What's the matter?"

They came to her and she slipped her arms around their waists, pulling them close. "Nothing. I'm fine. Some dirty old man on the phone, heavy breathing, that's all."

"Ooh, gross!"

"Yes. Anyway you'd better get going. Got your mobiles? Be back by ten. No later. And -"

"Be careful, yeah, yeah."

"Never mind 'yeah, yeah'."

They grabbed keys and bags, and slammed the door. The house was empty. She was alone. She picked up the phone and punched in the number.

"Hi, Lou. It's me. How are you?"

He replaced the receiver and made way for the next man in line. He went back to his cell, lost in thought. He shouldn't have done that. That was seriously stupid.

He should have hung up without speaking. Now he'd really landed William in it. What if things got so difficult for him, he could no longer visit? He shook his head. He had faith in him. William wouldn't desert him. Still, he would have a rough time with Olivia over this. All for a moment's idiocy. He lay down on his bed and looked up at the ceiling. That soft low voice was so like Eloise. He smiled. Olivia had recognised his voice. Maybe he hadn't changed all that much. He found this comforting, though he felt perhaps he shouldn't.

He was daydreaming about the Brooke girls half an hour later when Wally, from two doors along, put his head round the door.

"Eh, you left this in the phone."

He tossed a plastic phone card at Mark. It landed on his chest and he grabbed it. "Shit, thanks. It's my last one, as well. Appreciate it."

"See you do the same for me." This was a command, not a request. "Snooker later." Again, it wasn't a question.

The house was quiet and dark when Will got home at around ten thirty. Olivia and the girls must have decided on an early night. He flicked on the living room light.

"Jesus, Liv! You made me jump. What are you sitting in the dark for?" She looked at him, glass in hand. "Any wine left?" He looked about for the bottle. "Liv? Are the girls in bed already? Bit early for them, isn't it?" He nipped into the kitchen to get the almost-empty wine bottle and a glass. "Everything ok? They're not ill or anything? Liv? Olivia! Hello!" He waved at her in what he hoped was a comic fashion, and sat down. He poured a last glass from the bottle, and shook out the dregs. "Gee, thanks for saving me some. Had a

268

bad day, then?" She still didn't answer. "Olivia, I'm really not in the mood for this. Tell me what's up and get it over with." He waited. "You didn't answer me. Are the girls ok?"

Olivia swigged the last of her wine. "Yes, fine. The girls are fine."

"But you're not?"

"God, you're sharp. You're so sharp, Will."

"Ok, can we skip the sarcasm and get to the point?"

"The point, my love, is this. How long has that man been phoning you here?"

"What man?" But he knew.

"How long?"

"He doesn't call often. Only if he needs to tell me something about arrangements for visits or whatever." Olivia's face was pink. Was that anger or the wine? He pressed on. "He's supposed to phone when you're out."

"And that makes it ok, does it? Is that supposed to make me feel better?" She stood. "How dare you! How dare you let him phone this house? Do you really have so little respect for me? For my feelings?" She rubbed her hand against her forehead. When she spoke again her voice had diminished. "Do you really care so little about me now?"

"No, Livvy." He stood up and put his arms about her. "I'm sorry, love. It's not like that. I didn't know you'd feel so strongly about it." He rocked her gently. "I'll tell him not to call again, all right? It won't happen again, ok?" He kissed her hair and held her at arm's length so he could look at her. "Ok?"

He pulled that hang-dog face, the one that made her laugh. But she gazed back at him blankly. Her eyes were dry. His arms dropped to his sides.

"This is too much, Will. You've gone too far." Her voice was calm and measured. She wasn't drunk.

"Olivia -"

"No, I don't want to hear any more. I don't want to hear about how much he needs you, how sad he is, or how he's changed. I'm not interested. Don't you get it? He murdered my sister's child. That's all I'm interested in, Will. Don't you see? That's all I need to know."

"I know, I know -"

"But you don't. You don't know. You really don't understand. You haven't taken me seriously right from the start of all this. All you're interested in is you, Will Cooper. And your precious Mark. As long as you get to be with him, the rest of us can go to hell. Isn't that right?"

"No, Liv, please -"

"Enough." She paused, and began again, more quietly. "Enough, Will. I've had enough."

"What d'you mean?"

"I mean I want you to stop seeing him. I want you to stop all contact with him."

"I can't - "

"And if you *won't*, you can visit him from your mum's house, because you're not staying here."

"Olivia, you don't mean that. We need to talk about this. We can sort this out."

"No. We've talked, Will. We've talked and talked. And you've carried on seeing him regardless of how I feel, or how my family might feel." Her voice cracked at last. "You've made me lie to my sisters."

"I've never asked -"

"You know you have."

Will had no answer. She was right. He had made her lie. The entire bastard situation was dishonest. Olivia stepped toward him and laid a hand on his arm.

270

"Don't you understand, love? All this has left me feeling -" She looked about her, then she met his eyes and gave a little shrug. "It's left me feeling you love him more than you love me." She smiled faintly. There was pleading in her eyes.

"Of course I don't love him more than I love you." He saw her let out a breath, but he couldn't stop himself. He glanced at the ceramic elephant they'd bought in Kenya last year. "It's just -" Don't say it. He looked over her shoulder at their wedding photo on the mantelpiece. Don't say it, you fool. He felt her hand tense on his arm. "It's just I don't love him any less."

September
Chapter 31

For the second time in six months Mark found himself in new surroundings. The difference was hard to cope with. The regime was relaxed and friendly. The prison officers used first names with the inmates and among themselves. They seemed to spend any spare time, tea breaks and the like, socialising with the men. It wasn't unusual to see an officer sauntering along a corridor (there were no landings) slurping a cup of coffee. This would never have happened at Swainsea or Hartoft. A mug of hot coffee was a weapon to turn against an unwary screw. There was even a prisoners versus officers snooker league, which he soon discovered was the focus of much betting among inmates and staff alike.

And his cell. It wasn't a cell. It was a room, with a pine bed and a duvet. There were curtains. They matched the duvet. Bright green with yellow squiggles all over. And they were new. He could see the creases where they'd been folded in their packaging. They smelled of cardboard. He would never have believed, before his time inside, a clean duvet with matching curtains could move him to tears. As if that was not enough, the room had a lock, and he was given a key. He was able for the first time in eleven years to protect what was his. He would no longer have to stand ready to threaten or fight to avenge any imposition on his space and his stuff. He began to relax in a way that had not been possible for the longest time.

He waited nervously. This was William's first visit here. His first since the phone blunder. There was a snack bar in this visiting hall. He'd brought along some cash so he could buy drinks. He rose as William entered.

"Bit plush this, in't it?" William grinned at him and gripped his hand.

"It's all right, yes. Takes a bit of getting used to."

"I'll bet, after those other places."

"Can I get you a drink? Tea? Coffee?"

"Here, mate, let me." William reached into his jeans pocket which was a little inaccessible due to a definite paunch. Neither of them was getting younger.

"No, I'll get them. You sit down."

"Sure?"

"Sure." He went over to queue at the hatch. When his turn came, he called over: "D'you still eat Mars Bars?" He got an enthusiastic nod. William would always be his eighteen-year-old self. Even when he was ninety. He placed the tea and a couple of Mars bars on the table between them.

"Great. Just what the doctor ordered." William pushed a Mars bar toward him and opened the other.

"No, that's for your journey home."

"Oh, right. Cheers." William swallowed a mouthful of chocolate, and stuffed the spare bar into his jacket. "Won't say no. I missed my breakfast."

"Why's that?"

William looked away. "No reason. Just the usual."

Mark felt himself blush. William never spoke about it, but he'd sensed the growing rift between him

273

and Olivia. He was the cause of it. He wished there was something he could do to make things right. Something short of giving up William. He couldn't do that. He wasn't strong enough. He couldn't get through the next few months, a year maybe, without his support. But after that... after that, William would be free. He clasped his hands and squeezed until it hurt. "I haven't had chance to say sorry about that call to Olivia. I don't know what the hell got into me. Was she very angry?"

William sighed. "You have no idea. What were you thinking, you tosser?"

"I wasn't, I guess. And she sounds so like Eloise. You probably don't notice it -"

"Stop. If you go down that road, we're going to fall out big time, ok?"

"Ok."

"Have you asked about that counselling yet?"

"No, not yet."

"Come on, Mark! What're you playing at, man?"

"I don't know. I haven't felt ... I don't want to ... It's not easy."

"Of course it's not pigging *easy*. How can it be? But you've got to do it. You've got to get yourself ready for coming out. You've got to sort your head out."

"I know, I know. Bloody hell. Stop nagging me, will you? I'll sort it." William was worried about him, and he had only himself to blame. He shouldn't have shared with him some of his darker thoughts back at Hartoft. He'd clearly frightened him. He took a slurp of tea. "I've got my own key now."

"What, to your room?"

"Well, not to the front gate, idiot."

William laughed. "No, right."

274

"So I was thinking, if you do want to bring any books in, I can keep them safe now."

"Right, will do. You know I wanted to before. I don't mind if they walk."

"I know. But I felt bad, losing those others."

"Next time I'll bring in some texts from the course I'm teaching now. The Existential Novel. Have you read 'The Brothers Karamazov'?" Mark shook his head. "That's a real meaty one for you. I'll bring that first."

They settled into their usual rhythm. Why had William had let him off so lightly? They talked about the children, William's job, Ian Selby's plans for Mark to do some voluntary work in the community. Then William asked the question he'd been dreading.

"What about that dream? Is it still giving you jip?"

"You don't need to worry about that. It's not a big deal."

"It was the other week."

"I was tired, that was all."

"Are you sure that's all it was?"

William would take some convincing after the histrionics he'd treated him to on the last visit. He'd seriously let his guard down that day. Now he must do some damage limitation.

"Ok, I admit I'm not getting much sleep. That damned dream keeps waking me up. But I'll look into the counselling and I'll tell them all about it. I'm thinking that should make a difference. Maybe even stop it altogether." He laid his hand on William's. "So stop worrying, all right? I'm fine."

October-November
Chapter 32

"I'm sorry, Auntie Liv. I can't leave it." Olivia's hand tightened on the phone. She was tired. She did not want to deal with Patrick's crusading right now. He was still talking. "I've been thinking. Now don't get upset, but I'm thinking I might go and see Mark for myself."

"Patrick -" So much had happened since they last spoke. How could she explain it all to him? How could she tell him there was no marriage left to save?

"To see what's going on. Find out why Will's so pig-headed about all of this." His voice became softer. "What d'you reckon?"

"I don't know, love."

"I want to see how they are together. I want to see if Mark's - you know - if he's pulling the wool over his eyes. Taking advantage, like."

"Will's not stupid." She was surprised at the strength of her reaction. After all, the lad was only saying what she'd been thinking. "I don't want to spy on him, Patrick."

"It's not spying. I'll see if I can go with him next time he visits. All above board, don't worry. We need to settle this once and for all. I mean, it's possible … it is possible that -"

"Go on."

"It's possible Mark has changed. Like Will says. That he's not … like he was."

How could she respond to this? There was no way in which that man could change to become acceptable to her, but how could she make Patrick understand that? She was losing his support. He was leaning towards Will's point of view.

"Liv, I'm only trying to keep an open mind, look at all sides. We can't go on as we are, can we? And his release date can't be too far off now."

"God, don't."

"But we need to be realistic. They're not going to keep him inside for ever. We've got to accept that. Seems to me Will's managed to accept it and maybe we should, too?"

She was too tired to argue. "Do what you feel you have to, Patrick, but please understand, I don't want any part of it."

The days passed quickly now Mark was leaving the prison four times a week. Ian had worked hard to find him this volunteer placement with a local advice centre, and he was grateful. Despite his background in law, he had to study to keep up with changes in benefits and legislation, so he always had plenty to do, reading and learning, even on his days off. He spent any spare time in the gym, trying to get as fit as he could, ready for the outside. Also, with William's encouragement, he'd started a reading group which met fortnightly in the library. It was going well. Six people came last time. It was strange how the busier he got, the more he found to do. And it was phenomenal, this feeling of being occupied and useful, after so many years of merely surviving.

Keeping busy took his mind off the upcoming parole board hearing. Most of the time anyway. He would be invited to attend this one. The previous reviews had taken place without him, his only input being a written statement. But those reviews had not been so important. They didn't have to decide if he was fit for release. He would have preferred to submit yet another statement to this latest hearing, but Ian and Nick Webb, the lifer governor at Wrelton, both thought he was ready to make a favourable impression on the board if he attended. He wasn't so sure, but he had to trust their judgement.

The other thing he found himself trying not to think about was the visit. It had been planned for weeks. He'd been elated when William said Patrick intended to come. It was hard to get his head around. After what he'd done, two of the very few people he loved - the people he'd hurt so badly - wanted to see him. And Patrick, a policeman, had every reason not to want to be associated with a convict. Yet the prospect of seeing the boy - now a man - who'd helped drag him from the sea that day terrified him. Would he be angry? Would he judge him? Would he even remember that day? Of course he would. How old had he been? Sixteen? Surely he remembered. He couldn't bear to think about it. Dealing with that day back in his therapy sessions with Philip Dutton, and in his dreams, and even in his waking head, was one thing. Having the day made real and concrete by someone else who was there was quite another. He and William had never spoken of it.

As the day of the visit approached, he avoided sleep. He lay awake in the dark, willing himself to keep his eyes open, knowing he would be knackered at the advice centre the next day, but terrified of the purple that would envelop him the moment his eyes shut.

He lay awake thinking about Patrick and Eric. They were little lads when he met them at Rowan's

Well that first Christmas with Eloise. They must have been about five or six. Like a pair of Labrador pups, he remembered. All lolloping hands and feet, soft hair, and smelly. And those incredible bursts of energy. He'd never been around children, not since he was a child himself, and he was surprised how much he enjoyed their company. He got the same sense of acceptance and belonging from them that he'd found in William. That holiday, he'd spent far more time with the boys than with Eloise. He remembered how mad she'd been one night when he hauled blankets through from her bedroom to the boys' to make a tent to sleep in with them. In the end, he'd persuaded the lads to let a girl join their camp, and she'd won them over with a midnight feast. They'd gone camping for real the next summer. Just him with Patrick and Eric. That summer and all the summers after until - Until he no longer could.

Now he was to see the boy again. The boy grown into a man. Allowed to grow.

The day came. He spent most of the morning on the toilet. Bloody stomach cramps. With what felt like a huge act of will, he finally calmed himself down. He walked across to the visitors' block.

"Better late than never. We thought you weren't going to show," Tom, the reception officer, said.

"Shit, am I that late?" He'd lost track of the time.

"They're in the waiting room all ready for you."

He passed a hand over his mouth. "Ok. Can I go in, then?"

"Yep." Tom opened the door through to the visiting hall.

It was already full and noisy. Lots of chatter and small children shouting. He made his way to the only empty table. He caught the eye of the officer on the waiting room door. Before he had time to compose himself, William was striding through followed by a broad-shouldered young man with close-cropped bright red hair.

"Hi, Mark. How've you been? You're looking well." William clasped his hand. Then stood aside.

Patrick stepped forward. He had to look up into his face. He still had that same upturn of the mouth that gave him a playful look, even when he was serious. Like now.

"Hello, Uncle Mark. Long time …"

He offered his hand. Patrick gave it a brief, formal shake. He went cold.

"Sit down, please." He tried to keep his mouth from twisting. "So, Patrick. Thanks for coming. It's good to see you. You … you've … grown." That was lame. He stared at the table, aware of Patrick's eyes boring into him.

"I think we've both changed a lot since we last met. What d'you reckon?"

"Christ, I hope so, Patrick."

He looked at William who drummed his hands on the table with an unnecessary flourish and said: "How about I get us some drinks?" He wandered off, not waiting for an answer.

His mouth was dry. His stomach churning again. "So. You're in the police now?"

"Yeah. Cumbria Constabulary. Based in Carlisle." Patrick sat up and pulled his leather jacket straight. "Doing all right. Made sergeant last year."

"William told me. Do you enjoy it? Are you happy?" Patrick smiled for the first time and nodded. Despite the smile, there was something about him that took Mark straight back to those one-sided interviews with the police. Their open disgust. Their cold hostility.

He looked at Patrick and knew he was being judged still. And why not? The lad had every right to be cynical. To mistrust him. "Is there anything you want to say to me, Patrick? Anything you want to ask? You've come a long way to see me. I'll answer as honestly as I can."

Patrick held his gaze. "You're really fucking things up between Olivia and Will. You know that, don't you?"

He swallowed. "I do now." He glanced across to check William was still queuing. "What do you want me to do?"

Patrick seemed to relent a little. "He makes his own decisions, I guess. But I thought you should know. Olivia's never going to want to see you. Nor Eloise. Never. So don't even try, ok? You stay away from them. Is that clear?" Jesus. So much aggression. "Is that clear?" He nodded, but couldn't look at him. "Fair enough." Patrick glanced over at the servery. "Go on, then. Ask me some questions. Like you say, I've come a long way for this."

Eloise would never agree to see him. He knew this. It was no surprise. But it didn't stop the hurt to hear it said out loud. He was being been warned off by a man who could easily deliver on any threat he might make, and who was now insisting on making small talk. It was crazy. But he was desperate for news of the family. "Ok. Where d'you live now? Have you got a girlfriend? Are you married? Kids?"

Patrick laughed. He took off his jacket and swung it over the back of his chair. "In Carlisle. Yes. Not yet. And no."

"Patrick, I don't know what you want from me."

"Nothing, Uncle Mark. Absolutely nothing." He softened again. "Look, it's good to see you, ok? You just needed to know how things are. How they haven't forgotten. How I'm not going to let you hurt them again. All right?"

"Yes. Thanks."

"Shit. Don't thank me." He laughed as William returned with the coffees.

William seemed to be unaware of any tension. They chatted about Patrick's life. About his failed live-in relationship with Clare, who didn't deserve him, according to William. About his new girlfriend, Tish, who was gorgeous and funny and clever, and who he planned to marry, though she didn't know it yet. They talked about Eric who lived in London, close to their mother. He was a professional dancer in the West End. How could identical twins turn out so differently?

"We're not so different. We're still connected."

"Too right. Tell him about your ankles." William nudged him. "Listen to this."

"Shit, yeah. That was weird. Last year, I was working, policing a football match, and I got this right bad shooting pain in my foot. My ankle. Could hardly walk on it. But I hadn't twisted it. I mean I had dirty great boots on, so how could I? Anyway it swelled up that night. It was right painful. Then I get a call from Mum. All melodramatic, like - you know how she is. It turns out our Eric has fallen badly that afternoon in rehearsals and ripped the tendons in his foot and ankle. He was out of action for weeks. But I was right as rain the next day. What d'you reckon to that?"

"That's incredible. But, William, d'you remember that time when El - ?" He stopped. He'd forgotten the deal.

William glared at him. "Any news about the parole board?"

They talked on. Patrick seemed relaxed and friendly, but he was watching the two of them closely. He was looking out for his family. He'd turned out well.

Mark tried to play the gracious host, but for the rest of the visit, a small voice tormented him. It was tiny at first, almost imperceptible, but it grew stronger and more persistent. *You could have had a son like this. This is what you had. What you threw away.*

That night, he had the dream. The purple threatened to choke him. Suffocate him. The terror was unbearable. But this time was different, because when he jolted awake he knew what the dream was telling him. He understood at last. He stared into the dark, the vague shape of the window taking form as his eyes adapted. He passed a hand across his wet forehead. It was clear now and he was relieved. No more indecision. No more uncertainty. He knew now what his future held. He was glad.

He rolled onto his side and closed his eyes. He slept more peacefully than he had for many years.

December
Chapter 33

It was still dark on the M62. There was no need to go at this hour, but Will couldn't stand being in the house any longer than necessary. Not when Olivia was home. He shifted in his seat and swallowed the urge to weep. He'd done enough of that recently. It did no good. How had they come to this? Sleeping in the same bed, but only because there was nowhere else. Not without the girls noticing. But that was a joke. They weren't blind. What a bloody charade. He glanced in the mirror and overtook an artic labouring up the rise. This was all because of seeing Mark. He thumped the steering wheel. He'd fucked things up good and proper, and what the hell for? He didn't even enjoy the damned visits half the time.

He always looked forward to seeing Mark. He planned their time together. Thought of things to take him. Books, cds, or the odd dvd now he had a TV in his room. He enjoyed coming up with subjects to talk about, stuff to tell him. But the visits never lived up to his anticipation. In his imagination, they would sit chatting and laughing hour after hour without a care in the world. Much as they did back at university. Joking around and drinking tea and generally being God's gift to mankind. But the reality always disappointed, because Mark was different now. Fool. Of course he was different. He'd killed his own child and spent twelve years in prison for it. How could that not change him? But it was more than that. True, Mark had never responded to his visits as warmly as he'd hoped, but they'd rebuilt an intimacy of sorts, even if it *was* based mainly on Mark's vulnerability and dependence on him. The difference had come later. He couldn't pin it down. It felt like Mark was withdrawing, somehow. It felt dangerous. He flicked on the radio. Terry Wogan was bantering on in his inimitable fashion. He liked the Wogan Show. It made him laugh. But he rarely got to hear it. Olivia thought it was inane drivel. She preferred the Today programme. He switched it off. He wasn't in the mood for banter.

She accused him of being selfish. But what exactly was he supposed to be getting out of all this, aside from a wrecked marriage and a best friend who was rapidly losing interest in him? It wasn't as if this pigging journey every month was a bowl of cherries either. He would spend the first miles angry about the latest row with Olivia, and the last stretch worrying about the reception he'd get at the prison. The homeward drive was no better. Depression and exhaustion from keeping upbeat for Mark, mixed with dread of what new horrors awaited him at home. He could think of better ways to spend his time. Twice, recently, he'd been on the verge of telling Mark he could no longer see him. But something in his look - a frightening, naked need - had stopped him. Mark might be pulling away, but he wasn't done with him yet. A horn blared. He swerved back sharply into his lane as a car came down fast on his outside.

"Wanker!"

Concentrate, for God's sake. He turned on the radio again and retuned it. John Humphries was in full flow, lambasting some unfortunate about the parlous state of Britain's prison system. He glared at the radio.

There was a cd sticking out. He shoved it in. He needed something to occupy his mind. It was classical. Elgar, maybe. One of Olivia's. The heavy traffic ahead blurred. He brushed away the tears. The music was sombre. Soothing. He could see why she loved it so much. She said Elgar expressed the human soul in music. She was full of all that kind of shit. Why was he so angry with her? Sure, she was making his life hell, alternating unpredictably between the cold shoulder and vicious attacks. But none of this mess was her fault. She'd tolerated his betrayal for as long as she could bear. Then she'd snapped.

Maybe he should go home? He peered at the blue sign before it disappeared behind him. The next junction would land him in Halifax. He could turn around. Go home. Apologise. It wasn't too late. He could throw himself at her feet. Promise never to see Mark again. Simple. He hit the indicator when he saw the two-stroke marker. The tick-tick of the flasher seemed to slow time. There was the one-stroke marker. And there was the turn off to Halifax. He glanced at it as he sped past. Flashing lights behind reminded him to cancel the indicator. He could not turn back now. Olivia would be at work. No. He couldn't turn back because he had to see this through. To the end. He looked in the mirror. He wanted to get past the van in front but the lorry behind was right up his arse, blocking his view. Tosser. He had to face it. He was losing Mark. He was becoming a stranger. Their friendship was coming to an end. He didn't understand why or how. Or maybe he did.

Enough. This kind of thinking would get him nowhere.

He glanced at the folder on the passenger seat. He wasn't convinced Mark would appreciate the gesture, after all. The memories were too painful, surely? Inside the folder were details of the savings account he'd opened right after Mark was put away. In it, he'd deposited the £30,000 he made from the sale of Mark's vintage Jaguar, his pride and joy. When she gave him the keys and the logbook, Eloise had said: "Take it away. It's yours. Keep it or sell it, I don't care, as long as I never have to see it again." Olivia had wanted to invest the money for the children, but Eloise gave the car to him. In the midst of all that grief and anger and hate, he must have been thinking of the future. He'd insisted on putting the money away. They never touched it. He didn't tell Eloise what he'd done. She never asked. She had not even seemed to notice the car had gone. But then, she wasn't noticing much in those days. So now there was a tidy sum sitting in the bank to help Mark get back on his feet when he came out. He could set himself up with a fresh start. He patted the folder. Maybe he wasn't such a poor friend.

He ejected Elgar and tuned in to Wogan.

Mark could have stayed in his room. It was relatively quiet on the corridors at Wrelton. He could close his door and people - even the screws - respected his privacy. But he had got in the habit back at Swainsea of retreating to the chapel to do his thinking. He went to Doug Freeman, the principal officer.

"How long do you need, Mark?"

A good question. "About an hour?"

"Fine. Lock up, will you, and drop the key in at reception when you're done."

Not every prisoner was so trusted, and he strode to the chapel with head held high.

Once inside, he glanced back at the door. It was unlocked, and he had the key in his hand. This was a

287

novel problem. He didn't want to be disturbed. Should he lock it? He looked at the key. What if someone tried the door and found it locked from the inside? That could be enough to colour the parole board's judgement. No. He must not jeopardise this chance of release for the sake of a bit of peace and quiet. He thrust the key into his jeans' pocket and sat down on a plastic chair. He looked around. Not much wood or polish. It didn't feel like a church. Still, it was quiet and that was all he needed.

He sat forward, elbows resting on knees. He stared at the grey floor. That flash of understanding after his last purple dream had been a huge relief at the time, but in the cold light of day, it felt sinister. He had decided he would do it. He wouldn't go back on that. He had to do it. But he was afraid. Was this the only way? Should he not -? *No.* That little voice inside his head spoke up loud and clear. *It's best not to ask questions. It'll be easier that way. Less distressing. Less painful. All you need to know is you've made the decision. No whys and wherefores. Not necessary. Concentrate on the how. That's why you're here.*

The how.

His mouth was dry, his palms moist. The how. Put like that, it seemed so real. A done deal. *That's exactly what it is. You've already decided. There's nothing out there for you. No chance of forgiveness or reconciliation. No redemption. No peace of mind. No future. And there sure as hell is nothing for you on the inside. This is your only option.* But there must be other ways? Other choices? *No, nothing.* What about William? I've got William, at least. *You know that's not true. There's no way Olivia will allow you back into the family. No way. William's going to have to choose sooner or later. And he's going to choose his family. He*

288

has to. William couldn't risk everything he'd built for himself, his marriage, his family, to stay loyal to an undeserving friend.

It was one thing deciding to do it. It was quite another actually going through with it. He rocked to and fro.

"Oh God."

Come on. Pull yourself together, man. You can do this. You can. Make it quick, and you'll be none the wiser. It's not the dying you're afraid of, it's the pain. And it doesn't have to hurt. Not necessarily. Think. He stood up.

"Ok. Let's think."

He looked about the room for inspiration and saw the crucifix. There was a man who knew how to go out with a bang. Talk about melodrama. He patted his waist. No belt. Damn. If he'd only thought, he could have got it over with right now, maybe. He looked about. Yes. There was actually a coat hook on the back of the door. Unbelievable. He went over and tested his weight on it. It seemed strong enough. He sat down again.

Feverishly, he pulled the laces from his trainers. Exhilaration coursed through him. *This is it.* He looked at the laces in his hand. He needed to think this through. Was this what he wanted? It was pretty sordid. Surely he should do this in private? With dignity. He didn't want people finding him. Where was the dignity in that? Besides, it was a shit thing to do to anyone, to leave them to clear up his mess. And there was William to consider. He should prepare him. He owed him that.

So, for the time being, he overruled the little voice. He bent to relace his trainers. He must wait for the right opportunity. Probably on the outside. He'd waited twelve years. A few more months wouldn't hurt him. He sat up suddenly. Twelve years... Of course! He already knew of a quiet way. A just way. It would leave no remains.

2005
Chapter 34
Nine Days Before

The time came. Fifteen months after Mark arrived at the open prison, he was released. He shook hands with those prisoners and officers who had gathered, according to Wrelton tradition, to see him off. The reception officer, Tom, walked him to the gate.

"This is it, then, Mark. Last time through here."

"Yes."

"Good luck, mate. All the best."

"Thanks." They shook hands.

And that was it. He turned his back on the prison building and walked across the car park to where William waited by his car. He'd forgotten how his mousey hair glinted with auburn in the sunshine.

"All right, then?" William took his rucksack from him and slung it in the boot. "Next stop, Bolton. Home, yeah?"

"Christ, this is weird."

Suddenly the ground was dropping away from him. He clung to the roof of the car, the only solid thing. The dizziness passed. William pretended not to notice. He got in the car. He didn't look back. He was bewildered by the ease and speed of his release. They drove in silence.

They pulled up outside a tatty shop not far from Bolton town centre.

"This is it." William peered up at the dirty first-floor windows. "Home sweet home." Mark tried to hide his disappointment, but William saw it. "Look, it's not too late to change your mind. There's some nice new apartments gone up near us. You could easily afford the rent on one of them. I checked."

"No, really, this looks great. I'll be fine here."

He had asked William to find him something near the town centre with the lowest possible rent. He didn't want to break into the £30,000. This had irritated William. Of course, he couldn't explain he intended to leave that money intact for him and his family. It was his by right anyway. It would make a nice little college fund for the kids. He also couldn't tell him he would be in the flat no more than a couple of weeks.

Still, the reality of a dingy bedsit above a failing bike shop in the most rundown part of town was depressing. They climbed the sticky carpeted stairs, and William unlocked the door.

"It came furnished, so some of the stuff's a bit shabby, but we can soon replace it. New curtains, some rugs - I'll get the girls on to it, if you like. They're into all that. How d'you feel about pink and silver as a colour scheme?" Mark smiled. He walked through the small space. It smelled of blocked drains. William rubbed the grime on the window. "Oh, for Christ's sake, Mark. I can't leave you in this flea pit. Why don't you check into a hotel? Just for tonight. We can go flat hunting tomorrow. What d'you say?"

"No, this is fine." He dropped his rucksack on the bed (there was a distinct lack of bounce) and rummaged inside it. "Thanks, William. It'll do nicely. I've just come out of prison, remember. I'm not looking for the Ritz, am I?" With a flourish, he pulled out a packet of

PG Tips and a carton of milk. "Can I offer you a cuppa?"

The next morning, it was the silence that woke him. No one had banged on his door. No one had shouted in the corridor outside. He hadn't needed to pull the covers over his head to snatch a little extra sleep. He was disorientated at first. Where were his bright green curtains? Then he remembered. A rush of adrenaline coursed through him. He was on his own in the building. What if there was a fire? Who would raise the alarm? He leaped out of bed and sniffed about. No smoke. Just drains. He went for a pee in the tiny, smelly bathroom. He walked about the bedsit, taking long strides, for the simple pleasure of having so much space to himself. He made a cup of tea and sat down at the rickety dining table. *His* rickety dining table.

It was only then he recalled his dream. His buoyant mood evaporated. It had followed him here. He'd woken in the night, tangled in his duvet. Gasping for breath. Screaming, probably. The purple had found him here. He must finish this soon.

In the afternoon, William turned up with a trailer and some flat-packed furniture. Damn. Now he would have to dip into that money. William was so pleased with himself, so keen to help, he didn't have the heart to let him down.

"I thought the bed looks ok, but the mattress has to go, yeah? So a new one's being delivered today." William glanced at his watch. "Soon, hopefully. I went to Ikea for this lot. It's all pretty cheap, but at least it's clean and you can leave it here when you get somewhere better. They have sofas too, but I thought you might want to choose your own."

They spent a couple of hours humping old furniture down to the trailer, and putting together the new pieces. Mark was surprised to realise he was enjoying himself. Feeling happy, even.

"Bloody hell, William, do you call that straight? I said hold it straight. Now where's that bastard screw gone?"

William's face was red. "Hurry up. My shoulders're killing me, here."

"You want to get some exercise, my friend."

William laughed. "Piss off."

Mark sat back on his haunches. He couldn't find the vital missing screw. "Tea break?"

"How about a pint?"

Mark's stomach lurched. He'd not had a drink for years. Not since his first days locked up. The drink had got him by the throat back then. It had taken years to fight it off. It had taken him years to want to. The thought of walking into a pub full of free men… What would they think of him? What would they say?

"What about the mattress?"

"Oh yeah, I forgot that. Sod it. Let's go anyway. They can always deliver it another time. Come on. Let's wet your head."

They walked up the road to what might have become his local, eventually. The Swan was a graceful old building quite out of keeping with its dilapidated neighbours. No one turned to stare at him when they walked in. It was quiet. Some old blokes at the bar and a middle-aged couple huddled in secretive conversation at one of the tables. He had to remind himself this was not like prison. People wouldn't demand to know who he was, where he was from. They weren't interested. He relaxed a little. All the better to slip away when the time was right.

"What're you having?"

He scanned the range of beers on offer. "Guinness, please. Half."

"Eh, come off it, Mark. A half? You'll be asking for it in a lady's glass next." But he must have seen his discomfort. "Right you are. Half a Guinness coming up."

Will noticed how Mark stuck close to him as they entered the pub, and before then even, when they were walking up the road. Ian Selby had warned him Mark would find it hard to adjust to life outside. Walking in crowded streets, crossing roads, shopping, were all situations he was unused to and might be intimidated by. Selby said he would need lots of support to cope, initially. Christ, it was going to be like having another child to look after.

He picked up the drinks and nodded to a table in the corner. "We'll sit there."

Mark followed him, shadow-like.

That was Wednesday. On Friday, there was something wrong when Will got home at tea time. The back door was wide open. He heard his daughters shouting inside.

"Selfish little bitch! You're making things worse!"

"Leave me alone!"

As he walked in, a door upstairs slammed, shaking the whole house. He was nearly knocked off his feet by Annie. She stormed down the hall, her curly hair loose and flying.

"Whoa! What's going on?" He grabbed her by the shoulders as she barrelled into him.

"Dad... Hi!"

"Don't give me 'Hi'. What the hell's going on?"

"Nothing. It's Tess. She's being a right pain. She says she won't pull her weight." She screwed up her face and put on a high scratchy voice in cruel imitation of her sister. "She's like: why should I? And I'm like: you've got to. It's not fair if I have to do everything. Then she's like: I don't have to if I don't want to. And I'm like: yeah you do. Mum said so. And then she says: well Mum's not here, is she? And I'm like -"

Will threw up his hands. "Hold on, Annie. What's going on? Where *is* your mum?"

"Oh, right, yeah. You don't know."

"Know what?" Annie stared at her bare feet. She bit her lip. "Annie?"

She raised her head, her beautiful blue eyes sparkling with tears. "Mum's gone away." Her lip quivered slightly. "For a few days. To London. She said she's not sure where she'll stay. She couldn't get hold of Auntie Lou, so she said she'd head for Auntie Alex's. But she might end up with Eric. She'll phone when she knows where she'll be."

"London?"

"She said you'd be surprised. She said she's left some tea in the freezer. I've not looked yet. I've been too busy with that little witch." She jerked her head at the ceiling.

"London? But when did she decide this?"

"Dunno. She was all packed when I got in from college. She was waiting for me to get home. And Tess was kicking off because she wanted to go with her, but Mum wouldn't let her. Says she can't miss any school. That's why she's locked herself in the bathroom. You'll have to sort her out, Dad, because I'm not."

He walked through to the living room. It was strange. This was what he'd feared for months. Now it had happened, he couldn't believe it.

Olivia had left him.

Chapter 35
Two Days Before

It was hazy over the distant hills. Closer, the great dish at Jodrell Bank glinted in the winter sun. William bent over, his hands on his knees, catching his breath. Mark stretched and drank in the vista. He hadn't enjoyed such a wide open view for a long time. He raised his face to the biting wind. They'd had many happy times up here at Rivington Pike. He looked back down the slope they'd ascended with some effort. He saw the boys, Eric, Patrick and Hugo, rolling down, hurtling too fast to screaming laughter from the little girls. He remembered kneeling, arms around his young nieces, pointing out the shiny telescope dish away in the distance. Telling them it could talk to the stars. He saw the open-mouthed wonder on their pink-cheeked faces. Glancing up at the squat tower, he felt Eloise's hands slip into his coat pockets as she pulled him close in a snatched embrace. He breathed in the scent of her hair, his back against the cold stone wall.

That was all gone.

He sat on the steps of the tower and pulled some sandwiches from his pocket. They were a bit squashed, but still edible. William came over to join him. The auburn seemed to have been replaced with grey streaks. Could that happen so fast? He looked tired. Really tired.

William said: "Is this what you meant?"

"Yes, this is it, exactly. I needed to get out of four walls. Stretch my legs. Breathe some real air." He took a bite of cheese and pickle. "These are good. Did you make them?"

"Olivia was hardly likely to make us a picnic, was she, you fucking idiot?"

He was shocked. He knew he must resent him for what he'd done to their marriage. Now, it was beginning to feel like he hated him. It had been a week since his release. He had to get a move on. He gazed at the panorama before him. Across the Cheshire plain, he could make out the mountains of north Wales. That might be as good a place as any. He could catch a train.

William sat down beside him. "I'm sorry, mate. That was uncalled for. Yes, I made the butties. Eat your heart out, Nigella, eh?"

"Who?"

"You have so much to learn."

The wind picked up. He pulled his jacket closer about him. They were quite alone.

"William?"

"Mm?" He was tucking into the picnic with gusto.

"I'm grateful, you know. I know what you've sacrificed for my sake. I can never repay you for it, but I am grateful. Thank you."

William peered at him, screwing up his eyes against the wind. "What's this about, Mark?"

"Nothing. I just wanted you to know." He leaned sideways and gently pushed him with his shoulder. "I appreciate it."

"Ok. No worries." But William did look worried.

He cleared his throat, and tried to sound casual. "I might be going away for a while. Looking for work."

"What? But you can't. What about your probation conditions? You've got to reside at the registered address."

"Yeah, but I've discussed it with Selby -" He regretted saying this as soon as it was out of his mouth. William could easily check and probably would. He was chummy with Ian Selby. Why the hell was he making this up as he went along? He'd lain awake every night since his release planning this very conversation. If he raised William's suspicions now, it could all go pear-shaped. But he desperately wanted to talk to him about it. He wanted to explain himself, to ease the pain he knew William would suffer when he found out. He wanted to reassure himself he'd made the right decision. *You want to give William chance to talk you out of it, you selfish bastard.* He stood up. He shouldn't have said anything. "Yeah, Ian's fine with it." He clapped his hands. "Anyway, if we're all finished here, what do you say we tackle Winter Hill?"

William looked up at him, shielding his eyes from the sun. "Hang on a minute, Mark. What're you talking about? Ian can't ok a thing like that. It's part of the terms of your licence."

"Never mind. I was thinking aloud."

"But you said -"

"Forget it, ok? Are we walking, or what?"

William didn't move. "Talk to me."

He sat down again. He had no idea how he was going to explain. He took a deep breath. "I bumped into Olivia. Last Friday. In town." From the corner of his eye, he saw William's head jerk up. "Sorry. I should've told you before." He'd been going into Marks and Spencer. She was coming out. "She hates me, William." She'd stopped dead. Right in front of him. Her eyes were unflinching. Magnificent. He'd been terrified and

300

mesmerized. Was this what his Eloise looked like now? Copper hair faded, tiny wrinkles at her eyes and corners of her mouth? But still beautiful. Breathtaking. They'd stared at each other a long time. Finally, she opened her mouth to speak. She snapped it shut again. She stepped aside, and past him, and was gone. "I have to go away. It's not fair on her, me being here. It's not fair on you."

He raised a hand to quell William's objections. But no objections came. William stared out across the plain. Mark blinked back tears. He'd made the right decision, then. They sat in heavy silence until a couple of mountain bikers appeared in a spray of gravel and squeaking of brakes.

"I need to be getting back." William sounded tired and old. "Shall we make a move?"

Chapter 36
The Day

Thursday.

"All I'm asking you to do is sign it. You're witnessing my signature, that's all. See. You can read it. It's not committing you to anything. It's just a will."

He couldn't blame them for being suspicious. After all, he'd barely spoken to the shop guy before now. The other bloke was a customer and didn't know him from Adam.

"Why can't you get a solicitor to do it for you? What's the big hurry?"

The man, greasy-haired and unshaven, wasn't as dozy as he looked.

"I can't afford one. Look, the only thing that could happen - and it probably won't," he added quickly, as the man retreated behind his counter, "Is that you might be asked to confirm I was of sound mind when I signed this. That's all."

The bike shop owner was clearly not convinced, but Mark didn't have time to mess about. He had a train to catch. For fuck's sake. He should have done all this well before now.

"There's a pint in it for you, if that makes any difference?"

"Call it a tenner."

"Each." The random customer spoke up for the first time.

"Done." He held out the pen.

He ran back upstairs and read over the will one last time.

"This is the last will and testament of Mark Stuart Strachan … I appoint William Kenneth Cooper of etc etc to be the sole executor of this my will and if the aforesaid William Kenneth Cooper shall survive me for twenty eight days I give devise and bequeath the whole of my real and personal estate and effects unto him absolutely and beneficially.

If William Kenneth Cooper shall not survive me for the period aforesaid… I appoint Ian Selby of etc etc as executor and I give devise and bequeath the whole of my real and personal estate and effects to Olivia Jane Brooke of etc etc

In witness whereof I have hereunto set my hand …"

blah blah. That should cover it. There was nothing to argue with there. He carefully folded the paper. He had to grip his hands tight together to stop them shaking before he could put the will into the envelope. He was about to seal it when he decided to take one last look at the letter he wrote last night. He was surprised to see he'd pressed down so hard with the biro he'd ripped through the writing paper in places.

"William,

No need to explain to you, my friend. I'm doing what I should have done in the first place. It should have been me, not Rowan. It was the obvious solution if I hadn't been so blind. How different things would be now if only I'd been able to see.

Please let me do this. Don't come looking for me.

I'm sorry, William. I hope you can make things right."

It was unsigned, because he wasn't going to leave it. Best they didn't know for sure what he meant to do. Best he simply went away. Disappeared from their lives. He reread the letter, then screwed up the thin piece of paper. He rammed it in the bin under the remains of last night's takeaway. He hesitated, staring at the dirty lino. Was this right? Was this how it should be done? *You're leaving a will, for Christ's sake. What more do you need to say?* He started to seal the envelope. Shit, he'd nearly forgotten. He grabbed the savings account details from the table. He folded them and shoved them in the envelope along with the will. His hands were still trembling when he addressed it. It was seeing his friend's name flow from his pen that proved too much for him. He sank into the chair.

"William, phone me. Please. Phone me now. For God's sake, stop me."

But his brand new mobile phone, the one William had insisted he bought, the one he'd gone into town to buy the day he met Olivia, did not ring. He knew it wouldn't. William hadn't been in touch since they went up to Rivington Pike two days ago. So that was that. He went to the bathroom and washed his face. Then he pulled his rucksack from under the bed. He opened it up. It was large. Capacious. It would do. He threw one or two overnight things into the bottom, nowhere near filling it. He wanted to keep it as empty as possible. But he needed, for now, to feel like he would be showering and shaving in the morning. He pushed the envelope to the centre of the table. He made sure it could be seen from the door. He placed the mobile phone next to it. Then he left, locking the door and pushing the key through the letter box.

"Please, Lou. Put her on." Will's hand trembled as he held the phone. He hadn't slept again last night. His head thumped. His eyes were puffy and sore. He sobbed shamelessly down the line, but she wouldn't budge. Her voice sounded hard, unlike her. She knew.

"She doesn't want to talk to you. Not right now. Maybe in a few days." The line crackled: she'd put her hand over the receiver. She was talking to someone else - Olivia.

"Put her on, just for a minute." He raised his voice. "Liv? Livvy, please talk to me."

"Not now, Will." Eloise's coolness and indifference to his suffering were barely supportable. "Why don't you go to work? You'll feel better. Look, I've got to go. Bye." She hung up.

He sat on the bottom stair, phone in hand. He couldn't make himself move. He heard Tessa whisper from the top of the stairs: "Daddy? Are you all right?"

He heard her padding feet. He felt her slender arms about him. He leaned his head into hers and cried.

Mark was heading for Anglesey. Somewhere near Holyhead, most likely. As he approached the train station, he put on his new bob hat and pulled it well down. He didn't want anyone to remember a bald guy, with distinctive black eyebrows, buying a ticket to Bangor. He could have got the train straight to Holyhead but he'd decided to hitch the last part of the journey. There'd be plenty of lorries going to the ferry terminal on their way to Ireland. If William and Ian did track him down to Bangor, they wouldn't know where to go from there.

It would be a three-hour journey, with a quick change at Chester. On the platform, he kept his head down and stood apart from other travelers. He felt light-headed. Unconnected. Was he really going through with this? The train pulled in. His legs threatening to crumple beneath him. He managed to pull himself up into a carriage. He found a seat in a quiet corner where he could look out of the window.

The familiar names came and went. Deansgate. Oxford Road. Piccadilly. When they pulled into Navigation Road, he sat up. He'd forgotten the Chester train came this way. Navvie Road. His first primary school. That was before his parents, the original yuppies, moved away from Timperley. Sour milk and smacks from a hand with long scarlet nails. Next stop, Altrincham. His home town. He smiled. White and Swales record shop, every Friday after school. A single for 70p. The train swung into Hale station. This took him back earlier still, to the library on Saturday mornings. The smell of books and quiet reading. The thrill of reaching up and stamping his own book, if the nice library lady was there. He sat back, resting his head against the seat. He closed his eyes.

He opened them as the train, clunking and sighing, pulled into Chester. His eyelids were gummy and sore. He had to get that connection. He grabbed his rucksack and ran.

What made him choose Anglesey? His last journey was turning into an episode of 'All Our Yesterdays'. From Chester, it unravelled before him. A history of holidays. Prestatyn was that disastrous time when, to give Martha a break, they'd taken Patrick and Eric for a long weekend in a smelly caravan. The boys had both developed chicken pox, there was a landslide at the campsite and they'd crashed the car. Happy days. Rhyl predated the Brookes and Coopers. It was best not dwelt on. He blinked, hearing that hotel room door slam once more. And the key turn in the lock. No more time to waste on memories like that.

He leaned back, his cheek against the seat's course plush. He watched the sea. How was it going to feel? He should try to prepare himself. But he couldn't make it real.

Colwyn Bay. That little guesthouse Eloise always loved when they wanted to escape for a quiet weekend. Llandudno. Welsh Riviera. Enough said. Conwy. He smiled. Conwy was where they'd stayed at that batty guy's B&B. They were on a walking holiday. Him and Eloise, William and Olivia. They happened upon this place. The owner was totally unprepared for guests, but took them in anyway. It was straight out of Fawlty Towers. The guy was taller than Mark. Spindly and more than a little mad. They'd sat for half an hour waiting for their breakfasts, the smell of frying bacon wafting through from the kitchen, along with the occasional curse. Eventually, Mark had gone to the door through which their host had disappeared. He'd peeped through a spy hole in it. He'd fallen back in surprise at seeing a bright blue eye staring at him. At once, the door flung open. He found himself nose to nose with Basil Fawlty, arms piled with platefuls of congealing Full English. Basil had sidestepped him and served the cold breakfast with panache. Why, and for how long, he'd been waiting behind that door letting their breakfast go cold was a source of hilarious speculation for years afterwards. The train pulled into Penmaenmawr. He gazed down on the beach. He remembered Hugo's excitement at discovering the cannon washed up on the sweeping expanse of sand. And three-year-old Annie's disgust at being made to trudge through wind and rain in mack and soggy wellies to look at a stupid chunk of rusty metal.

The train arrived at Bangor. His body was heavy as lead. He willed himself to his feet.

Will snatched the phone on the first ring.

"Will? Ian Selby. Sorry to bother you, but have you seen Mark yet today? I'm in Manchester. I've been trying to get hold of him, but he's not answering his mobile."

Not what he'd been hoping to hear. He could do without this. "No. I've not seen him for a couple of days, to be honest with you."

He sensed Selby's disapproval. Well, he could fuck off. Right now he had enough on his plate.

"I thought … My understanding was that you would see him every day for the first couple of weeks? If I'd known, I would have been in touch earlier."

Selby's anxiety finally registered with him. "I could meet you at his flat in half an hour?"

Will's hand shook. His spare key was sticky in the unfamiliar lock. Mark wasn't answering his phone. He hadn't come to the door. Will felt sick. What was he going to find inside? The first thing he saw was the door key on the floor. Relief washed over him.

"Looks like he's gone," he said to Selby over his shoulder. "He did say something about looking for work. Come on in."

Mark couldn't take his eyes off the lorry's odometer. The miles clicked by so fast. He wanted to shout: "Slow down! Stop!" He sat passively, watching his life click away. Mile by mile. The steady roll of the numbers had a hypnotic effect. With each click he retreated further inside his own head. Burrowing deeper. Hunkering down as far as he could from reality. He was on his own now. The world outside had nothing to do with him. As in a dream, he saw they had crossed the embankment onto the little island.

"Anywhere here will do, thanks."

The driver pulled over. He jumped down from the cab and threw his rucksack over his shoulder. He tried to focus. Looking through his eyes - his own eyes, he reminded himself - was like looking through binoculars. He peered out of the casing of his skull. His body was no longer part of him. He was inside his head only. Curious. He was reminded of another time, another place, when he'd felt this way. He lacked the energy to pursue that thought further. Just as well. There was only now. He knew what he had to do.

He turned off the main road and picked up a good pace. It would start to go dark soon. He wanted this over with. After about a mile, he passed a stone circle close to the road. He spared it barely a glance. Another mile on, the road ended in a sandy car park. It was empty. *Good. Perfect.* His bowels seemed not to agree. He plodded over to the cliff top. It was about thirty feet down to the stony beach. He walked a bit. Peered over the edge. Wiped his mouth. His legs did not want to do his bidding. It was like driving a tank, making this body move to his instructions. He looked along the cliff. There was a little headland. Beyond that, a small sandy beach. Quite deserted. *Come on, then. Get a bloody move on before someone turns up.* He could make out, in the growing twilight, a rough path zigzagging down to the rocks below.

Selby picked up the envelope. He handed it to Will. "Why would he leave his mobile?"

Will opened it and read. He sank onto the bed. It was not possible. Mark wouldn't do that to him. He couldn't. Not after all he'd done for him. After all he had lost. He'd sacrificed his marriage for him. Had that not been enough? He couldn't have done more. Surely he could see that? He couldn't leave him like this.

"Will? May I?" Selby took the papers from his slackened grip, and glanced through them. "Fuck. This is bad. This is really bad. Where might he have gone, Will? Think, man!"

Selby took out his mobile and started making calls. Will felt hollow. He wanted to reach out and grab Mark. Bring him back to safety. He wanted to tell him - tell him what? That it was ok? That everything was going to be ok? He clamped his hands to his face. Where would he go … to do this? He had no one. So it had to be a place. Home? To the cottage, or up onto the moors? Or maybe to his childhood home? Had there been a place? Anywhere important to him as a boy? Yorkshire. Yes! Rowan's Well. Back to where he - Will sprang to his feet. Maybe he'd left some clue. A bus or train timetable. A scribbled note. Anything. They might still be able to stop him. He opened drawers. He looked under the bed. The rucksack was gone. Was that a good sign? He went into the kitchen. The bin was overflowing with wrappers from an Indian takeaway. He pulled them out. Dropped them on the floor. He plunged his hand into the bin. Pulled out a screwed up sheet of paper. It was written on in a heavy hand.

He held onto hope a few moments more.

Chapter 37

The sun is setting. The sky has turned a shade of indigo that has its origins, impossibly, in the yellows and oranges of a sun-streaked early evening. The sea is quiet. Calm. Still. Grey as iron, it seeps up the colour-drained beach. Apart from the creep of the tide, nothing stirs on the sands. Not even a seagull breaks the stillness. The tide crawls its way higher. Quietly. Undisturbed.

There is movement. From round the headland appears a man. Walking with purpose. He is tall. He covers the wet sand quickly. He is slim. Fit-looking. A bald man in his fifties. Or maybe his forties. He is alone. The beach is empty. The guarding cliffs are deserted. He is unobserved. Unaccounted for.

The rucksack on his back is bulky. It drags at his shoulders. He strides on, oblivious to its weight. He follows the water's edge, some yards away from it. He looks straight ahead. Not out to sea. Purposeful.

Where the sands disappear round another spur in the cliffs, the tide has risen to meet the rock face. The way is blocked. He strides on regardless. Perhaps he does not see the tide is coming in. It is so quiet. So calm. He walks on until he can no longer ignore the water splashing over his boots.

He slows. Reluctantly, it seems. His stride is broken. He stops. Passes a hand over his forehead. He glances to his left, up at the cliff wall, and then back over his shoulder at the way he has come. The cliff is steep and crumbly, but not impossible to climb. The beach behind him is disappearing under the tide that moves like spilled mercury. His decision is made. Was made long ago. He eases his thumbs under the too-tight straps. He shrugs his shoulders sharply to adjust the weight of the rucksack. With a deep sigh, that no one hears, he lifts himself to his full height. Shoulders back. Chin high.

He turns to face his horizon.

Acknowledgements

Thanks to Susan Johnson, Caroline Cattermole and Nikki Treherne for sharing with me their particular fields of expertise. All accuracies are due to them. Any inaccuracies are mine alone.

Thanks to the MTG Collective for their unstinting honesty and wise counsel.

Thanks to Jill Rowe for helping me remember football, though she has probably forgotten she did so.

Thanks to Mike Martin (www.redherringcg.com) for the cover design.

And finally, thanks to Harry Harter. For everything.

CJ Harter
July 2013